HIDDEN THRONES

BOOK ONE

RUSS SCALZO

OUT OF THE STACK PUBLISHING

HIDDEN THRONES

Book I

RUSS SCALZO

"Put on the full armor of God so that you can take your stand against the devil's schemes. For our struggle is not against flesh and blood, but against the rulers, against the authorities, against the powers of this dark world and against the spiritual forces of evil in the heavenly realms."

Ephesians 6:11&12

Hidden Thrones is a work of fiction. Names, characters, places, and incidents either are the product of the author's imagination or are used fictitiously. Any resemblance to actual persons, living or dead, events, or locales is entirely coincidental.

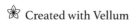

CONTACT INFORMATION

Listen to Chronicles of the End Times

Available on:
Alexa, ITunes, Google Play, Spreaker, iHeartRadio

To receive "Chronicles of the End Times"
Podcast direct to your email.
JOIN HERE!

Follow Russ on Facebook.
www.facebook.com/RussScalzoAuthor

BOOKS BY RUSS SCALZO

On the Edge of Time
Scalzo/Mamchak
Book One
Book Two

Hidden Thrones Series
1: Hidden Thrones
2: Open Warfare
3: Face to Face
4: The Hammer Falls
5: The Cup of Iniquity
6: Many Crowns
7: Redemption

Dedication

I am blessed to have an incredible loving wife who knows the power of prayer, three beautiful daughters, five amazing grandchildren and a kid brother with whom I share many awesome memories. However, none of this would have been possible without Helen and Russell, my amazing mother and father. I dedicate this book to them. They now look upon the Lord they loved and followed all of their lives, and share in the rewards of a life filled of faith.

Thank you, Jesus for all you have done and continue to do in all of our lives.

1

THE OSLOW HOUSE

The driver of the car slowly navigated up the long, twisting stone driveway. He had to be careful not to drive too fast because of the thick, tall pine trees that towered over both sides of the narrow passageway. A strong wind blew the giant trees from side to side, creating strange and ominous shadows on the ground. It was a clear night except for the occasional harmless cloud dashing by a brilliant full moon. The car stopped a hundred feet from an old, three-story Victorian house. The young couple sat staring as the moon washed over the old house, giving it an eerie appearance that rivaled any Hollywood movie set, but that didn't bother Tom and Louise. After all, that's why they came.

Tom stepped out of the car first. He stood six feet, three inches tall, weighed two hundred and ten muscular pounds, with jet-black hair. All the girls said he was drop-dead gorgeous. The passenger door opened, and Louise got out, holding a large blanket. Looking up into the wind, she brushed her long blonde hair out of her eyes. Louise was all that Tom was in a seventeen-year-old girl kind of way. Beautiful of face and body. She had it all and had no problem showing it off. Every boy at Blackstone High, Virginia, dreamed about her, and they would trade places with Tom any day, any time.

Aside from Hollywood looks, they had something else in common. They were totally and outrageously out of control. Tom and Louise did anything they wanted whenever they wanted. Caught having sex in one of the back-stair hallways at school in their junior year, they refused to apologize for their actions and even had the audacity to ask the principal what the big deal was? That was just the tip of the iceberg compared to some of their more infamous exploits.

It was their senior year, and they had every intention of making it memorable. The Oslow House was, by everybody's account, haunted. There was no doubt about it. Year after year, kids would pull up to the house and drive away, too scared to go in. Many said they did, but no one ever had the guts to do it. There was one case where a kid ran onto the porch but then took off in a panic when he said he saw a tall, dark figure coming toward him.

The Oslow House had been empty for over thirty years. The Oslows, a couple in their late forties, were mysteriously murdered in this house thirty-one years ago this very day. Tom and Louise knew it was the anniversary date of the murder and had planned this escapade for some time.

Louise walked over to Tom, grabbed him by the belt, and pulled him tight against her waist. Reaching up, she gave him a long passionate kiss, saying, "Let's do this thing, babe."

Tom looked down at her, grinning, "All the way, Lou. All the way."

The two strolled toward the house. The swing on its big wraparound porch swayed in the night wind with a foreboding squeak that only turned them on even more. As they stepped onto the porch, they smiled at each other and then opened the door. It was solid wood and heavy, but no challenge for Tom's strength. He pushed the door open, and they walked inside.

The room was dark except for the moonlight streaming through the broken glass windows. It was difficult to see much of anything except shadows of old furniture and pictures that still hung over the fireplace, just as the Oslows had left it thirty years ago. Louise laid the blanket on the floor and took her shirt off. Tom followed her lead. They planned on going for it right in the old house, defying every frightening story they had been told. Arrogance was their forte. They fell to the floor and embraced feverishly and passionately. Suddenly, Tom thought he heard footsteps coming down the stairs from the second floor. He turned his head to see what it was. Looking puzzled, Louise prodded, "Come on, babe. What's wrong?"

Then she heard it too. They both jumped to their feet. Tom looked up and saw a tall, dark figure descending the steps. Louise stepped back and let out a blood-curdling scream. Tom looked for something to use as a weapon, and, grabbing the fireplace poker, he stepped in front of Louise as they both stepped back towards the door.

The figure stopped at the landing and growled, "Well, look who we have here. I know you two very well." The voice was low and menacing, shaking Tom and Louise to their very core.

"You don't know us!" Louise shouted, her voice quivering. Clinging tighter to Tom.

"Oh, but I do, Thomas Stockshire and Louise Crowder. I've been watching you for some time. You are in *my* house now."

Though scared out of his mind, Tom still had enough arrogance to shout, "Oh yeah? Then come and get us, jackass!"

The figure floated towards Tom without touching the ground. In less than a second, it was in Tom's face. Tom swung the iron poker, but it passed right through the creature. Tom's eyes widened, and sweat sprang from every pore of his body.

Louise screamed and ran to the door, shouting to Tom, "What are you doing? Run!"

Tom felt himself lift off the ground. In an absolute panic, he flailed away at the dark figure in vain. Stunned, Louise bolted out the door and ran for the car. The creature let out a thundering roar and flung Tom headfirst into the brick wall above the fireplace. His body fell lifelessly to the floor. The creature moved to the door and let out a sound so awful that it shook the surrounding trees. Louise got to the car and began frantically locking every door by hand. Searching for the keys, she realized, in despair, that Tom had them in his pocket. Grabbing her handbag, she fumbled until she found her phone and shakily dialed 911.

"911. What is your emergency?"

Louise screamed into her phone, "Please help! We are being attacked!"

"Ma'am, I need you to calm down. Where are you?"

"We're at the old Oslow House off of Conway Street! I think it killed my boyfriend!"

"Ma'am, the police are on their way. What attacked you? Was it an animal?"

"I don't know what it was. It wasn't human!"

"Are you in the house now?"

"No. I'm in the car, but I don't have the keys." Louise looked toward the house and screamed into her phone, "Oh my God!"

"What is it? Are you still there? Ma'am?"

"It's coming! It's coming! Help me, please! Oh my God!"

The creature was standing outside her car door. It peered through the window, staring at her. Louise frozen in fear, her eyes locked with the creature's. Its eyes were like deep, dark, endless holes. Paralyzed with fear, she dimly heard the voice on the phone repeating the same question.

"Ma'am, are you there? Are you there?"

Louise raised the phone to her ear and said in terror, "Oh God—it's here. It's here..."

The 911 operator did her best to stay calm, but the pitch of her voice was getting higher and higher. "What's there? Tell me what's happening. The police are almost to you. Stay with me. Ma'am, are you there?"

There was no answer. Then a click, then silence—nothing but dead silence.

2

DARKNESS REVEALED

J ack Bennett sat at his desk, typing madly, surrounded by piles of papers and books. His monitor and keyboard, the only things visible in the middle of a mountain of clutter. He was working on his latest blog series, "The Growing Evil on Planet Earth," when his cell phone started vibrating at the corner of his desk. He looked at it and drew a deep breath. Not recognizing the number, he let it ring. Jack frequently got calls from local police departments and various government branches in DC to investigate unexplainable and mysterious activity, but rarely at this time of night.

It started ringing a second time. Against his better judgment, Jack picked up. He swung his chair around, facing a literal wall of books on subjects ranging from ancient Babylonian religions to the latest reports on present-day paranormal activity. Jack was a bibliophile. He didn't merely love reading books; he loved the smell of them. Some say the reason the smell is so appealing is that it has a hint of vanilla. The scientific explanation for the vanilla-like scent is that almost all wood-based paper contains lignin, closely related to vanillin. It releases chemical compounds into the air that mix to form a unique scent as it decomposes.

Jack thought it smelled like coffee... his second obsession. To be accurate, he had three obsessions. The third was the most important one, Jesus. In the middle of his library sat a large Bible. In fact, Jack had an entire shelf of Bibles of various translations and age from all over the world. This particular Bible contained hundreds of scribbled notes and comments that he had written over his many years of travel and research. It was his secret weapon. Taking a deep breath, Jack answered,

"Hello, this is Bennett."

"Jack, it's Frank. We need you to come down to the old Oslow House right away."

Frank Lederman was an FBI agent stationed in Washington, DC, assigned to the newly formed Paranormal Division. The nation's capital was a mere forty-five-minute drive from Jack's house, so he and Frank saw a lot of each other. Frank investigated paranormal activity, a new fascination in Washington. This night, the Blackstone, Virginia Police Department, needed him to look into a most unusual case.

"Frank, is this a new cell number? I almost didn't pick up. You realize it's 12:30 in the morning, don't you?" Jack retorted, sounding exhausted. "Whatever it is, can't it wait until the sun comes up?"

"No, it can't, and besides, I know you aren't sleeping. You're probably sitting at that mountain of former trees you call a desk, pounding away on your keyboard. This is a weird one, Jack, and I mean weird."

"Let me guess—more kids messing around at that old house again?" Jack quipped with a bored look on his face.

"Not quite. We have a homicide on our hands this time. Two young kids from Blackstone High—one dead and one in complete shock."

Jack spun around in his chair, resting his elbows on the pile of paper on his desk. He had heard countless rumors through the years about that house, but never took them too seriously. But murder got his attention big-time. "Okay, I'll be there in twenty minutes." He quickly changed his shirt, grabbed a bottle of water, and headed out the door.

Jack had just turned forty a couple of weeks before. At five feet eleven inches, he was not overly tall or handsome, but nice-looking. He kept himself in relatively good shape by playing softball when he had the chance. Jack had never married and wasn't really much for socializing. Not that he didn't enjoy the company of a woman. Over the years, there had been a couple of ladies, but there was no one special at present. For now, he was content to dedicate himself to his work, or as Jack liked to put it—his calling.

It was a short drive to the Oslows. Everyone in town knew the history of the old house and avoided it like the plague. Jack drove up the narrow driveway and parked next to one of the three police cars with their lights flashing. It was a sobering scene. Jack watched as the ambulance slowly pulled away with young Tom Stockshire lying lifeless inside. Jack had seen many strange things over the years, but he never got used to the death of anyone so young.

Frank walked up to him and urged, "Thanks for coming, Jack. You need to see this."

They made their way onto the porch and into the house. The main room was a buzz of activity. Large floodlights lit up the once dark and eerie room. A forensic team was hard at work, taking pictures and collecting evidence. Jack looked around and immediately noticed the blood on the brick wall above the fireplace and a large blood pool on the floor below.

He drew a deep breath. "Okay, what have you got so far?"

Frank tilted his head to the side. "Not much, the girl is the one who called it in. Apparently, she ran to the car and locked herself in but couldn't get away. We found the keys in the vic's pocket. She was in a nearly catatonic state when we got here. We found hair and fragments from the victim's scalp embedded in the brick above the fireplace. It appears he hit the wall with incredible force, then fell on the floor and bled out. Most likely killed on impact."

"Was the girl attacked physically?"

Frank shook his head. "No, but she's not able to talk. I mean, she's gone, like nobody home. We tried to get her to say something, but she just stared into space and kept repeating, He's coming. He's coming."

Jack leaned in and asked, "Who's coming?"

Frank gave him a look. "I don't know, Jack. If I knew, I wouldn't have called you."

Hmm, Jack thought. "Have you searched the rest of the house?"

"Yeah. Nothing."

Jack turned, looked around, and looked up. "This ceiling has to be at least ten feet high."

"Eleven to be exact," Frank remarked, revealing the tape measure in his hand.

"So, the question is—who or what would have had the strength to throw someone that hard and that high to cause that kind of damage?"

"Exactly. Plus, our vic was 6'3" and had to weigh at least 200 pounds. There are no bears around here, and no other marks on the body."

Jack instinctively felt something. He spun his head and studied the staircase. He sensed this was no ordinary murder case. Something supernatural and extremely evil had transpired here, and he was determined to find out what it was, but that would be for another day. He turned to Frank. "We need to talk to the girl as soon as possible. We need to know what she saw and find out who she thinks is coming. How about the 911 call? Do you have that?"

"Yeah, I've got it here on my phone. You're going to love this." Frank said cynically. "Give me a minute, and I'll play it for you."

Frank knew Jack well enough to recognize when he sensed something weird. "You feel something, don't you?" Frank shook his head. "Damn! I hate when you get that look on your face." Frank hit play. Jack knew what he was looking for—and then he heard it.

"We're at the old Oslow house off of Conway Street! I think it killed my boyfriend!"

"Ma'am, the police are on their way. What attacked you? Was it an animal?"

"I don't know what it was. It wasn't human!"

Jack looked up at Frank. "You're right. I need to talk to that girl. This is a strange one."

3

HEALING AND HOPE

The next morning, Jack drove to the hospital. He needed to speak to the girl. He had encountered something similar to this event the year before in upstate New York, and he was certain the second victim was right. Whatever attacked her boyfriend wasn't human.

He took the elevator to the third floor. The doors opened on the nurses' station. Approaching the desk, Jack introduced himself.

"Hello, my name is Jack Bennett. I am a special consultant for the FBI. I'm here to see Louise Crowder."

The nurse didn't have to check her list. Everyone on the floor knew what room Louise was in. The nurse replied, "You won't get much out of her. She's in pretty bad shape. Her parents are with her right now. I'll ask them if you can see her."

Jack nodded, but he knew nothing was going to keep him from

talking with the girl. He needed to see her face and look into her eyes. They would tell the story even if she couldn't.

The nurse stuck her head in the room, then stepped out into the hallway and motioned for him to come.

Louise's father, Steven Crowder, met Jack at the door. Mr. Crowder was the vice president of Halls Technology Group, a high-tech think tank that made most of its money in government contracts. He reached out and shook Jack's hand as he walked in.

The nurse did the introductions. "Mr. and Mrs. Crowder, this is Jack Bennett..."

Mr. Crowder interrupted. "Hello. Introductions are unnecessary. You're Jack Bennett, the consultant I've heard so much about. It's a pleasure to meet you, but I'm afraid Lou will not be much help. She is still unresponsive. The doctor says it is going to be a long road back."

"I understand," Jack said compassionately. "If you would allow me, I would like to have a minute with her. It's important to the case."

Sitting next to her daughter's bed, Louise's mother glanced at her husband and shook her head: "No!" Mr. Crowder walked over to his wife, and gently put his arm around her. "Let's give him a minute, honey. We will stand right outside the door. It will be all right."

Mrs. Crowder looked at Jack. "She won't even respond to us! You're wasting your time." She stood up and allowed her husband to lead her into the hallway.

Jack gently approached Louise. She was awake but appeared to be completely unaware of her surroundings. Her eyes remained fixed on the ceiling over her bed. Every muscle in her body frozen in fear. Jack reached out, touched her hand, and, in a calming tone, said, "Hi Louise. My name is Jack. I need to ask you a few questions, okay?"

Her eyes widened, and her head snapped to the left. She looked straight at Jack and responded in a low whisper. "He's coming. That's what it said. He's coming."

Jack sensed the Lord was touching her. He leaned a little closer. "Who is coming, Louise?"

Her eyes closed, then opened in a look of absolute terror. "The spirit of Babylon. He's coming."

Louise continued staring at him. The fear in her eyes told Jack all he needed to know. She glared at him, not blinking, not moving a muscle.

Jack knew very well what Louise meant. The spirit of Babylon was a biblical reference, meaning a spirit of rebellion. It was the one Jack had been writing about. This spirit had a long, ugly history starting with the rebellion in Heaven when Lucifer gathered a third of the angels attempting to overthrow God. Defeated and banished from heaven an eternity ago. Jack recalled several ancient scripts.

Isaiah 14:12-13 came to mind: "How you have fallen from heaven, O morning star, son of the dawn! You have been cast down to the earth, you who once laid low the nations! You said in your heart, I will ascend above the tops of the clouds; I will make myself like the Most High."

Jack recalled Ezekiel 20:14: "You were anointed as a guardian cherub, for so I ordained you. You were on the holy mount of God; you walked among the fiery stones blameless in your ways from the day you were created till wickedness was found in you."

Jack knew what he was up against. Louise was under the influence of a great evil. His heart broke to see this young girl so bound and distraught. Jack could not leave without asking the Lord to free her from the darkness that entombed her. He leaned in, took her hand,

and said in a low gentle voice, "Louise, I am going to pray for you. Okay?"

Louise didn't say a word. Her eyes fixed on him. Louise squeezed his hand tighter and tighter. The desperation in her eyes cut Jack to the heart. He had to be careful, but there was no way he was going to leave her in this state. Only Frank knew about Jack's secret weapon, and how he solved all the mysterious cases they assigned him to. If anyone else found out about it, they would label Jack as a religious freak and he would lose his position, along with the opportunities the government sent his way.

Jack looked up towards heaven and prayed, "Father, by the authority you have given me, in the name of Jesus, your son, I release this child from the bondage of evil and fear."

Suddenly, Louise sat up. Her eyes softened, then brightened. She looked around the room, then back at Jack. Louise gasped, took a couple of quick breaths, then grabbed onto Jack's arm and wept. She cried, "Thank you! Oh, my God! Thank you!"

Jack smiled and quickly responded, "Jesus loves you, Louise. Stay close to him."

Instantly, the hospital room door flew open and in came Mr. Crowder, with his wife right behind him.

Mrs. Crowder ran to Louise. "What happened? Are you all right?" Turning to her husband, she yelled, "I knew we shouldn't have left her alone!"

Louise, with tears streaming down her face, shouted, "Mom, Dad, I'm all right, I'm all right! This man prayed for me, and set me free! It's like a door opened up, and I walked out into the sunlight."

Upon hearing this, Mrs. Crowder turned around to thank the

mysterious man who had given her daughter back to her, but he was gone. She looked down and there on the bed was a small card. It read, "Who the son sets free is free indeed." John 8:36.

Jack got out of the elevator on the ground floor and headed for the parking lot. It wasn't necessary to hang around. God did the work, so how could he take any credit? Besides, he didn't want that kind of thing to get around just yet. He had to keep his secret agent status. He was on a mission, and nothing was going to get in his way, neither the seen nor the unseen.

4

HISTORY LESSON

C J's Street Café was a great place to get a quick bite and a strong cup of coffee. Frank Lederman loved CJ's because he could get out of the office, sit outside, and enjoy some fresh air while observing the people hustling by. It was a beautiful spring day with a light breeze and warm sunshine. The type of day that induces a heavy dose of spring fever.

Frank enjoyed reading people, and he was good at it. That's what made him such an excellent agent. He took a sip of his hot black coffee and patiently waited for his buddy Jack to arrive, hoping to hear some good news about his hospital visit.

He spied Jack walking leisurely down the street. Frank shook his head and smiled. He couldn't figure out how Jack remained so laid back and calm, even under the most bizarre circumstances. Jack pulled out a chair and sat down across from Frank. Smiling, he caught the eye of the server and placed his order.

"Hi there. Coffee, please, cream and sugar, and an egg bagel toasted with butter. Thanks."

Frank looked at him and teased, "You know, you should drink your coffee black. You ruin it with all that crap."

"You think? Maybe a little sugar would improve your disposition."

Frank lifted his cup in a mocking toast. "Hilarious! So, what did you find out? When we got there, the girl was so scared she couldn't talk at all. I hope you fared better."

"Well, it is as I suspected. Louise was right. The thing that attacked her boyfriend wasn't human. It was a demon."

Knowing Jack, Frank figured it would be something he didn't really want to hear about.

"A demon. Of course! What else could it have been?" Frank shook his head. "The girl actually spoke to you? Why am I surprised?"

"She's going to be fine. The creature told her that the spirit of Babylon was coming. It's a biblical reference to the spirit of rebellion that, according to my research, has been growing stronger since the early 1960s. Over the last ten years, it has grown exponentially."

Jack paused for a moment as the server arrived with his coffee and bagel.

"You know I hate this crap. It gives me the creeps." Frank was not a fan. "Why can't it be some madman that I can track down and put in the slammer? With you, it's always got to be a spirit or a demon or whatever. Geez, Jack—now what?"

Jack knew he had to get Frank back on familiar turf. "I need you to pull the file on the Oslows. I've got a feeling it starts there. What do you know about them?"

"It was before my time, but the story goes they were into some strange stuff. They belonged to some weird secret society called The Sons of Marod or Moorod or something like that."

Jack interrupted, "Could it be The Sons of Nimrod?"

"Yeah, that's it—Nimrod. The Sons of Nimrod. You've heard of it? Wait a minute." A big smile broke out on Frank's face. "Of course you have."

Jack was excited. "That explains a lot. The Sons of Nimrod are an organization based in the Middle East. They believe in a world without religion, a world where everyone is free to live any way they want, no rules, no boundaries. The Sons of Nimrod are waiting for a new world leader, one they believe is coming soon."

Frank motioned to the server for a refill. "I got a feeling I'm going to need more caffeine. So, who is this Nimrod character?"

"This is why you need to read the Bible. Nimrod was the first leader and king in recorded history. According to the ancient historian Josephus, Nimrod excited the people of his day to have contempt for God. He was the grandson of Ham, the son of Noah. He persuaded the people not to give God credit for their lives or contentment, but to believe that it was their own courage and intelligence that brought them happiness.

"Nimrod set out to build himself an empire. He began conquering cities and forming a tyrannical government. He intended to turn men from their fear of God into a constant dependence on *his* power. Nimrod declared he would get revenge on God if He should ever drown the world again. To do this, he would need to build a tower so high that the waters could not reach its top. He built the tower of Babel near ancient Babylon. He promised he would avenge his forefathers, destroyed by the flood.

"What is even more interesting in what the Jewish historian Josephus wrote is precisely what we find in the Gilgamesh epics. Gilgamesh also set up tyranny. He opposed God and did all that he could to get the people to forsake Him. Many believe Gilgamesh and Nimrod are one and the same. The name Nimrod probably has to do with the Hebrew word marad, meaning 'to be rebellious' or 'we will revolt.'

"Interesting, but what does that have to do with us?"

Jack took a sip of his coffee. He liked it hot. "They worshipped all these gods in ancient Babylon, and that's the meaning of what the demon told Louise. The Spirit of Babylon is returning."

Frank marveled at Jack's knowledge. He stared at him for a moment, then responded. "Wow! Why is it that every time I'm with you, I feel like I'm back in class at the university? So this Nimrod, or Gilgamesh guy, was a real person, and this organization believes he is coming back?"

"He was a real person. However, they don't believe he is the one coming back, but another that will walk in his footsteps."

The subject intrigued Frank. "The Sons of Nimrod, are they mentioned in the Bible?"

"No. No one is really sure when they got started. Some say the early 1700s."

"So, this demon thing that is or was in the Oslow House—you think it had something to do with their deaths?"

"Absolutely. I'm sure the Oslows did not know what they were getting into. They invited the demon in, and it killed them. I can't prove it, but I'm sure that's what happened."

"Okay, so now we're back to what?"

"Well, I have to pray about it, but it feels like the next step is to go back to the house."

"Back to the house and do what?"

"I'm going to have to confront this thing."

Frank had a bad feeling that Jack was going to say that. "Are you crazy? You can't go walking in there by yourself. Whatever that thing is, it just picked up a 200-pound kid and threw him across the room to his death."

"If I do, it will be God who confronts it. Don't worry about me. I'll give you a call tonight and keep you updated. In the meantime, please get me that file on the Oslows."

Frank shook his head in disbelief. "Ok... but I don't like it."

5

PROPOSITION AND PREPARATION

The local police station was jammed with the usual low-end criminals. The agency prioritized partnering with local police to help carry out investigations and assess local and regional crime threats. It was not unusual for Frank to walk in and out of the station. They knew him well and furnished him with a place to work when he needed it. Frank walked through the chaos, sat down at his desk, logged into the computer, and pulled up the Oslow files.

He began reading when he heard, "Hey, Frank! Where have you been, man? Long time, no see."

It was Donny Westleton. Not one of Frank's favorites. Donny was obnoxiously loud and excessively nosey. He thought of himself as a top-notch detective and a real ladies' man. He was neither.

Donny, looking over Frank's shoulder, snickered, "The Oslow file? What the hell are you looking at that for? You Feds thinking of going cold case on us or somethin'?"

Frank swung his chair around. "Just checking a few things out, that's all. A very interesting case."

"I wouldn't get too wrapped up in that one. That's one case better left alone. You know what I'm saying? Unless you're writing a book or somethin'?" Donny laughed out loud. "You writin' a book, Frank?"

"Don't you have a crime to solve?" Frank paused for a moment and then sarcastically finished, "... or somethin'?"

Donny shot him a quick chin flick and walked away.

Close by, Detective Heidi Macaulay stood listening intently. Heidi was thirty-five years old, five-nine, and extremely good-looking. She was a highly respected detective and had more street smarts than most, and—she had a thing for Frank. Heidi waited for the right moment and then slowly walked over to Frank's desk. She was trouble, in more ways than one.

"I couldn't help but hear Donny being his normal jackass self. Checking out the Oslow murders, huh? It's awful what happened to those two kids. Weird, right?"

Frank looked up at and thought, 'Wow! She looks great today, but then, she always looks great.'

Heidi had been after Frank ever since his divorce two years ago, and even before that, but Frank knew it would not be a good move to get involved with a fellow cop, especially Heidi. Clearing his throat, he said, "Yeah, very weird."

"Donny is annoying, but he might be right about this one. Some things are better left alone. It was thirty years ago. The guys who worked that case are long gone. From everything I've heard, it's nothing I'd want to get into."

Frank wondered, 'What's this all about? Something's not right. Why is everyone trying to push me away from this case?'

He didn't like the way it all felt. "Well, I'm not really getting into it. I'm just curious, that's all."

Heidi sat down on the corner of Frank's desk and leaned in, her long brown hair falling around her face, framing her incredible green eyes. "Wanna grab some lunch today? I got some time."

Frank took a deep breath and politely replied, "I have a ton of work to do, and besides, I don't really think that would be a good idea. You know people talk."

"Let them talk! They're gonna do it, anyway. So, what!"

"No thanks. I'm really buried."

Heidi stood up, straightened her dress. Making sure she gave Frank something to look at, while shooting him a look that could melt steel. "Maybe another time?"

Frank nodded and went back to work. Once she was out of sight, he took another deep breath, exhaled slowly and thought, 'Wow, I gotta get outta here.'

He pulled out a small USB drive, copied the Oslow file, put it in his pocket, and left. He needed to get that file to Jack ASAP. Only God knew what he was going to do next, and whatever it was, Frank wanted to be there.

* * *

It was 6:00 p.m. Jack had spent an hour in prayer. He relied on his conversations with God for wisdom, direction, and strength. He voiced his concerns, even though God already knew them all. The silence was sacred to him, a time to listen with mind, heart, and soul.

Jack knew beyond any shadow of a doubt that he was to confront and remove the demon from the house that it had called home for over thirty years. He grabbed his Bible off the desk and headed out the door. As Jack was getting ready to pull out, Frank roared up the driveway in typical FBI fashion. Jack got out of his car and stood with his arms folded, waiting. Frank meant well, but this was one task he needed to do alone.

"Hey! I got the thumb drive with all the Oslow files. Where are you going?" Before Jack could answer, he added, "Wait, are you going to the house?"

"Yeah, I have to take care of this. And Frank, I have to do it alone."

"Are you sure? You might need backup."

Not that Frank really wanted to be there. He had seen Jack do this kind of thing only once before. If he hadn't, maybe he would have pushed the issue further. But he had. Frank wasn't really a believer, but he acknowledged that an invisible world existed that he didn't understand, and Jack did.

"Don't worry. I wouldn't go if I didn't have backup."

Frank wasn't exactly sure what he meant by that, but knowing Jack; it had to be something to do with God. He tossed the USB drive to Jack, who gave Frank a reassuring nod, smiled, and headed off to do what God had called him to do—confront the demon at the Oslow House.

6
CONFRONTATION

The setting sun gave way to darkness as Jack pulled up in front of the Oslow House. He turned off the motor, sat there for a moment, and said a silent prayer. Jack opened up his Bible to a chapter he knew well, II Corinthians 10, and read verses three and four out loud.

"For though we live in the world, we do not wage war as the world does. The weapons we fight with are not the weapons of the world. On the contrary, the weapons we have been given have divine power to demolish strongholds."

Jack knew this was a major stronghold that needed to be torn down and destroyed. It had cost one naïve and rebellious young man his life. Jack knew this kind of evil had a broad influence and not limited to this one house, but affected the entire area. Strengthened by his faith and the gifts God had given him, he got out of the car and headed for the front door.

He slowly pushed the heavy wooden door open. Its old, worn hinges chanted a foreboding chorus of creaks and moans. Looking around, Jack felt a cold penetrating dampness emanating from the stairway that led to the second floor. He knew he wouldn't have to search for the Demon, for the Lord would draw the foul creature to him.

Suddenly, the air became heavy. Jack could feel the atmosphere changing. A thick gray mist slowly cascaded down the steps. Jack took a deep breath and prayed, Jesus, this is all you. A loud bloodcurdling scream shook the house and jolted Jack's senses. Then—there it was. The creature stood ten feet in front of him, hovering over the lower landing of the stairway. Jack's eyes grew wide, and his heart pounded in his chest. The creature's appearance was terrifying. The demon's eyes glowed reddish-orange, and its skin was like that of a lizard. It had two large black wings, with what appeared to be thin red lines similar to veins running through them. It glared at Jack, then reared back its ugly head. Opening its mouth wider than what seemed possible, let out a terrifying sound that started low and guttural and rose to a high pitch squeal that shattered the remaining glass panes in the windows. Jack knew it would do all it could to strike fear into his heart, hoping it would shake his faith and paralyze him, preventing him from completing his mission.

Jack felt a new strength coming over him, one he had come to rely on. Then it spoke. Its voice was defiant, deep, and raspy. "Jack Bennett! This is MY home. They invited here me, and here is where I'm going to stay! You can't move me. I am a prince, not like the others you have dealt with. I have dominion in this area."

Jack suddenly felt a new presence enter the room. It was powerful, and it was growing stronger by the second. Feeling his faith rise, Jack stood firm, and with renewed confidence, declared, "I did not come here on my strength, and I did not come here to talk, but to remove you from this place. In the name of the Lord Jesus Christ, the son of the living God, I bind your power. It is the Lord Himself who casts you from this place!"

At that, the demon let out a howl, the likes of which Jack had never heard before. In a violent rage, it circled the room, stopping right in front of Jack, inches from his face. Indignation radiated from its fiery eyes. In a desperate last attempt to hold its ground, the demon let out an anguished roar, then shrieked, "I am Gadreel! I will not be moved!"

Suddenly, Jack felt a surge of power. It was as if God himself was speaking through him. He glared at Gadreel and proclaimed, "Gadreel, in the name of Jesus Christ, the King of Kings and Lord of Lords, I command you to leave this place! To Gadreel's shock and amazement, he was no longer in control. He was instantly and fiercely plucked up, and in a flash, he was gone.

Jack stood stunned and alone in the middle of the pitch-black room. The silence was deafening. He wasted no time in getting out of the house. Taking his phone out of his pocket, he made his way to the door. His job completed. As soon as he got back in his car, Jack broke out into a cold sweat. Taking one more look at the house, Jack took a deep breath and silently thanked God for his faithfulness. He picked one of his favorite worship music and cranked it up.

Jack knew in his heart this was going to be a long fight, but for now, he rested in the peace and power of his God, and that was as sweet as it gets.

7

MEETINGS AND METHODS

S pringtime in Washington DC is always beautiful, especially with the National Cherry Blossom Festival, a tradition that showcases the beautiful gift of 3,000 cherry trees the city of Tokyo gave to the US Capitol. It is also when a secret society, the Sons of Nimrod, come together for their annual meeting. This time of year, DC was jammed with visitors, making it the perfect time for certain high-profile individuals to fly in for a quiet, clandestine meeting.

The Hotel Palomar was a six-minute walk from the DuPont Circle Metro Station and about two miles from the National Mall. It was the location where the society had met for the last twenty-five years. It had every amenity, including a private conference room that fit their purposes to a T.

Outside, in front of the hotel, a long black limousine pulled up. A door on each side of the limo opened, and two large men in black suits got out. They were typical federal agent types, the kind that looked like they could handle any situation. They quickly scanned the area, then opened the second set of doors. Two well-dressed men stepped out. The agents escorted them into the lobby of the Hotel Palomar.

Senators Ray Hollson and George R. Wellsenburg made their way through the lobby, oblivious to the beautiful artwork displayed on nearly every wall. At forty-eight, Hollson was the younger of the two, whereas Wellsenburg sixty-one, was a seasoned politician. Turning left, they walked through double doors and proceeded down the hall to the boardroom. Senator Wellsenburg was the last to enter. He gave his bodyguards a few last-minute instructions and then went in, shutting the door behind him. After a few cordial greetings, Wellsenburg addressed the group.

"Gentlemen, it is good to see all of you here today. It is also my pleasure to welcome two new members to the society. Richard Donlum, Vice President of Donlum Aircraft, and Roger Stillerman, CEO of Spacetech. Both are major financial contributors to our cause. Let us begin with a reminder of our purpose and goals. As the Sons of Nimrod, it is our mission to reduce the influence of religion, and mention of God, from government and the public square. It is our intent to facilitate the establishment of a new world order under one world leader."

Senator Wellsenburg took a sip of water and then continued, "Previous presidents had made promises 'to fundamentally transform the United States.' Although we have made some progress, there is still have much to accomplish. I'm sure we all feel a certain amount of satisfaction knowing that we are moving closer to transforming America into a more modern and secular society, a land where religion is only tolerated within the walls of a church or private establishment. Our ultimate aim is to expunge it from society."

At this, everyone in the room applauded vigorously. Wellsenburg smiled. "Senator Ray Hollson will now bring us up to date on our latest accomplishments."

Hollson pulled a file from his briefcase and set it on the table.

"Good evening, gentlemen. We have accomplished much in the last few years. I will present you with the highlights. After dinner, you will each receive a copy of the entire brief."

Wellsenburg gave him a nod, and he began.

"Since removing prayer from public schools on June 25, 1962, we have made some modest gains. We are moving quickly and decisively to introduce a worldwide digital currency that will not only eliminate the need for cash, but for the phrase 'In God We Trust' on our currency. As you are aware, the capitalized form in God we trust first appeared on the two-cent piece in 1864; printed on paper currency in 1957. A law ill-advisedly passed in July 1955 by a joint resolution of the 84th Congress and approved by President Dwight Eisenhower. We will also continue our campaign to remove offensive Bible references from all public and government buildings.

"In February 2009, we eliminated the conscience protections that allowed pro-life Christian doctors and nurses in federally funded hospitals to opt-out of performing abortions and other procedures they consider immoral.

"We are moving forward to remove the phrase 'endowed by their Creator' from the Declaration of Independence. Per our instructions, past presidents omitted it on at least seven different occasions."

"In February 2012, the Air Force removed the Latin word for God,

Deus, from the logo of the Rapid Capabilities Office, and also removed the Latin motto, which means 'doing God's work with other people's money.' The new logo reads, doing miracles with other people's money.' This is a small step, but is a step in the right direction."

Once again, all in attendance responded with rousing applause.

The senator continued, "Finally, we are always endeavoring to support and appoint judges that will propagate our ideas and vision. Thank you."

Senator Wellsenburg again stood up and addressed the group.

"Thank you, Senator Hollson. Before enjoying a wonderful dinner, I have asked one of our newer members, Dante Adal, to give us a few moments. He has some fascinating insight into how we might attain even greater success."

At the end of the table sat Dante Adal. Impeccably dressed in his flawlessly tailored Kiton $60,000 suit. Dante was a tall and lean man that few knew well. He had recently joined the society, and in that brief time, had provided more funds for the cause than anyone else. He was a successful entrepreneur from southern California with a mysteriously vague history, but was welcomed with open arms once they heard him speak. Those in attendance that day said there was something mystical, even mesmerizing, about him. Some used the word spellbinding.

Senator Wellsenburg instantly became Dante's biggest fan. He even suggested that he consider running for office. Someone with that kind of ability to influence would be invaluable to the society. Consequently, the good senator also enjoyed a rise in his stock investments and other holdings since he became involved with Mr. Adal. Wellsenburg's holdings now totaled $250 million, making him the wealthiest US senator. The many meetings aboard on Dante's private jet had mysteriously gone unnoticed by some on Capitol Hill. Those who had remained silent. Mr. Dante Adal proved to be very influential, indeed.

Dante got up and walked slowly and confidently to the small podium in front of the room. Wellsenburg shook his hand, and Dante turned to speak.

"My fellow Sons of Nimrod, I appreciate the opportunity to speak with you tonight. There is an element that would desire us to fail in our endeavors and who would rejoice to see our society abolished. This element of which I speak, you know all too well. I speak tonight of a certain sect of Christianity that believes their God has given them powers to oppose us and destroy our mission."

Dante took a moment to look around the room, his piercing eyes assessing each one in attendance. What he saw pleased him. All eyes were now fixed on him in great anticipation of what he was going to say next.

He continued, "As some of you know, I have certain gifts and abilities that enable me to sense when the ideals of our organization are being attacked. The threat to our society is real. It is a growing concern of mine. It is imperative we act now. I have a plan that will strike fear into the hearts of our enemies and discourage them from ever getting in our way again. Senator Wellsenburg invited me to share with you tonight and request your permission to implement that plan."

By now, Dante had every person in the room completely engrossed in his words. Dante glanced at Wellsenburg for final approval before detailing his plan.

"We face some of the same obstacles our namesake and coming

world leader, Nimrod, the descendant of Ham, experienced. They must be stopped! There are those I am affiliated with who, on my order, can hunt down and, shall we say, discourage our opposition. Because of their covert nature, they can operate in complete darkness, leaving no trace or trail that would lead back to us."

Roger Greystone, a long-time member and celebrated Free Thinker, raised his right hand slightly and caught Dante's attention. Greystone was a formidable opponent by human standards, but he did not know who or what he was dealing with this time.

"This seems to me to be an extremely dangerous enterprise. Who are these people you are referring to? What kind of experience do they have, and what assurances do we have that this won't blow up in our faces?"

Dante's face grew stern, and his eyes narrowed. He did not appreciate Greystone's questions or the tone in which he asked them, and would have made an example of him in front of everyone. But before Dante could answer, Senator Wellsenburg rose to his feet, "I can vouch for all Mr. Adal is saying. His associates are more than capable." The Senator had no idea who Dante's associates were, yet somehow he believed Adal could do whatever he claimed. Dante's demeanor slowly tempered. Collecting himself, he added, "I understand your apprehension, Mr. Greystone, but as the Senator stated, my associates can handle any situation that might arise. They have been doing so for, let's say," a frightening smile crawled across his face, "forever."

Greystone had no intention of letting this newcomer go on and on without a challenge. "With all due respect to the senator, I would like to know more details about this plan. How is this going to be accomplished? What type of discouragement are we talking about?

You used the term 'hunt down.' That hardly sounds like harassment or discouragement. To me, it sounds a bit more like assassination. What are we getting ourselves into here?"

At that moment, there were some in the room who believed they saw Dante's eyes turned an eerie, orangey-red, but it was so fleeting, each dismissed it as a reflection from the lights above the podium. Dante put both of his hands flat down on the podium and leaned forward, his eyes fixed on Greystone.

"Some things are better left unsaid, don't you think, Mr. Greystone? Let's call it plausible deniability. However, you seem to have many questions the others do not have, so maybe we should meet one-on-one after the meeting, and I will endeavor to answer your questions."

Senator Hollson, like Wellsenburg, eager to see the Sons of Nimrod move forward, took the bait, not knowing what Dante was capable of. Wellsenburg's charismatic guest speaker had spun his web and his victims were powerless. He quickly stood up, walked over, and shook his hand. "Thank you, Dante." Looking around the room, he asked, "Are there any more questions?" Hollson scanned the gathering, waited a few more seconds, then said, "Is there a motion from the floor to take a vote?"

Several hands went up. "Mr. Donlum?

"Yes, Senator Hollson. I so move."

"Thank you. Do we have a second?"

"Thank you, Mr. Waverly. We have a second. By a show of hands, how many vote to move forward with Mr. Adal's plan of action?"

A quick look around the room told Greystone that he was the only dissident, so he reluctantly joined the others. He hated Adal for many reasons, but predominantly for taking his spot as the Society's most influential voice.

"It is unanimous. Well done! I am sure we are all ready for some dinner, so let's enjoy the rest of the evening."

Senator Wellsenburg turned to Dante. "When will you contact your people?"

Dante locked eyes with him and firmly replied, "It is already done."

8

STRANGERS

The early morning sun bathed Jack in its warmth as he sat on his old-style wraparound porch, coffee in hand. It was a beautiful morning. He could still feel the touch of God on him from the night before. There was nothing to compare it to. God had used him to cast a demon prince out of the town of Blackstone. The air seemed lighter, and the birds sang louder. There was an obvious change in the atmosphere.

Jack took another sip of coffee and checked his podcast stats on his phone. His new series, "The Growing Evil on Planet Earth," was getting a lot of attention - ten thousand listens this week alone. Jack opened his favorite news app. He liked to keep up with world events, especially in the Middle East. It served only to underline what he already knew was coming. His phone rang.

"Can't a man have a few moments to himself?"

Frank joked, "All you have is time to yourself. We need to meet. I need an update on the case. I have a report to write, you know. Besides, we have a new event."

"A report! You've got to be kidding."

"Yeah, you know how it goes. We've got it logged in as a paranormal event, so they want your report. You want to get paid, don't you?"

"Frank, you know how I feel about getting paid for what I do. I don't do it for the money."

"You know that, and I know that. Look at it this way—you get to do what God wants you to do and pay your bills at the same time! You're always saying that God will provide, so there you go."

"Oh, so now you're quoting me! You know I donate most of that money, right?"

"That's your business, my friend. My business is to get the report and keep everybody happy."

Jack smiled, "Fine. CJ's in an hour?"

"That's what I'm talking about."

Jack swallowed his last sip of coffee and went inside to change. He needed to write a few notes for this evening's podcast.

Forty-five minutes later, he was on his way to meet Frank when he saw a young man walking along the road with his thumb out, looking for a ride. Jack liked to pick up hitchhikers. It allowed him to share his faith. He pulled the car over, rolled down the passenger side window, and hollered out, "Where you headed?"

The young man looked over and said, "Just up a ways."

Jack responded, "Jump in! I can give you a lift into town if that works."

The young man smiled and got in the car. As they started down the road, Jack immediately sensed something very unusual about this hitchhiker. The young man sat staring at him with a wide, radiant smile on his face. Jack felt a little uncomfortable. Finally, he glanced over at him and introduced himself. "My name is Jack. Beautiful day, huh?"

"Yes, very nice. I can sense a different, let's say a spirit, in the air today."

That got Jack's attention big time. 'A different spirit in the air?' He thought, 'Okay, let's take this a little further.' "It has a lighter, brighter feeling to it. The Lord is good."

The young man smiled and said, "Yes. The Lord IS good, Jack Bennett."

Jack's eyes widened. "Hey, how do you know my last name? Do you listen to my podcasts?"

"We know all about you, Jack. You're famous where I come from."

Jack laughed. "Oh yeah, and where would that be?"

"I don't have time to get into that right now. I have a message for you from the Lord."

Jack thought, 'a message? Who does this guy think he is? A prophet?'

The young man continued, "The days are getting darker. You must be on guard. Forces on the rise that wish to suppress and throw the truth of God's Word to the ground and trample on it. Even now, they are gathering and preparing to destroy the faith of God's people through fear and despair."

Every word the young man spoke pierced Jack's heart. There was no doubt in his mind that this was coming from the Lord. Jack questioned him, "How do you know this?"

"You are highly favored, Jack Bennett. Do not fear. All will be revealed to you. For now, you only need to know that it is true. You must gather men and women of like faith to pray and ask God for help. If you do, God Almighty will fight this battle for you, but you must not delay."

Jack's heart was pounding in his chest. His mind was racing. "I want to believe you, but I don't know who you are or where you're from. Who am I supposed to contact? I'm not sure how to proceed."

"Right now, you are on your way to meet your friend. While you are there, a woman will come up to you wearing a gold cross around her neck and a gold ring with a dove on it, and ask if you are Jack Bennett. She is the one who will help you. The favor of God is upon her. Listen to her, for I have told her about you."

Jack could hardly believe what was happening. He finally asked, "What's your name?"

"My name is not important. Do what I have told you, and victory will be yours. You must occupy until He comes."

Jack turned his head, and the young man was gone. Jack's heart leaped in his chest. 'Dear sweet Lord! He was an angel. I just talked to an angel!'

He could hardly drive. He glanced at the passenger seat at least half a dozen times. His heart was racing. 'Frank is going to freak out when I tell him this one.' What about this mysterious woman he was supposed to meet? Jack let the events of the last couple of days roll over in his mind. 'What is happening, Lord? I am humbled by your presence in my life.'

* * *

Jack found a parking spot right in front of CJ's. He was so excited he didn't know what to do with himself. He couldn't move fast enough, nearly falling over his own feet getting out of the car. Frank, sitting at his favorite table, had an unobstructed view of Jack's entrance. He began shaking his head and thought, 'Now what?' Never wanting to miss an opportunity to take a poke at his old friend, he quipped, "Drinking already? I thought you didn't do that kind of thing anymore?"

Jack, slightly out of breath, sat down across from Frank, ignoring his comment. Emily Richardson, their regular server, saw Jack come in and went over to their table. Emily knew them both.

"Hello, Mr. Bennett! Are you ok?"

"Ah—yes Emily, I'm fine. How—how are you?"

"I'm fine, thank you. I like that shirt you're wearing. It's very nice." Emily paused, then asked, "So, what can I get for you today?"

"I need a large cup of coffee, Emily. Oh, and thanks! It's not really new or anything, but thanks anyway."

Jack waited until she left and said, "You will not believe what just happened to me."

Frank laughed out loud. "You're kidding, right? You just had it out last night with some kind of demon-creature thing. What the hell could be more bizarre than that? And by the way, that girl likes you—and she's a Christian. You're always telling me you would only date a Christian, so..."

Jack, half-listening, stunned and a little annoyed, said, "What? Emily? You're crazy! Besides, she's ten years younger than me." He couldn't believe Frank went there. He had something out-of-this-world to share, and Frank wasn't listening. Jack took a deep breath and collected himself. "I can't talk to you about that now. I've got something to tell you that will blow your mind."

Just then, Emily brought Jack's coffee and put it on the table. "Is there anything else, Mr. Bennett?"

"No, thank you, not right now."

Emily made eye contact with him and held it just long enough to let him know she was interested. She gave him a big smile. "Okay! Just let me know if you need anything."

Jack nodded politely; he was completely oblivious to it all. As Emily walked away, a big grin grew across Frank's face.

Jack gave him his famous if-looks-could-kill stare and said, "Just shut up."

Frank laughed. "Okay, so what's this mind-blowing news?"

"Well," Jack paused and re-adjusted his chair. Leaning in, he said, "I have to warn you, this might sound a little over the top, even for me."

Frank interrupted, "You're killing me. This is getting painful. Please, just spit it out."

Jack cautiously looked around. "I was just talking to an angel."

Frank just sat there, staring at him with a blank look on his face. "What? Like a real-life-heaven-type-angel?"

Jack could hardly contain himself. He began talking faster. "Yeah, like a real-life-heaven-type-angel. I was on my way here, and I saw this guy hitchhiking along the side of the road, so I stopped and gave him a ride. He seemed to know all about me. He told me some powerful evil was coming, and I had to get people praying to overcome it, and if I did, God would come and fight for us."

Frank's head was spinning. He had experienced a lot of what he called, "wild and crazy Jack stuff," but this? Seeing and talking to angels? Frank put his elbows on the table and, resting his chin on his hands, said, "Look, hanging with you these last few years has taught me that anything is possible. I trust you, buddy. Really. But maybe this entire episode last night has got you looking for things that aren't there. You know what I mean?"

"Frank, there is nothing wrong with me. I've never felt better. I saw what I saw, okay? What's the problem? I know Jews believe in angels."

"Yeah, a couple a thousand years ago, maybe. Okay, okay." Frank folded his arms and leaned back in his chair. "What did he look like? Did he say anything else?"

"He looked like a regular guy. Here's the clincher. He knew I was coming here to meet you. He told me when I got here; a woman would come up to me and ask if I was Jack Bennett. He also said she would have a gold cross around her neck and a gold ring with a dove on it. She is the one who will help me."

Frank looked unnerved. "Let me get this straight. The angel knew you were coming to meet me? Did he say my name?"

Jack breathed deep. "No, he didn't say your name, but he knew you were my friend."

Frank, still not convinced, thought a second, then said, "I don't know, Jack. No one has come up to you yet. Did he say how long you had to wait?"

"No, but I haven't been here that long. I'm not losing it. Trust me."

Frank motioned for the check. "I wish I could stay, but I gotta go. I hope she shows up, whoever she is. I have a meeting in an hour in the D.C. office. Not to get off the subject, but I need that report today. I don't need my boss chewing me out again."

"Yeah, okay. I think I'm going to wait here a little longer. You know, just to be sure."

Jack caught Emily's eye. He raised his coffee cup slightly. She nodded with a smile. Frank stood up to leave, took one step, and froze. Jack, seeing the look on his face and was about to turn when suddenly, a woman's hand gently fell on his shoulder. He pivoted. Then he saw it. The ring with the image of a dove.

He looked up at her. She was about fifty years old, nicely dressed, and, around her neck, was the gold cross, just like the angel told him, but it wasn't only the ring and the gold cross that grabbed Jack's attention. It was her eyes. They sparkled with incredible joy. She looked at him apologetically and said, "Please excuse me for interrupting, but I need to know, are you, Jack Bennett?"

Frank stood there in shock and disbelief. He took hold of the back of his chair, slid it out, and sat back down, his eyes locked in on the mysterious scene playing out in front of him.

Jack responded, his heart pounding. "Yes, I'm Jack Bennett. Who are you?"

"My name is Conni Riser," she said with a smile. "I was told to come here and ask for you by..." she paused for a moment, feeling rather nervous and somewhat embarrassed.

The pause was just long enough for Jack to say, "An angel?"

The woman exhaled and broke into a wide smile. "Yes! Yes, an angel. You saw him too?"

"Yes, he told me you would come and what to look for. Where are you from?"

"I lead a large prayer meeting in High Point, about twenty miles from here. We have been praying for you without really knowing who you were. I guess we have a lot to talk about."

Slowly coming out of his daze, Frank excused himself. "I really have to go."

Jack stood up. "Oh, sorry! Conni, this is my good friend, Frank Lederman. He is a special agent with the federal government."

"Hello, Mr. Lederman. Nice to meet you."

Frank, in a haze of disbelief, said, "Nice to meet you, Mrs. Riser. Please sit down. You can call me Frank."

"Mrs. Riser makes me feel old. Conni works fine for me as well."

Frank stood stunned and motionless. With a look of amazement, he said, "Okay, then. I'll talk to you later."

Jack gave him a halfhearted wave and turned his attention to Conni. They started talking immediately. Frank started down the sidewalk, got about twenty feet, pulled his phone out of his jacket pocket, and began frantically waving it in the air for Jack to call him.

Frank, walking away, said to himself, 'You gotta love that guy!'

9

MARDUK

It had been a long flight back to Los Angeles from his meeting with the Sons of Nimrod in Washington. Dante hated flying, at least in the conventional way, but he knew it was a necessary nuisance, at least for now. He stayed busy during the flight back, confirming his plans for the next phase. Now that he was back at his desk, there was much to do. He loved sitting in his luxurious office suite, stories above downtown LA. The City National Plaza, a twin tower skyscraper complex on South Flower Street, provided the view he was most used to. The rent was exorbitant, but that didn't matter to Dante, because he had income streams from many sources, including those not of this world. There wasn't a pie he didn't have his finger in, and his connections didn't end there. The worlds he dabbled in were far more interesting than any mortal could imagine. In fact, he had invited a long-time associate to meet him in his office this morning. He also had a long flight. Dante leaned back in his chair and patiently waited for his guest to arrive. He did not have to wait long, for he could now feel the atmosphere changing all around him. A pleasant and familiar feeling, he thought.

Dante swung his chair around, anticipating his associate's entrance. A murky mist filled the room. It twisted and turned around every piece of furniture, falling like a curtain over the large glass window behind Dante's cherry wood desk. Ghostly streams of light pierced the green, swirling mist, creating an ominous, nightmarish scene. Followed by the sound of moist bits of leather unfolding. The mist separated around the figure, revealing his ten-foot frame. The tips of his jet-black wings brushed ever so slightly against the ceiling. His large, yellowish cat-like eyes moved left to right as he scanned his unfamiliar surroundings.

"Marduk, welcome to the city of angels," he said with a smirk.

"Dante." His voice was deep and throaty, a menacing sound to most, but one Dante gladly welcomed.

"I am eager to hear the updates from Europe and the Middle East. How are things in Geneva at CERN?"

As if stretching, Marduk rotated his head from one side to the other. "Shiva the Destroyer is monitoring that. It was so good of them to put his image right in front of the building. Mortals are so compliant."

"We are making progress in the Middle East, I see."

"Things are going well for us there. That pot is so easy to stir. Our plans to inspire an Arab invasion of Israel are moving forward nicely. We are making headway in many places in the EU." Marduk paused. "Something alarming has occurred right here in the United States. There has been an angelic incursion."

Dante, disgusted but not surprised, said, "Let me guess. Uriel, The Light of God?"

Marduk winced. The mere mention of his name was painful. "Yes, he has appeared to two humans."

"What was said?"

"We do not know, but there's something else. A believer named Jack Bennett has forcefully removed Prince Gadreel from the Oslow house in Blackstone."

The news jolted Dante to his very core. He slammed his fist down on his desk in a fit of rage. Normally, he sensed such things. That he hadn't enraged him all the more.

"What! How can that be? We haven't seen that kind of faith in a long time. He must be stopped. We can't afford to have that spread to the others."

Attempting to pacify him, Marduk offered, "You could not see it coming, because there was a prayer cover over him, and I fear it is growing stronger."

"You fear! Fear is what WE should put into THEM!"

Dante could barely control himself. He knew this could put a kink in his plans and his ability to influence the Society. Although his promise to them was merely a sidebar to his overall goal and strategy.

Marduk's eyes glowed brighter. "Do you want me to go to Blackstone tonight, My Prince?"

"No, not now. It's too dangerous. First, we must discourage the prayer warriors. As long as they keep praying, we are vulnerable. We must create roadblocks at every turn. We must do all we can to hinder them from getting together. I will send the spirits of pride and envy. They have proven to be very dependable in these situations. After all, humans do such a wonderful job of tearing each other apart, don't you think?"

Marduk bowed his head in compliance. "Will that be all, My Lord?"

Dante sat back in his chair, looking out over the city. "Yes—for now. Return to Syria. You are doing well there. You and the others must continue influencing and inspiring the weak and high-minded. There is so much more we need to accomplish."

Marduk bowed his head, then slowly wrapped his wings around his ten-foot frame. His large glowing eyes peered through the darkness. In one violent motion, he spun around and vanished. Like a dark grey robe, the trailing mist disappeared behind him. In a moment, all was back as before. Dante Adal sat down in his chair and stared out at the city. Planning—always planning.

10

BLOGS AND BECKONINGS

It was six o'clock in the morning, and Jack was already hard at work. He was busy banging out Part Two of his blog series, "The Growing Evil on Planet Earth." He would have loved to share his experience with the angel, but he knew better. That would have to wait for another day. 'Maybe Part Twenty?' he thought with a smile. His mission to reach as many people as possible with the truth about paranormal activity had only begun.

The Spirit of Lawlessness and Rebellion

By: Jack Bennett

We read in II Thessalonians 2:3-7 that a spirit of lawlessness and rebellion is coming. It reads: "Don't let anyone deceive you in any way, for that day will not come until the rebellion occurs and the man of lawlessness is revealed, the man doomed to destruction.

For the secret power of lawlessness is already at work; but the one who now holds it back will continue to do so until he is taken out of the way."

The Greek word for rebellion is apostasia, and is the source of our English word apostasy. It means the defection from the truth or falling away from the truth.

In our world today, there is a great rebellion underway. Our country is moving further and further away from the truth. But the genuine issue is about us—you and me. Where are we in all this? Evil is rising all over the world. Are we praying? Do we believe in prayer anymore? Does prayer work, or is it just a desperate attempt to console us when nothing else works?

Terrorist groups are getting more ruthless, their attacks more brazen. After one extremist group dominates the news with threats of attacks, another one surfaces with a different, more harrowing claim.

Then there's the ever-present threat of al-Qaeda, the brutality of Boko Haram, and the looming Taliban. Did you know the United States has a list of 59 designated terror groups?

The family is under attack in new ways. Our children are at risk, and violence is on the rise. The enemy knows if he can indoctrinate the up-and-coming generation to his ways, he can change the world.

Folks, we need to pray. Prayer moves the hand of God. Join me, and let's commit to asking God to help us tear down the strongholds of evil worldwide and in our own country.

The apostle Paul tells us we have the power to demolish evil strongholds, so let's get together and make a difference. Yes, prayer works. The problem is not God—it's you and me.

Through it all, we need to live and love like Jesus. In an ever changing world, we need to be people of faith. We need to get better, not bitter.

Until next time,

Jack Bennett

Jack hit the enter key, posted the update. His face was still glowing from his meeting with Conni—it was beautiful and uplifting. He was looking forward to meeting her prayer group that evening. They prayed for him when they didn't even know who he was or what he was about to face. The way the Holy Spirit leads and guides His people to pray amazed him.

On the flip side of things, he had been thinking about what Frank had said about the server at CJ's, Emily. He had kept himself so busy that he never gave dating much thought. The idea scared him out of his mind. There had been a few women over the years, but certainly nothing serious. There was one he deeply loved. They were engaged until one cold rainy night fifteen years ago a drunk driver took her out of his life for good. After that, he buried himself in his work. His heartache led him down a path he might have never found. It brought him to a place of revelation, where the Lord was waiting to heal and restore him.

Jack knew what prayer could do, and he was determined to teach the truth to anyone who would listen. Including Frank, though until now, he had had little success. 'Emily?' he thought, 'Huh, I wonder.'

Jack let his mind wander, but it was short-lived. His cell phone jolted him back to reality. It was Frank.

Jack answered, "Hey, Frank. What's up?"

"Hey, did you have time to look at those files I gave you?"

"Oh, no, I didn't. Sorry. I'll look right now. I just finished updating my blog, so check it out."

"Okay, let me know what you think. The Oslows were into some bizarre stuff, man. I'm talking off the wall. And hey, you never told me how things went with that lady, Conni. How weird was that? I'm sorry I didn't believe you at first. You must admit, talking with angels sounds pretty wild. I'll tell you Jack—you get involved with the weirdest shi-stuff."

Frank always tried to cut down a little on his cursing when talking with Jack. Jack never mentioned it; it was just something Frank felt compelled to do.

Jack smiled, "No worries. I still can't believe it. You don't hear that kind of thing too often. Right? Anyway, I am heading over to High Point tonight to meet with her prayer group."

"Are you gonna tell them about the angel and all that demon stuff?"

Jack laughed out loud. "I'm not sure exactly. I'll have to see how the Lord leads."

"Well, that should make for an interesting evening."

As they were talking, Jack saw something in the files that caught his eye. Halfway down the second page, the report stated that Mr. Oslow had meetings with Senator Wellsenburg in DC on several occasions. The last time they met was two days before he and his wife were found dead in their home.

After a few seconds of silence, Frank picked up on the fact that Jack was preoccupied. "Are you still with me?" he asked.

"Yeah, I was reading this. What's up with the connection between the Oslows and Senator Wellsenburg?"

"Not sure. Do you think he is part of the same secret society? They had no other connection according to the report, no business or personal ties that anyone discovered. Wellsenburg was a rookie senator. He was barely thirty years old. Of course, now he is one of the most influential members of the Senate."

"Why wasn't that checked out?"

"I'll look into it, but it won't be easy. Wellsenburg is pretty well insulated. I'm sure I will hit a ton of roadblocks along the way."

Jack smiled and urged, "That's never stopped you before."

Frank laughed. "True, my friend, true. I'm heading back to Washington today anyway, so I'll see what I can find out. You still owe me a breakfast at CJ's, remember! Let's get together tomorrow morning, say 9:00 a.m. I should be back by then."

At the mention of CJ's, Emily's face came into view. He wondered, 'Wow, where did that come from?'

"Sure, I can do that. We'll have plenty to talk about."

"Okay, good. See you then."

11

THREATS

It was 7:30 p.m. when Jack pulled up to Liberty Church, a historic wooden building surrounded by woods. The landmark building built in 1812, empty for over fifty years, was now enjoying a spiritual renovation. When they first met, Conni told Jack how God would speak to her about leading a prayer meeting there that would tear down strongholds and lead many to Christ. She was about to find out how.

Jack pulled into the parking lot. He thought about the deep-rooted history woven in and through the old church. At one time, God moved mightily here, and now it was happening again. He made his way up the steps where Conni and some of her prayer team met him with open arms.

"Welcome, Jack! So good to have you here tonight! Everyone is excited to hear from you." Conni motioned to one of her friends, "Patty, this is Jack Bennett, the man I was telling you about."

"It is a pleasure to meet you, Jack. I've heard so much about you already. I feel like we are old friends."

Jack extended his hand. "Patty, so nice to meet you. Thank you for all your prayers. I am overwhelmed and humbled."

"It is exciting. God is moving in our midst. We meet downstairs in the fellowship hall. We'll get started in a few minutes."

"Looking forward to it."

Jack was feeling a little nervous as he followed them downstairs. It was a large room, sixty feet wide by seventy-five long. Conni had set up fifty folding chairs in the middle of the room on the old-style black and white vinyl tile floor. There were several tables set-up with refreshments. Coffee, tea, and some homemade baked goods. There were three small basement windows on each side, and double doors all the way in the back that led to the rear parking lot.

Jack was more comfortable writing or recording his podcast than speaking in public. He wasn't one to shout and jump around. He just spoke normally and let the Lord do the rest.

Conni opened in prayer, then introduced Jack. "Tonight, I am blessed to have a special guest who has an important message for all of us. Please welcome my friend and author, Jack Bennett."

Jack received a warm welcome. The group consisted mostly of women. Jack estimated the average age to be fifty. He was pleased to see several young people in the group. In Jack's experience, attendance at prayer meetings usually topped out at ten or twelve. Jack knew God had used dedicated women of prayer to accomplish His purposes down through history. The origins of the World Day of Prayer dates back to the 19th century. It originated with Christian women from the United States and Canada.

"Thank you so much. It is a true honor to share with you tonight. First, I would like to thank all of you who prayed for me over the past few weeks. When Conni told me, it blessed me to no end. Thank you for being sensitive to the Holy Spirit. Only God knew what I was going to face and what I would need. He is so faithful."

"To see so many dedicated to prayer is amazing. Prayer moves the hand of God. If we wish to be blessed and victorious, we must continue to seek the Lord. What I have to tell you tonight is difficult to hear and, I suppose, to believe. Yesterday, on my way to meet a friend for breakfast, I saw a man hitchhiking. Now, I don't recommend any of you ladies doing this, but I have made it a practice to give hitchhikers a ride when possible to speak to them about the love of God. Except this one was very different. This hitchhiker turned out to be—an angel."

The reaction was mixed. Some "oohs" and "ahs," others stared at Jack as if he had two heads.

Jack pressed on, "I know you don't hear that kind of thing every day, but I can assure you it is true. Remember the book of Hebrews 13:2, 'Do not forget to entertain strangers, for by so doing, some people have entertained angels without knowing it.' It was an experience I will never forget. The most vital part of what I am about to tell you is what the angel told me. He said the days were getting darker, and we must be on guard. There are forces rising that wish to suppress and throw the truth of God's Word to the ground and trample on it. Even now, they are gathering and preparing to destroy the faith of God's people through fear and despair. The angel told me to gather people of like faith together to pray. The Lord desires to move among us, but we must be obedient to His call. Although the times are changing, there are many who need Christ. We must never forget our mission. If God is for us, who can be against us?

At that, all in attendance stood to their feet and applauded in agreement. Jack knew it wasn't for him, but praise unto the Lord.

As Everyone sat back down, Jack noticed two people standing in the back of the room. He had a feeling they weren't part of the group. They kept to themselves and carried on a conversation, whispering to one another the whole time he was speaking. It was clear they disapproved of what was happening. Jack planned on asking Conni about them afterward.

Jack continued with renewed vigor. "Who are these forces? The apostle Paul said it best." 'Our struggle is not against flesh and blood, but against the rulers, against the authorities, against the powers of this dark world, and against the spiritual forces of evil in the heavenly realms.'

"These dark rulers are infiltrating our world at every level. We see the horrific acts of terror in America and worldwide, but this is only the beginning. We have failed as the people of God in doing battle on our knees, but it is not too late. It is, however, all-out spiritual warfare that is needed. Some have folded their hands in defeat; others are barely hanging on, desperately waiting for the Lord's return. I can only echo the words of Jesus himself—'Occupy until I come.' The issues we face are not political but spiritual. We cannot defeat the enemy with clever speeches and new laws. Only prayer can win this battle. We cannot do it on our own.

"Remember the words of the Apostle Paul. 'I know what it is to be in need, and I know what it is to have plenty. I have learned the secret of being content in any and every situation, whether well fed or hungry, whether living in plenty or in want. I can do all things through Christ who gives me strength.' "

Jack panned the audience, checking the reaction of the two mystery observers. "I have faced these forces before, and they are formidable, but through the power of God, we can and will prevail. We must never forget, Jesus is Lord of all!"

Applause broke out all around the room.

Conni led the group in a worship song before prayer. As soon as the group started singing, the two visitors headed for the back door. Jack needed no special insight or gift to see they were up to no good. He would find out soon enough. For now, Jack's only desire was to enjoy worship and join everyone in prayer.

* * *

After prayer, everyone stayed for refreshments, eager to talk with Jack about his experiences, specifically the visit from the angel. Conni was so pleased. "That was wonderful. Your message inspired and energized everyone. I know I am truly blessed."

"Thank you. I hope so. We need as many people praying as possible." Jack glanced at the doors in the back of the room. "Who were those two people standing in the back?"

"I noticed them as well. I have never seen them before."

"They appeared to be a little out of sorts, if you know what I mean."

Conni looked around the room, "Phyllis—she knows everyone around here. Hold on. I'll get her."

Conni motioned to Phyllis. She made her way over to where Jack and Conni were standing, coffee cup in hand. "Phyllis, Jack asked me about the two people standing in the back tonight. Do you know them?"

"Oh yes, I believe they are on the historical committee. They handle how Liberty Church and other historic buildings in the county get used. I thought it rather strange that they were here, because—how should I put this? They're really not religious people, if you know what I mean." Phyllis, realizing how that may have sounded, quickly added, "Not that they couldn't be. I mean, everyone is welcome here."

Jack put Phyllis at ease. "No, you're right, Phyllis. I don't believe they approved of what was going on. They looked a little perturbed to me."

"If that's true, we might be in a bit of trouble. They have a lot of sway in the county."

Conni looked a little concerned, but kept her composure. "God called us here. I know that for sure. We need to keep praying and believe it will all work out."

"Conni, thank you for inviting me. I will keep you and the group in prayer."

"God bless you Jack."

Jack left through the double doors at the back of the room. When he got to the top of the steps, he saw two people off in the distance talking. It was the same two people from downstairs. It was difficult to see with only four old, dimly lit streetlights hanging over the parking lot, but it was them. A man and a woman. Once they saw Jack, they moved quickly, meeting him at his car.

"Mr. Bennett, we have a serious matter we would like to discuss with you."

Jack looked them up and down, checking for a weapon. Working with Frank taught him always to be aware and suspicious.

"You have me at a disadvantage. A serious matter, you say? And who are you...?"

"Our names are not important. What is important is that the people we represent do not want to see you here again. You are an instigator. A trouble maker if you will, Mr. Bennett. Your kind is not welcome here."

"Really? What is my kind, and who exactly is it I'm making trouble for?"

"I believe you know what we are talking about. The people we represent are powerful. You don't want to piss them off, Mr. Bennett. It would be very unwise. Besides, you wouldn't want anything to happen to your new friends here in High Point, would you?"

Jack's eyes widened. He wanted to rip into both of them. Suddenly felt a presence he recognized and had dealt with many times before. He needed to be careful and to answer wisely. Then again, a little sarcasm couldn't hurt.

"That's quite a threat coming from the historical society. Is this common practice in this area, or should I feel special?"

Their eyes grew wide, then narrowed. The woman snidely replied, "So, you know who we are?"

Jack glared at them and said, "In more ways than you know."

"We are fully aware of who you are and what you do. So, I suggest you be very careful from now on. Bad things can happen to good people."

"Well, I guess you guys have nothing to worry about then," Jack replied with a smirk. Jack could be very sarcastic. He wasn't perfect. God was still working on him. In this case, the temptation was too great. "Hey, I really would love to stay and chat, but I have an appointment with Jesus when I get back. You've heard of Him, haven't you? Lord of Lords? King of Kings? You know, all that kind of stuff. I would say have a good night, but why bother with formalities when you're making threats, right?"

Jack opened the door of his car, got in, rolled down the window. "You guys really need to read the Bible. It doesn't work out well for you. I would seriously consider switching sides. If either of you should decide to change your mind, I suppose you know how to reach me." Jack gave them a sharp grin and pulled out of the parking lot. The mysterious couple clothed in darkness stood there speechless, watching Jack drive away. Once Jack got a mile down the road, he took a deep breath. A bead of sweat formed on his forehead. Jack thought, 'Never let the devil see you sweat.' He started his meeting with Jesus in the car.

12

THE FIRST STEP

A steady rain fell on Bath Avenue as Jack walked into CJ's. They would eat inside this morning. Normally, Frank would sit at the table impatiently looking down at his watch, but not this morning. Jack had too much on his mind to sleep. He had spent most of the night praying off and on, thinking about his newfound friends and enemies. There was much to discuss. Jack found a table by the window and fell deep into thought.

Emily, standing nearby, anxiously waited. With her pad in hand, she approached Jack. "Hi, Mr. Bennett! Can I get you something while you wait?"

She had never seen Jack come in by himself before, so she naturally assumed he was meeting Frank or someone else.

Startled, Jack replied, "Oh, I'm sorry. Yes, please. I'll have a cup of coffee—and please call me Jack."

Emily gave him a big smile. "Okay—Jack."

In all the craziness, he had forgotten about Emily. He thought, 'What am I going to do about that? Am I going to do anything? I guess asking her to call me Jack is a start.'

Frank came bursting through the door, shaking the water off his jacket. Spying Jack, he walked over and sat down. "Hey! I can't believe you beat me here," Frank laughed. "What's gonna happen next?"

"That's a good question."

"Oh, you got news. Okay, so what have you got?"

Emily arrived with Jack's coffee. Turning her attention to Frank. "Good morning! What can I get you?"

"I'm starving! I'll have two eggs, home fries, and bacon. Crisp. And lots of coffee."

"And you, Jack?"

Frank's radar instantly went up. He was dying to say something, but held his tongue for the moment.

Jack ignored Frank's inquiring look. "I'll have the Masala Omelet and a refill on the coffee, please."

As soon as Emily walked away, Frank dove in. "And you, Jack?" He said, mimicking Emily's voice. "Well, have we decided?"

"I'm thinking. Let's leave it at that." He changed the subject. "How did you make out in Washington?"

"Well, considering I had less than twenty-four hours, not too bad. I found out that the good senator had a D.C. meeting on the down-low a few days ago with some real heavy hitters in the business world, including another U.S. senator. It seems he belongs to some secret society—so secret nobody knows what it's all about."

"What about the Oslows?"

"That's where it gets interesting. It turns out they were big contributors to his campaign back in the day. Not sure how that all connects. That will take some time to dig through."

Emily brought their order and refilled Frank's cup first. She glanced at Jack and then poured his coffee. For the first time, Jack noticed her eyes. They were a deep blue and seemed to sparkle, especially when she looked at him. He always thought she was pretty, just never thought of her in this way. He wasn't sure why it had taken him so long to catch on, but there was no doubt about it. Emily was interested. Though intrigued, the thought unnerved him.

"Wow—talk about a connection. I can feel the heat from here."

Jack glanced at Emily, standing at the counter. "This is new ground for me. I'm going to take it slow." He cleared his throat. "Okay, back to the Oslows. I went over those files you sent me. Did you get a good look at them?"

"I didn't have the chance. I was in a hurry to get out of the station. It was getting strange."

"Heidi again? You better stay out of there altogether. That's not the girl for you, pal."

Frank immediately pictured her leaning over his desk. "I know, but she's got it all going on."

Jack gave him a stern look. "Run, my friend. Run as fast as you can."

"Yeah, yeah - don't worry. Cause it's never gonna happen. So, what did you find in the report?"

"Are you ready for this? The Oslows were originally from Iraq. They owned the house for ten years before their deaths. They originally bought it with cash. $545,000. We knew they belonged to a Middle Eastern group called the Sons of Nimrod, but we didn't know that they were helping Saddam Hussein finance the rebuilding of

Babylon. Once built, they had plans to reinstate worship to the ancient gods of Mesopotamia, including human sacrifice."

"Human sacrifice? Saddam Hussein?" Frank had a bewildered look on his face. "Don't tell me this was on the report?"

"No, not that part. I sent a few emails to some folks know in Kuwait. They supplied that info. Remember, this goes back aways."

"So, the Oslows were Iraqis? I'm guessing Oslow wasn't their real name."

"No, their real last name was Sahar."

Frank thought for a moment. "Okay. So, let's put this all together. They came to America over forty years ago, then somewhere along the line, they connected with yet-to-be-elected Senator Wellsenburg and helped him win a Senate seat. Bizarre."

"A few minutes ago, you mentioned Wellsenburg was part of a secret society. What if Wellsenburg, in a roundabout way, sold his soul to the devil to win the Senate race? You told me yourself months ago that he has grown in power year after year and has his eye on the White House."

Frank's head was spinning. "You really think that? I mean, is that even possible?"

Jack nodded. "It happens all the time. Maybe not to this degree, but in different ways every day."

"Now that I think of it, it fits with what the demon creature said to the girl."

Jack looked down for a second, then quietly repeated, "The spirit of Babylon is coming." He leaned back in his chair. "There's more."

Frank took a deep breath. "Of course there is. What else?"

"Last night at the prayer meeting, there were two people, a man, and a woman, standing in the back of the room the whole time I was speaking. The woman was taking notes, and the man was talking on the phone. The same two people were waiting for me outside in the parking lot after the meeting. They came over as I was getting into my car and threatened the prayer group and me. They said they worked for powerful people who did not want to see me back there again. Frank, I got the same vibe from them I got when I entered the Oslow House. It was weird, bizarre."

Frank thought, 'How dare they threaten a prayer group and someone like Jack!' He wished he could have been there.

"Are you kidding? Man, what were their names?"

"I didn't get their names. They wouldn't tell me."

You could see the steam coming off Frank's head. "I'll find out who they are and pay them a brief visit. Don't you worry."

"Slow down, buddy. I don't think that's a good idea. I appreciate your concern, but there is more to this than meets the eye. Somehow, all these pieces fit together."

Frank took a deep breath. "So, you think this has something to do with the Sons of Nimrod, and maybe even Senator Wellsenburg?"

Jack looked back at him. "Don't you?"

Frank pushed aside his empty coffee cup and rested his elbows on the table, and began nervously massaging his forehead with his fingers. "I don't get it. Why should anyone in Washington care about a prayer meeting in some small town? I mean, no offense, but why would they care about Jack Bennett? Are you sure this just wasn't some bent-out-of-shape, small-town officials playing God?"

Jack leaned forward. "Frank, I'm telling you, it goes deeper than flesh and blood. I can sense it! Trust me on this one."

"Okay. I trust your premonitions, feelings or whatever. You know more about this stuff than I do. So, what's our next step?"

"I'm not sure. Let's give it a couple of days. I need to pray about this and think it through."

"It's Tuesday. We should meet again on Thursday to compare notes. If you find out anything before then, call me. I'll snoop around Washington and see what I can find out. Until then, you watch your back. In the meantime…" Frank glanced at Emily and then back at Jack, "Keep moving forward, if you know what I mean."

Jack picked up the check and gave Frank a look. "I'll talk to you later."

Emily was standing by the counter when Jack walked over to pay the bill.

"How was everything?" she asked, looking straight into his eyes.

Jack stood there, speechless. The longest few seconds of his life. His heartbeat quickened. He knew he had to make his move. It was now or never. "Good, as usual. Ah—I was wondering—that is, if you don't have any plans, would you like to have dinner on Friday?" Emily's eyes immediately brightened. 'Finally!' She thought. "Sure! I mean, yes. That would be very nice."

"Great. "

They shared phone numbers. Jack instantly felt lighter. "How about I pick you up at seven? Is Regina's okay? Do you like Italian food? They are the best around."

"Sounds wonderful. Seven it is."

Jack was all smiles as he walked out to his car. It had finally stopped raining, but it didn't matter. It could have been snowing, and he wouldn't have noticed. Jack had a date.

13

GETTING READY

Back in L.A., Dante Adal awaited a report from one of his foul-spirited henchmen. He liked to use them for what he called "Stage 1 Intimidations"—threats and minor hindrances. These types of spirits worked well through individuals who displayed a similar state of mind. When possible, the spirits would actually inhabit their hosts without their knowledge. This was the most profitable scenario for many reasons. These ambassadors of hate could come and go as they pleased. Operating in this way gave Dante a wide range of options, given there was no shortage of disenchanted and defenseless souls to choose from.

A slight gust of sulfur-scented air crossed over Dante's desk as an emaciated ghostly image materialized in the center of the room. Dante placed his hands flat on his desk, leaned forward, and demanded, "What do you have to report?"

"I have done as you asked, Master," the voice said in a garbled, whispered tone.

"Jack Bennett has been warned, but I do not believe he will back off. This one is different. The Spirit of the Holy One is strong in him."

Dante stood up straight and growled, "All flesh is the same. We will have to take it to the next level. What about the prayer meeting? Is it being shut down?"

"I have stirred the two you chose. They will do their worst to have them thrown out of the old church. It seems the historical society will do our bidding, as you suggested."

"Excellent. Ah yes, jealousy and bitterness—two of my most delightful tools. Keep up the good work." Dante snickered. The phrase amused him. "Make sure that happens. You may go. I will deal with this Jack Bennett in person."

With that, the spirit vanished into thin air. Dante knew he had to move slowly and methodically if he was going to destroy this uprising and avoid any confrontation with angelic forces, particularly Uriel. He would have to be sly and deceptive, but then again, that was his nature.

* * *

Jack finished his Wednesday morning blog update and walked out onto the front porch and plopped down in his favorite chair. This was the place he liked to pray, meditate, and just plain zone out. The view from the front porch was beautiful and serene. Jack's house set back a good two hundred feet from the road, separated by a line of black oak trees that came with the property and four flowering dogwoods he planted himself.

Jack thought hard about all that had happened over the past week, including his encounters with Emily. However, foremost in his mind was the heated spiritual battle he was now engaged in. Well aware that this fight would be lengthy and difficult, Jack comforted himself, knowing that the reward would be great. The words of God's holy messenger resounded in his spirit as Jack contemplated all that God was about to do. It didn't mean he wasn't concerned. Jack was well aware of his limitations and the enemy's plan.

The last thing the king of darkness wanted was a group of on-fire Christians praying in unity and agreeing on something—anything. Since the beginning of time, his strategy has been the same: divide and conquer. Through the years, his success, including separating the church into denominations, had fostered rivalries and ungodly dissension among believers. Jack often said that, if possible, Satan would have us arguing over how many angels could fit on the head of a pin.

Jesus said, "A house divided against itself cannot stand." Jack knew this and had always taught and encouraged unity. His favorite scripture was in the gospel of John, 17:21. "That all of them may be one, Father, just as you are in me and I am in you. May they also be in us so that the world may believe that you have sent me."

Next to prayer, unity is the most powerful weapon in the church's arsenal, and when believers are together, it has the power to change the world. The mere thought of it caused the Enemy to tremble. That was what was so incredible about Conni's prayer group. Jack knew that dividing them was the first thing the enemy would try to do. If Satan and his forces could cause friction between the believers and get them to walk away, he would be on his way to victory.

The ring of Jack's cell phone interrupted his thoughts. It was Conni. He had a feeling it was not good news.

He answered, "Hi, Conni. What's going on?"

"Hi, Jack. I heard from the historical society today." Her voice was stressed and obviously disturbed. "They told me we couldn't use the church anymore for our prayer meetings."

Jack could feel his blood pressure rising. "What was their reasoning for that decision?"

"They said the building wasn't safe enough for large gatherings, but you and I both know what's really going on. Obviously, those two people you pointed out to me had something to do with it. The historical society would have never approved it in the beginning if there were structural problems."

Jack felt awful. He thought. 'If I hadn't gone there and spoken, maybe none of this would have happened.'

"Yes, we know who's behind this. I feel bad, Conni. I might have brought this down on you and your group."

"They couldn't have known you were coming. I think this was in the works for a while."

Jack stood up and paced from one end of the porch to the other.

"There is something I didn't tell you." Jack drew a deep breath and continued, "When I left the other night, those same two people were waiting for me in the parking lot. They came up to me when I was getting in my car, threatening that if I came back, something bad was going to happen to me, or you, or both of us. They told me they worked for powerful people who wanted me to stay away."

Jack could tell Conni was a little shaken. She took a couple of seconds to respond.

"Wow, that is awful. Who do those people think they are?" Conni shifted from shaken to furious in a heartbeat. "We should fight this thing!"

"I feel the same way, Conni, but they have authority over all those historical buildings. We would have to prove that the building is safe, and even then, they could still deny us access. We need to find another place for you to gather. Does anyone in the group have a home church that will let you use their building?"

"Well, as you saw, the group is diverse. Very few of them go to the same church. That's what makes it unique. The gathering was interdenominational. You know how it is. Churches are so territorial. I'll ask around, but honestly, that's why we chose Liberty. It was our only option."

None of what Conni said was news to Jack, but it bothered him to hear it. Jack needed to encourage Conni to move ahead. Without prayer, they would be in trouble.

"This is the age of technology, Conni. We can still get together and pray, just not in the same place. Email everyone and tell them what's going on. Ask them to pray that God will provide a place to get together. We are not in this alone. This is God's battle, not ours."

"Okay, I can do that. If I send you the group's email addresses, would you mind sending them an encouraging word? I think they would like to hear from you as well."

"Absolutely. It would be my pleasure. Anything I can do to help."

Conni thanked Jack and said goodbye. She felt so much better after talking to him. Jack had a way of encouraging people, a gift Conni was very thankful for. She was well aware of what was at stake. The spiritual world was very real to her. She had prayed over many disturbed and spiritually harassed people in her life and knew what prayer could do. For years, most of her family saw her as some religious freak, especially when she tried to share her God experiences with them.

Although she never married and had no children of her own, Conni loved kids. She volunteered as a Care Coordinator with the local children's hospital, bringing toys and treats for many sick children. When the opportunity presented itself, she prayed with them and their parents. Conni had touched many lives over the years, and she planned to continue doing so as long as the Lord allowed.

Jack laid his phone down on the table next to his chair and said some prayers of his own.

He just got started when the phone rang again. "Hey, Frank."

"We won't be able to get together tomorrow. We have another case. I will need you on this one too. You will not believe where this one is. High Point. I think it's the same church your friend Conni holds those prayer meetings."

Jack straightened. "What? No way! I was just there. What's going on?"

"They say the lights are going on and off at night, chairs are flying around, and strange sounds are coming from the steeple. It's scaring the hell out of the neighborhood." Frank caught himself and quickly apologized for his phrasing. "Oh, sorry. You know what I mean."

Jack half-smiled. "You don't have to apologize. Unfortunately, Hell is a real place. I need to be in on this one."

"I had a feeling you might say that. Meet me there tonight, say, at seven o'clock. I need to clear some things up in D.C. first. Plus, I know you—you'll want to see if things go bump in the night."

"Okay, see you there."

Jack leaned back in his chair and stared straight ahead. He couldn't remember a time when things were this crazy. 'We are truly in the last days. The spirit world is manifesting itself, and the fight is moving into the open.'

He bowed his head and prayed, "Father, strengthen your people for the battle ahead."

14

THEN THERE WERE TWO

A heavy mist fell as Jack turned into the parking lot of the old Liberty Church. Frank was sitting in his car with the motor running, talking on the phone. The church was dark. The two old-style streetlights were no match for the gloomy weather. Jack waited, then joined him in his car.

"Well, here we are again. Have you seen anything unusual since you've been here?"

"No, but then it's just now getting dark, and nothing happens until it's dark, right?" Frank half-joked. "Of course, this fog isn't helping. I hate this kind of weather. I brought two big LED flashlights. It looks like we're gonna need them."

Jack looked puzzled. "What for? The lights were working when I was here last."

"Yeah, about that—the historical society had the power shut off earlier today. Last night the local cops came by, and when they saw the lights flickering on and off, they figured there must be a short in the electrical system somewhere, sooo...we are working in the dark tonight, my friend."

"Great. They couldn't wait one more day? Didn't they know you were coming?"

Frank gave Jack a sarcastic look. "What? You expect the federal and local agencies actually to communicate?"

Jack shook his head in disgust. "Unbelievable. Well, let's get started."

They got out of the car and walked up the long, gray slate sidewalk that led to a small wooden front porch. Out of habit, Frank passed his hand over his gun. He liked to make sure it was ready to go, just in case. Jack made his way onto the porch and reached out to open one of the large double wooden doors.

"Hey, I should go first. I'm the federal agent with the gun," Frank insisted.

"I thought the cops already went through this place?"

"I don't trust anyone except myself and God." He added, "And, occasionally, you."

"God? Really?" Jack commented with a smile. "Interesting."

Jack yielded, Frank led, both brandishing flashlights burning brightly. Jack tried the light switch, but Frank was right—the power was off.

"I'll check the attic. That's where they say the sounds were coming from."

Frank looked at Jack like he was insane.

"No way! Don't you watch any movies? That's what all those morons do. Oh, let's split up," he said mockingly. "No. We are staying together, especially after all I've seen working with you—no way. That's not gonna happen."

Jack rolled his eyes. "You watch too much TV. I feel like I'm back in high school sneaking around old abandoned houses. Fine, we'll go together."

Shocked, Frank said, "You, Jack Bennett, broke into houses?"

Jack peered at him. "Just keep walking."

The two men climbed the stairs slowly and methodically. Frank murmured. "Forget about wackos or goblins. These old rickety stairs will probably kill us first." The attic went on forever. It was difficult to distinguish anything. It appeared to be empty.

Suddenly, Jack felt something that disturbed him. It was the same familiar feeling he always got when something evil was about to appear.

"Frank, I'm sensing someone or something is here."

Just then, there was a wolf-like howl and a powerful gust of wind. Frank felt something brush by him that gave him a chill up and down his spine. He turned quickly, moving his flashlight all around, hoping to get a glimpse of whatever it was.

Jack spun around. "Did you hear that?"

"Hear it? I felt it! It brushed right by me. Very creepy. I think it headed back down the steps."

Frank pointed his flashlight at the staircase, revealing a trail of reddish—orange smoke swirling around the top of the steps. Jack saw it too. They looked at each other and carefully headed back down to the first floor. Once again, they heard what sounded like a combination of growling and howling. Jack noticed a wisp of red smoke rising from the basement. They slowly made their way downstairs, flashlights in hand. Frank braced his gun and flashlight tight in his hands, sweeping the room from one side to the other. Jack was right alongside him, searching meticulously for what he knew was not human.

"I don't think that gun is going to do us any good, Frank."

"Well, I'm not putting it down—you can bet on that. You have your weapons, and I have mine."

A ghostly plume of red smoke twisted and turned, then hung in mid-air, growing larger until a dense reddish-orange fog filled the room with. Jack and Frank cautiously watched the supernatural event unfolding in front of them. Suddenly, horrific, deep guttural sounds leaped from within the swirling smoldering cloud. It grew louder and more intense. In vain, Jack and Frank covered their ears. Two glowing red eyes slowly burned through the thick, churning mist. Then—there it was. A large, menacing figure with massive jet-black wings stood before them. It had a dragon's head, its reptilian body covered in scales like a snake. Jack watched in shock and amazement as the creature slowly stretched out its wings until it filled the entire room. Strapped to its side was a large pewter-colored sword that reached the floor.

This was not the first time Frank had seen crazy-weird-Jack-stuff, but it had always been at a distance, and it was never this evil or ominous. Frank could feel all the air being sucked out of the room, making it increasingly difficult to breathe.

The creature scowled at Frank and then quickly dismissed him as non-threatening. The being slowly turned its attention to Jack, tilting its head from one side to the other as if examining an opponent or prey. Finally, it spoke. Each word out of its mouth was long and labored. "Well, if it isn't Jack Bennett. I knew you would come if I put on a little show for everyone."

Frank could not move, his hand frozen on his weapon. His whole body seemed to be paralyzed, but not with fear.

Jack knew this was no ordinary demon. Something in the higher realm. Possibly a fallen angel. But Jack knew he served no ordinary God. Fear should have paralyzed him by now, but the Spirit inside him wouldn't allow it. He looked the creature in the eye, stood firm, and said, "You have no right to be here."

It glared back at him, challenging him venomously. "Oh, but I do. I brought this place down fifty years ago. The leadership was more concerned about preserving the building than about saving their souls. They invited me here with all their petty bickering and backbiting. It was satisfying to watch them tear themselves apart. I can't have you and the others re-sanctifying this place. They gave it to me, and I don't plan on giving it back. It is—MINE!"

Jack knew all demons were liars, but in this case, there was a measure of spiritual truth in what it said. He stood his ground. The scripture came to him, 'Having done all to stand, stand, therefore.'

Jack responded with confidence, "The Lord intends to take this place back. It was dedicated to Him, and it will be again. I stand in His name, the name of the Lord Jesus Christ."

With that, the creature winced and repelled backward. The name of Jesus seemed to penetrate it like hot flaming arrows. Taking a deep breath, the creature spat back at Jack with fury, "I am the prince of the entire region you call the United States! You cannot cast me out. I will destroy this country from the inside out, and there is nothing you can do about it. You cannot stop it. It is well underway."

The creature reached down, drew its sword from its sheath, and raised it high in the air. Holding it out in front of Frank, he then put it to his throat. Taunting Jack, he spat, "You may be protected, but I can do away with this one." Frank's eyes grew wide, and he felt helpless, still frozen by an invisible force.

Jack cried out at the top of his lungs, "Father! In the name of Jesus Christ, your Son. Remove this demon from this place!"

Suddenly, white hot, blinding streams of light ripped through the darkness and fill the room. Like strikes of lightning, they seemed to come from every conceivable direction. The reddish-orange mist quickly dissolved as the pure bright light filled the basement and the entire building. The creature jerked backward, holding his sword out in front of him in a defensive posture as another figure emerged. An angel of light holding his own sword that pulsated with the holy fire. It was so intense, Jack and Frank had to turn away.

Although clothed in spectacular glory, Jack recognized his face as the hitchhiker he had picked up. He had little to reference, given that it was the only angel he had ever seen, but he had a witness in his spirit that it was.

Frank, still frozen in position, his arms outstretched, holding on tight to his weapon, felt the blood flowing back into his arms and legs. Jack guided Frank's arms back down to his sides. There was clearly no need or use for earthly weapons here.

The creature moaned in agonizing disapproval, "U r i e l, we meet again."

Uriel's voice was authoritative and brimming with confidence. "Yes, Dante. The Lord sent me to remind you that, once again, you have overstepped. These belong to Him."

Dante growled and pointed his sword at Frank. "Not this one!"

"Do not presume you know the plans of the Lord. Only He can read the hearts of men."

"Why does he bother with such fools?" Dante retorted.

"His ways are not our ways, and they are definitely not your ways. The Lord is reclaiming what is His, for His glory and His honor." Uriel then commanded the creature with authority, "I command you by the Almighty One, the keeper of the keys of life and death, to leave this place and never return!"

Dante winced and bowed his head. Then added, "You can't help them. Mortals are such fools. They live only to serve themselves. You cannot prevent the inevitable."

Uriel raised his sword, glared into Dante's red glowing eyes, and shouted, "Enough! The Lord God has spoken!"

Dante shrieked in anger and frustration. The sound of his voice rattled every loose board and pane of glass in the building. He glared at Jack, then suddenly, he was gone. Uriel stood alone, surrounded by white-hot streams of light. He looked at Jack and smiled. "Thanks for the ride, Jack."

Uriel glanced at Frank, raised his eyebrows, and looked back at Jack. He smiled again and shot up through the building like a rocket into the night sky. The room went dark, the only light emanating from the flashlights lying on the floor.

Jack smirked. "This would be a good time to make that commitment to the Lord we've talked about."

Frank stared at him in stunned silence. A slow smile formed on Jack's face, growing wider and wider until he couldn't hold it in any longer. It was as if all the pent-up tension of the last few days was pouring out of him in a cleansing flood of joy and laughter.

Frank smiled nervously, breathing deeply. He carefully put his gun back in its holster. Jack's laughter was contagious, but Frank could only muster a much-subdued chuckle.

Frank didn't speak a word until they got outside. Standing in the parking lot, still tingling all over, Frank said, "Okay, so what do I have to do? I mean, besides changing my underwear?"

Jack continued laughing, partly due to what Frank said and the incredible joy of the moment.

Becoming more serious, Jack answered, "I'll tell you what—I know this is an extremely private matter for you, considering your Jewish roots and all. I know you pretty well, so I think you should get in your car and talk to the Lord the same as you would talk to me or anyone else. Reflect on your life. Ask Jesus to forgive you for every sin and wrong thing you have ever done. Ask the Lord to give you a new start and to come in and fill your heart with the assurance of His mercy and love. I guarantee you will feel the change. Call me and let me know how you do."

At first, Frank just stared at him, not knowing where to begin. Finally, he said, "Okay. I can do that. The Lord and I have a lot to talk about." He paused, then said, "This is a night I will never forget. Geez, Jack, what was that?"

"Frank, I will not pretend that I know. All I can say is that this Dante is obviously a powerful fallen angel from what we heard in there. It seems he is going to play a major role in the last days. We have kicked over a huge hornet's nest."

Frank was still in shock. He looked around, then glanced up at the night sky. "All these years—I had no idea this stuff existed."

"Don't feel bad. Most people live their whole lives without realizing there's more to life than what we see with the natural eye."

"Do you think the prayer group will get to come back now?"

"Well, if I were a betting man, I'd be all over that one. I don't know when or how, but my money is on God."

Frank stood motionless, staring at the church as if in a trance. Jack reached over and gave him a man hug. He looked like he needed it.

"Talk to God, my friend. Your Messiah is waiting for you."

Frank took another deep breath and got into his car. He rolled down the window and said, "I'm gonna have some crazy dreams tonight."

Jack nodded. "You and me both, brother. Now it's time to head home." As Jack pulled away, he thought he heard the bell ringing in the church steeple. He listened again and then shook his head. 'No,' he thought, 'that couldn't be.' Suddenly, a wave of goosebumps came over him. It made the hair on his arms stand on end. He smiled and whispered, "Oh, yes, it could be!"

15

THE DATE

Thursday came and went without incident, except for the long-awaited call from Frank. He told Jack all about the incredible experience he had driving home the night before and how he never thought something like this could happen to him. Frank truly felt the weight of the world lift off him when he prayed. He took the day off to rest and to read his Bible, which Jack had given him as a gift a few weeks after they started working together.

Jack couldn't be happier. He felt like it was happening to him all over again. He was so happy for his friend. Before they hung up, Jack prayed with Frank and then jokingly said, "Now we really have something to talk about."

Jack was looking forward to introducing Frank to some of his friends from church, many of who had been praying for him for years.

Now it was Friday morning, which meant that Friday night was only hours away. Jack was more than a little nervous about his dinner with Emily. It had been a long time since he had been on an official date. Jack wasn't much for going out, although he had attended his share of social events, prompted mostly by his publisher. She was constantly encouraging him to be more interactive with the reading public, especially the women. But this—well, this was the real deal.

Jack had picked Regina's for its food and great atmosphere. Slightly upscale, yet casual. Most fine dining establishments made him uncomfortable. Jack wanted to step beyond the small talk and find out more about Emily, her interests, how she came to Christ, and what she was looking for in life. These were the things Jack really liked to talk about. He couldn't imagine how awkward it would be to go back to CJ's if things didn't work out. His mind filled with scenarios, good and bad. For now, he would do his best to take a deep breath, decompress, and stay positive.

* * *

Jack pulled up to Emily's apartment building, shut off the car, and collected himself. He thought, 'Come on! I have fought with demons and talked with an angel. How hard could this be?'

He walked up to the apartment building and hit the buzzer. Emily's excited voice came through the speaker. "Hi, Jack! I'll be right down."

"Okay," he answered. Jack scanned the neighborhood as he waited. It was a quiet part of town. A two-story apartment building, well kept and in a pleasant neighborhood. The door swung open, and Emily walked out, looking beautiful. He thought to himself, 'Jack, try not to screw this up!'

"Hi," Emily greeted him with a smile. "I see you found the place, with no problem."

"Oh, yeah!" Jack replied, trying not to sound nervous. "GPS - never leave home without it."

As they drove off, Jack said, "Regina's is only a few miles from here. Have you ever been there?"

"No, but everybody I know loves it there. I'm a big lasagna fan. I lived on Italian food back in New York. That's where my family's from - Brooklyn, actually."

"Brooklyn? Wow, I would never have guessed. I never pick up on an accent."

"It comes out once in a while. I've been in Virginia for about eight years now."

"How long have you been at CJ's?"

"Only about three months. The owners are nice, and the tips aren't bad. You seem to like it there, too. You and..." she paused. "Frank, right?"

Jack laughed, "Yeah, Frank. We work together. We like to meet there and discuss—business, I guess."

"If you don't mind me saying so, your conversations look—intense. Not that I hear anything, really. It just looks like you're very into whatever it is you're discussing."

Jack flashed a smile. "We get intense sometimes. I guess you could say that it's a complicated job."

Jack could now see Reginas coming up on the right. "Here we are. We have a reservation for 7:30."

Jack escorted Emily to the hostess station. The young lady

confirmed their reservation and showed them to their table. It was the perfect spot beside a large window overlooking the flower gardens.

The server promptly came over and asked, "Can I get you something to drink?" Emily smiled. "A glass of iced tea would be fine, please."

Jack took note and added, "I'll have the same." Jack would occasionally have a glass of red wine, but he didn't know how Emily felt about it, so he followed her lead.

"So, from Brooklyn, New York to Blackstone, Virginia. What made that happen?"

"Well, I went to George Mason University in Fairfax right out of high school. I was there for a couple of years and kind of bailed out. I've been in the area ever since."

Jack's mind quickly figured out that Emily was younger than he thought. She didn't look older, but he somehow convinced himself that she was at least thirty years old.

"If you don't mind me asking, what kept you from going back home to New York?"

"Well, I met a guy I thought was really cool, and," she added sarcastically, "big shocker—he was a musician and in a band! I dropped out of school to go with him on tour - not the smartest thing I ever did. It didn't end well. I wasted two years of my life with him. To make things worse, my parents completely freaked out when I dropped out of the university, and we kind of stopped talking after that."

She looked at Jack and thought, 'He'll probably be glad when this date's over.' Emily sighed, "Pretty awful, huh?"

The server brought their drinks, and Jack told her they needed a few more minutes to look at the menu. She nodded and left them to decide.

Trying not to make her feel worse, Jack said, "Hey, things happen. I get it. We all go through stuff, that's for sure."

"It's okay. We talk twice a month now. They would like to see me go back to school, but I have to make a living, and I'm not sure what I want to do just yet. The best thing was after I left him and was at my worst; the Lord came into my life, which convinced my family I went from bad to worse. If you know what I mean."

Jack sighed sympathetically. "Believe me, I know. It's a shame you had to go through all that, but God has His ways. I've never been able to figure them out, but He always has our best interests at heart."

Emily nodded. It was time to change the subject. "Well, enough about me. How about you? I hear you are an author. What kinds of things do you write about?"

Jack could only think, 'Wow! If she thought her life was a little crazy, just wait until she hears about what I do.'

Jack took a sip of iced tea and answered, "I study and write about paranormal activity, and, occasionally, the government will bring me in as a consultant on unusual and difficult cases."

Jack waited for her reaction. Emily stared at him for a moment. He could feel the sweat building up on the back of his neck. 'Really, Jack? You opened with that? God, I'm blowing this for sure.'

"Wow! That's amazing. How did you get into that?"

Immediately, Jack could feel the anxiety draining from his face.

"That's a long story. Maybe we should order first." Jack motioned for the server, and they placed their order. Emily ordered her lasagna and Jack, his favorite. Ravioli. Very interested in hearing Jack's story, Emily kept the conversation going. "So, you were about to tell me how you got into this paranormal stuff?"

"Right. Well, it might not be a pleasant dinner conversation now that I think about it. I don't want to get all heavy-duty on you." He tried to deter her from the subject, but the look in her eyes told him she was eager to hear about it.

"I don't mind! I think it's really cool. Please, I've been on dates that were just plain awful and filled with long, boring conversations. If you don't mind talking about it, I would love to hear it."

Jack was still hesitant, yet he felt comfortable talking with her. "Well–okay. But I warn you. It has a very sad beginning." Jack drew a deep breath and then exhaled. Emily mimicked him and braced herself.

Jack continued, "It started fifteen years ago when my girlfriend Susan, who I was about to propose to, until a drunk driver took her life. It devastated me and I drifted along in a daze for quite some time."

Taken aback. Emily felt terrible. That is so sad. "Oh, my goodness! Are you okay talking about it?"

"I'm fine. It was a long time ago. It is a little awkward being that it's our first date and all, but it actually feels good to talk about it."

"No, please. Don't think like that. Life is real. It must have been so hard for you. I can't imagine losing someone like that."

"It was pretty tough. I tried to stay connected to the family, but it was difficult. Her sister Renée was into mediums and psychics and all kinds of weird stuff. She was bent on talking to her dead sister. She dragged me along with her to all kinds of readings and séances, trying to contact her. It was awful. Every place we went, all they did was take her money and lie to her. I mean, I didn't know the Lord then, but even I could see all they were doing was ripping her off. I tried to tell her it was a bad idea, but she wanted to try one more, so I went along with it, making her promise it would be the last one. We ended up at a carnival that advertised a woman who could tell the future and talk to departed family members and friends. Well, as soon as the woman got going, I got a very uneasy feeling. There was something very different about this one. Suddenly, we heard voices whispering. It seemed like it was coming from everywhere. And just when I thought it couldn't get any weirder, the woman spoke in a man's voice. It was deep and gravelly. Nothing like I had ever heard before. It shook me to my core. I grabbed Renée, and we got out of there in a hurry.

"When we got out, we saw this guy handing out pamphlets about the Lord. He told us the woman we saw was very evil, and we needed to look to the living for answers, not the dead. He asked us if we wanted to accept Jesus as our savior and handed us a pamphlet. Renée took the pamphlet, looked at it for a minute, then crumpled it up and threw it on the ground. She grabbed my hand and tried to get me to leave, but I wanted to hear more. I told her to go ahead, and that I was going to stay and talk to him some more."

Mesmerized, Emily couldn't take her eyes off of Jack. The server brought the food just in time. Jack was happy for the opportunity to change the subject. "Thank you! This looks great."

"Can I get you anything else?"

Jack checked with Emily. "No, I'm good," she said with a smile.

Jack leaned over and asked, "Is it okay if I say a quick blessing over the food?"

"Of course! Please, do."

Emily thought, 'This guy is too good to be true.'

Jack said a quick prayer and smiled. "Okay, enough talking - let's eat."

After commenting on how exceptional the dinner was, Emily leaned in and asked, "If you don't mind, please continue. I love listening to you."

Jack hadn't talked about this topic for years and for a lot of reasons. However, this felt like the right time and the right person with whom to share it.

"Okay. Well, I stayed and talked to this guy for an hour or more, asking him all kinds of questions. Finally, he asked me if I would like to pray with him and ask Christ to come into my life. At that point, I was ready—I had lost the girl I loved and hoped to marry, and done running around looking for answers in all the wrong places. That day, God changed my life. From that day on, I attended Bible classes, studied every day, and grabbed everything I could get my hands on about paranormal activity. I didn't realize it, but God was preparing me for something extraordinary. Now, I get to investigate cases for the federal government and reveal to others what the unseen world is really about." Jack smiled, "That's my story, and that's what I write about." Relieved to have finally shared his story with someone. Jack studied Emily anxiously, awaiting her reaction.

Emily sat back in her chair, taking it all in. After a brief pause, she responded, "That is amazing! The Lord has surely been with you. I think what you do is fascinating."

Jack, somewhat relieved, smiled and thought, 'That's just the tip of the iceberg.'

When they finished eating, Jack suggested they get dessert at a little ice cream place that made it all from scratch. Emily agreed, and off they went. Afterward, they went for a long walk, enjoying each other's company and their ice cream.

It was late when they turned for home. Jack pulled in front of Emily's apartment and shut off the engine. They sat in the car, talking and laughing for another hour.

Neither wanted the night to end. Emily, checking the time, said,. "Wow! It's later than I thought. I wish I didn't have to go. Unfortunately, I have to get up at 5 a.m. for work."

Emily moved a little closer to Jack, smiled, and whispered, "I had a great time. I can't remember the last time I enjoyed myself so much."

Jack smiled back. "Me too. I would love to see you again. Can I call you?"

Emily's mind was spinning. 'Is he kidding?'

"I would love that."

Jack couldn't believe he hadn't noticed her before this. She was truly beautiful from head to toe. He gazed into her sparkling, deep blue eyes and gently brushed a lock of her long blonde hair away from her face. They leaned into each other and kissed. They felt it instantly. The chemistry, the connection, the spark—it was undeniable!

Emily whispered, "I really like you, Jack Bennett."

Jack stared into her eyes, then kissed her again. "I really like you too, Emily Richardson. I will call you tomorrow after work."

Jack opened the car door and walked Emily to the front of her building. They stood briefly face-to-face. Jack couldn't resist. He kissed her again. "Goodnight."

"Goodnight, Jack Bennett." She loved saying his name. She had envisioned this night many times. There was something special about him. There was no explaining it—and she wasn't about to try.

Jack strolled back to his car. Emily was pretty beyond words, and so easy to talk to. Jack never saw this coming. It stirred up feelings he hadn't had in years. He knew this wasn't the best time to start a new relationship. Still, his feelings for Emily were real and exhilarating.

16

MR. THERION

Dante sat glaring out his window overlooking downtown LA. He was still fuming from his encounter with Uriel. He wanted so much to destroy Jack Bennett and his cohorts. Dante was so angry that it was difficult for him to keep his mortal form. The thought of two such weak beings getting the best of him was more than he could stomach. He got up and paced back and forth, breathing deeply and exhaling slowly. The intercom on his desk rang once, then twice. He reluctantly punched the button.

"Mr. Adal, there is a Mr. Therion here to see you."

His countenance changed abruptly, and an uncontrollable feeling of dread came over him. "Ah—yes, send him in."

The door opened, and a tall, stern-faced, dark-haired man walked in, carrying an ebony walking stick. It had a handle of pure gold in the shape of a viper's head. He walked in without saying a word and sat in the high-back leather chair directly across from Dante.

The room turned darker and an undeniable heaviness fell like a blanket over Dante's office and the entire building. Dante silently and submissively sat down behind his desk. Therion's laser-like stare bore into him. "I will not tolerate failure. I expect you to be sly and deceitful, not out of control and foolish."

"Master—I, I..."

"No excuses." His voice went right through Dante. Therion stared at him in raging silence. Dante wasn't sure what to do or what was going to happen next. If he were capable, he would have been sweating.

Finally, Therion broke his silence. "That is not the way we do things. Confrontation with the light is for a later time. We do what we have done for ages. Undermine and appeal to the flesh and get them to turn on each other. Or have you forgotten how many congregations and ministers we have destroyed with that approach? We do not appear to these mortals in our true form. We cannot give them proof of our existence. They don't believe in us, and that is to our advantage. It took years for us to develop and plant those seeds in their minds."

Petrified, Dante shakily responded, "Yes, master. I lost myself in my anger and outrage."

"You will lose more than that if you continue to disobey me. Pride, my prince—pride, is the secret weapon. Make them feel superior to everyone else. Pump them up and fatten them for the fall. That is how we win. Divide and conquer. It is a foolproof plan. We are making progress all over the world. Hate is on the rise. Even my lesser spirits are gaining ground. Every day there are more and more random attacks of violence.

Look at the Middle East! It is a virtual playground for hatred and abomination, and all in the name of God. If they're not killing in the name of God, they're blaming and cursing God for everything that happens to them. Either way, we win. Whether it is airline pilots diving their jets into buildings, or people randomly turning on members of their own families, one constant must remain. Invisibility. No one ever reports seeing demons or dark angelic beings behind it, all because we don't really exist. We are only myths and legends created by authors with vivid imaginations. I hope you fully understand." Therion paused. "Do you, Dante?"

Dante bowed. "I understand, master. It won't happen again."

"See that it doesn't. It has already cost me. A soul has crossed over into the light. Don't give them a reason to believe. It is prosperity that will divide them. The rich get richer, and the poor get poorer. Get it? Above all else, keep them from praying. It's bad enough we will have to fight to get that church back from the prayer group. No more setbacks, the countdown to the end of days has begun—we must keep them in the dark. Evolution, aliens, big bang, cosmic inflation—I don't give a damn what they choose to believe."

"Yes, my lord."

Therion rose from his chair and walked toward the door. Turning to Dante, he said, "I have to say, I enjoy occasionally walking among them in this way. They are so self-centered and puffed up. It's rather encouraging."

Therion gave Dante one more look and walked out the door.

Dante sat back down and closed his eyes. He had dodged a very serious bullet but needed to be smarter and a great deal more careful. He would take the advice of his master and pit them against each other. In fact, he had just the perfect person in mind—arrogant, prideful, and just right for foiling the prayer group in High Point. He couldn't let this small wild fire spread to other regions of his domain. There were only two phrases that struck fear into his heart. Revival and Spiritual Awakening. Dante knew his job was to keep the Christians happy and satisfied, so they would sleep right through the day until the rise of the Dark One. By then, it would be too late. As he gazed out his window on the world below, he studied his reflection in the glass. An evil smirk slowly grew across his face.

He thought, 'They will all soon bow to me.' Dante caught himself and nervously looked around the room. His smile grew larger and more sinister as he corrected himself. 'I mean to the master.' It was only a matter of time.

17

THE DAY AFTER

Jack was up, showered, and working at his desk by 8:00 a.m. His thoughts were many and diverse. It was hard for him to concentrate on any one thing. What a week it had been! Every aspect of his life was flying by at an accelerated rate. There were angels, demons, Frank, and then there was Emily.

He stopped typing for a minute and stared straight ahead. His mind kept going back to Emily and their incredible first date. He really wanted to go down to CJ's, but he felt weird about it, so he waited and call her after she got off from work. Never in a million years did Jack think he could feel this way about a woman again. Somewhere in the back of his mind, he always thought that he would stay single, dedicating his life to his calling and ministry, but now he wasn't so sure. Maybe there was room for a woman in his life. Sure, it was only their first date, and God knows the whole thing could blow up and be history in a week two, but it sure felt good to have someone to talk to.

He took a sip of his now not-so-hot coffee and, while putting it in the microwave, he received a text message alert. It was Conni.

Good morning, Jack! This goes under the headline, "Believe It or Not." I got a phone call from the historical society last night. They are sending an electrician to the church on Monday, and if there are no issues with the electricity, they will allow us to use the church for prayer again. Unbelievable, right? I'll let you know what happens. God is good. God bless!

"Wow! Lord, you are amazing!"

He grabbed his re-heated coffee and headed back to his desk. Sitting down, Jack reread the message. He could hardly believe it himself. It had only been two days since their encounter with Dante, and Uriel and God had already solved the problem. Jack marveled at God's providence and the effects of His power and love. Jack thought of the scripture in Isaiah, "For my thoughts are not your thoughts, neither are your ways my ways, says the Lord. For as the heavens are higher than the earth, so are my ways higher than your ways, and my thoughts than your thoughts."

As the day wore on, Jack finished his blog post and jumped back into working on his new book while quietly counting the minutes until Emily would get home from work. He couldn't help wondering how she was feeling about their date. Maybe she was having second thoughts. Maybe she had decided he was a little too old for her. He checked himself. 'It is God, or it's not.'

Jack's phone rang. "Hey, Frank. How are you feeling today? Great, I hope."

"Hey, Jack. Yeah, feeling pretty good. I have to keep reminding myself that it really happened. I want to sit and talk with you for a while before I walk into this church tomorrow morning. Are you doing anything tonight? I can come by and hang for a while if you have the time."

Jack's first thought was, 'No way.' He was really looking forward to seeing Emily again. However, this was big. He had been praying for Frank since the day they started working together. Jack knew what his answer had to be.

"Sure, bud. We'll order in and talk about Jesus tonight."

"Great, man. I'll be at your place around six."

"Okay, brother. See you then."

Jack hung up and thought, 'Brother? That just flowed out, but now he really is my brother in the Lord. God—what You do is beyond words.'

The time had finally come to make the call. It was 2:30 p.m. Jack figured Emily was home by now. It rang once... twice... three times. He started getting nervous.

On the fourth ring, she answered. "Hi, Jack."

"Hi, Emily. How was work?"

"It was okay. Glad to be home. How was your day?"

Trying to sound nonchalant, he said, "Oh, just catching up on a few things."

They were both searching for assurances, not knowing how to get there. Jack jumped in. "I had a great time last night."

Emily let out a silent sigh of relief. "Oh, so did I."

Jack wanted so badly to ask her out tonight, but he knew at this point it was more important to spend time with Frank. "I was hoping we could catch a movie tonight and spend some more time together, but something came up that I really have to do. Are you working tomorrow?"

"No, I don't work Sundays anymore unless they really get jammed up. What did you have in mind?"

"Well, I know you have your own church you go to, but I was wondering if you would like to go to church with me tomorrow?"

Emily was smiling from ear to ear. "Sure, I would love that. What time?"

"We could go to the first service at 9 a.m. and then come back to my place for a late breakfast. I could fix you something to eat for a change."

"That sounds wonderful. You cook?"

"Well, I make an exceptional breakfast. Beyond that, it can get a little dangerous."

Emily laughed. "Okay, breakfast it is! What time should I be ready? Oh, and what do people wear at your church?"

"It is very casual. No one gets too dressed up. We meet in the high school auditorium. Pastor Eli launched this church four years ago, and God has blessed it. We already have nearly three hundred people in attendance. I'll pick you up at 8:30."

"That sounds wonderful. I'll be ready. And Jack—I really had a great time last night."

Jack's smile grew wider. "I am so happy to hear that. I did too. I'm really looking forward to seeing you again."

Emily was beaming. "Not as much as I am, Jack Bennett. See you at 8:30."

Jack walked onto the front porch and dropped into his favorite chair. The smile would linger on his face for hours.

18

AFTER GLOW

J ack was checking his email when Frank pulled into the driveway. He looked at his watch and smiled. It was exactly six o'clock. He knew how pumped Frank would be, which made him feel good, even though Emily was still on his mind. The newness of Frank's experience with the Lord reminded him of his own and how amazed he was when he realized how much God loved him.

It was a pleasant spring evening, so he left the front door open. Jack loved the feeling of spring. It was exhilarating. The birth of new life, the eternal hope of new beginnings. It seemed even more fitting tonight, considering all that was going on.

Frank, accompanied by a refreshing light breeze, came bursting through the screen door. "Hey, Jack! How are you, man? Great day, huh? I love this weather!"

Jack wasn't used to seeing Frank this happy. He gave him a big hug and said, "Doing great, my friend. And I see you are too."

"Unbelievable is all I can say. I can't get enough, you know? I've been reading like a maniac. I have experienced so much with you, especially the other night. I feel like I'm living the Bible in real-time." Frank's eyes were open wide and gleaming with new life.

Jack laughed out loud. "I've never heard it put that way. That is awesome. Come in the kitchen, my friend. I ordered a pizza. It came a few minutes ago. I knew you would be hungry and on time."

They walked into the kitchen, with Frank talking a mile a minute.

"Thanks, man. So, here I am. One of those born again, Jesus freaks, I used to think was so weird. I mean, before I met you, that is."

Jack just kept smiling. "Glad I could help."

They sat down at the table. Jack opened the pizza box. "What do you say we pray before we eat?"

"You'll get no argument from me."

Both men bowed their heads as Jack prayed, "Father, we thank You for bringing us together and for all You have done for both of us. We thank You for this food. Bless our time together, in Jesus' name, amen."

Frank started with a question before Jack could take a bite of his first slice.

"I read in the gospel of John that Jesus said no one can see the kingdom of God unless he is born again. That is so real to me now. I understand it because I can sense and feel Him in my life. Before, it was just a story to me, you know? Like I used to say to you all the time, 'Whatever works for you. It didn't seem real or even possible."

Jack couldn't believe what was coming out of Frank's mouth. It was so cool to hear him talk like this.

"It is personal. You can't have my experience, and I can't have yours.

There are over seven billion people on earth, and God has a personal experience waiting for each one if they would turn to Him and receive it."

Frank was merely warming up. "I also read about Jesus casting out demons. That's what you do, right?"

"Well, yeah. I don't do it myself, though. It is the power of God in me that does it. Jesus said, 'Anyone who has faith in Me will do what I have been doing and even greater things because I am going to the Father.' When he rose from the dead, he gave us power over the darkness and the world."

"Why doesn't every Christian do what you do?"

Jack took a deep breath and picked up another piece of pizza. "Frank, I want you to know that I'm not anything special. All I do is try to stay close to the Lord and do what He says. Anybody who does that can do what I have done. Jesus walks beside me, and without that, I have nothing. Jesus said, 'I have given you authority to trample on snakes and scorpions and to overcome all the power of the enemy; nothing will harm you.' But He reminds us we should not rejoice, that the spirits submit to us, but rejoice that our names are written in heaven. That's the most important thing."

Frank's eyes grew wide. "That demon thing the other night. It knew who you were. I mean, it knew your name! That is way too freaky, man. When I heard that, I was blown away. You say you're nothing special, but what's up with that?"

Jack smiled and opened his Bible to the book of Acts, chapter 19. "There is a story about seven sons of a chief priest who went around trying to cast demons out of people. I guess they thought they were special because of their father's position. They used the name of Jesus and the apostle Paul's name to do this, but one day the evil spirit answered them and said, 'Jesus I know, and I know about Paul, but who are you?' Then the man who had the evil spirit jumped on them and gave them such a beating that they ran out of the house naked and bleeding. The point is the devil and his demons know who is walking the walk vs. talking the talk. We are all special to God, and, as long as we stay connected and close to Him, we have power over the darkness."

"Why wouldn't all Christians want to stay close to Him? I've never felt better in my whole life."

"Things happen. Life gets in the way. You know that. We all get busy and focused on our own lives. If we're not careful, the concerns of this world will overwhelm us. Sometimes God gets crowded out. I don't think anyone does it intentionally. Most of the time, we don't even realize it's happening. The other night, you saw an example of how powerful the darkness is. The enemy is sly and deceitful, and if we stop praying, we lose our way. It's a battle, but it is a battle we can win."

Frank sighed with relief. "I still can't believe this is all happening. I feel like Neo in The Matrix. It's like a hidden world, and, suddenly, I can see into another dimension."

"It is pretty wild. We have to watch what we say to other people. You know, like the agency. They have been a significant source for me over the years. God has opened doors I never thought possible. Share your newfound faith in Christ, but for now, stay away from talking about demons and angels."

Frank laughed. "I get it. They would lock us up and throw away the key. I don't know how you do it. How weird is it to be a part of a covert agency, centered on the study of paranormal activity, and not be able to report the truth?"

Jack shrugged his shoulders. "I know. In God's timing, we will have our opportunity, but we need to be cautious. If they label us religious fanatics, we would be out of the loop and out of a job. Until then, we share our faith in Christ and tread carefully."

The conversation went on for hours. Jack answered as many questions as possible, explaining the meaning of many Bible verses to Frank's delight. They talked about all their experiences together and, of course, just before Frank left, the subject of Emily came up.

"So, how did you do asking Emily out—or didn't you?"

Jack shook his head. "I did. We had a great time! In fact, I'm picking her up for church tomorrow morning."

"Really? You like her, huh? I knew you would. She's a babe."

Jack laughed. "Yes, Frank. She's a babe. She is also a lovely girl. We are just getting to know one another. It's a process."

Frank stood up from the table. "A process? Oh, brother. It's not a process." With his arms crossed and pressing his Bible close to his chest, he mockingly said, "It's love, my man. It's love."

Jack rolled his eyes. "Go home! It's late. Remember, service is at 9:00 am."

Frank laughed. "Okay, I'll be there. I'll meet you in the parking lot."

Frank opened the car door and looked back at Jack. "Thanks for praying for me all that time. You're a good friend. And hey, I'm telling you, man, don't blow this one. That Emily, she's a keeper."

Jack raised his arm and pointed towards the end of the driveway without saying a word. He did not want to hear any more words of wisdom from Frank. At least for tonight.

19

A DAY OF REST

It was another beautiful morning in Eastern Virginia. The thermometer read seventy-two degrees, and there was a warm, gentle breeze blowing from the Southwest. Jack was up early, excited to introduce Frank and Emily to his friends at church. He was a little nervous, hoping they would both enjoy the service and anxiously counting the minutes until he would see Emily again.

Finally, it was time to go. Jack jumped in the car and headed off. It was a short drive, but long enough to pray for Frank and Emily. Jack desperately wanted them to feel comfortable and enjoy the service. He pulled up to Emily's apartment building exactly at 8:30 and started up the sidewalk. Emily stepped out of the door. She had been waiting and watching from her second-story window for the last fifteen minutes. Jack's eyes immediately lit up upon seeing her. She had on a beautiful floral-print dress and a white half-sleeve sweater. Her hair, her eyes, everything about her was beautiful. It was like he was seeing her for the first time.

"Hi! I'm ready," she said, glowing.

"Wow, you look great!"

He opened the door for her, walked around to the driver's side, and slid behind the wheel.

"I hope you like the service today. Pastor Eli is a laid-back guy. He usually teaches in jeans and a t-shirt. I think you will like him. He really knows the Word. My buddy Frank is coming for the first time today, as well. He just came to the Lord last week. He is a little nervous, but extremely excited."

"That's awesome. God is really doing a lot of new things lately."

Jack agreed. "Yeah, I guess you could say that."

It wasn't long before they were pulling into the parking lot. Jack immediately spied Frank standing by his car. "What an incredible day!" Frank shouted. "Hi, Emily! I'm Frank. So good to see you outside of CJ's."

"Hi, Frank. I'm glad to be here. This is new for you, too, I hear."

"Yes, it feels strange, but right."

Jack took Emily's hand, and they all headed up the steps to the front of the school. Jack felt like he was floating on air with his new girl and his best friend in tow.

Jack introduced Frank and Emily to a few folks on the way in. The service was about t begin. The ushers directed them to three available seats. Jack positioned himself between them so he could answer any questions they might have. As the worship band kicked in, he looked over at Frank - he was smiling from ear to ear.

Frank leaned in. "I never thought it was going to be so cool. I love it."

Emily was already clapping her hands to the music and worshipping the Lord. Jack thought, 'Can it get any better than this?'

Pastor Eli concluded his message with a challenge to the congregation to follow close to the Lord and stay faithful to their weekly small group meetings held in various homes throughout the community. Jack didn't know everyone, but they knew him. It was obvious to all, especially the ladies, that Jack Bennett had a lovely young woman sitting next to him. After the service, Jack took great delight in introducing his guests to several friends in the congregation. Pastor Eli was in his usual place, greeting each one at the door as they left.

He spied Jack, "Hey, Jack! Good to see you. Who's the young lady?"

"Good morning, Pastor. This is Emily Richardson."

Pastor Eli reached out his hand and greeted her. "Good to meet you, Emily. I hope you enjoyed the service."

"It was wonderful, Pastor. I loved everything about it."

Before Jack could introduce Frank, Pastor Eli jumped in.

"And this must be Frank. I've heard a lot about you over the past few years. When I saw you come in, I said to myself, that has to be Frank Lederman. We've been praying for you for quite some time."

"I appreciate that... more than you know, Pastor."

Pastor Eli put his hand on Jack's shoulder. "You stick with Jesus and this guy, and you'll be all right."

"I plan on it," Frank said with a smile. "It was great to meet you."

Eli's hand remained on Jack's shoulder. "Let's get together for lunch this week. I want to catch up with you and discuss a few things."

"No problem! The sooner, the better. It's going to be a busy week. How about tomorrow morning? Is that possible?"

"Normally, I am not available on Mondays, but that works for me. Let's do it. Is your place all right? Say at ten o'clock?"

"My place it is. See you then." They hugged each other, and Jack headed out into the parking lot. It wasn't unusual for them to meet and discuss church business. They had been close friends for years.

As they made their way back to their cars, Frank said. "You were right. I never pictured church this way. It was outstanding. Unfortunately, I have to get back to DC this afternoon. The FBI never rests. Not even on the Lord's day."

Jack reached out and hugged him. "I can't tell you how great it was having you in service this morning. God is so faithful. I'll talk to you tomorrow."

"Sounds good."

Frank said goodbye to Emily and drove off to Washington.

"What do you say, ready for some breakfast?"

"Absolutely."

* * *

Emily made herself comfortable as Jack began his assault on the kitchen. After a nice breakfast of Jack's famous waffles and bacon, they went out onto the front porch and curled up on Jack's new outdoor sofa, enjoying the beautiful surroundings and the fresh air.

"I love your place. It's so peaceful here."

"Thanks. I loved it the first day the realtor showed it. Privacy is important to me. Despite what most people think, I guess I'm a bit of a recluse."

"Really? You don't come off that way."

Jack sighed. "That's good to know. I don't want you to think I'm weird or anything. Other than what I've already told you."

Emily chuckled, "On the contrary, I find you very interesting." She thought, more than you know, Jack Bennett. Handsome, sensitive, and humble.

"There are a few layers to me, I suppose." Jack put his arm around her, and Emily intuitively laid her head on his shoulder. For the next few minutes, they sat silently, resting in each other's arms, enjoying the moment. Emily was thrilled. Guys like Jack were a rare find. That he was older somehow made her feel more secure. He had a quiet confidence that reassured her. She had met no one like Jack before. Emily's thoughts ran to Friday night and the tender way their lips blended. She wanted to kiss him now, but she would wait for him to make the first move.

Jack gently put his hand under Emily's chin, lifted her head, gazed into her incredible blue eyes, tilted his head slightly, and kissed her. Emily responded with a kiss of her own, both discovering and enjoying a deeper connection than before. Jack opened his eyes as a gentle breeze blew Emily's dress. He glanced down at her legs. She was very beautiful. His thoughts quickly ran to places he didn't want them to go. Jack realized he needed to slow it down. He couldn't allow his feelings to get the best of him. Jack was not under any delusion. He knew he was as prone to temptation as anyone else. To Jack, any other way of thinking was foolish. He often quoted I Corinthians 10:12, 'So, if you think you are standing firm, be careful that you don't fall!'

Jack certainly didn't want to do anything that would offend or lead Emily to go down the wrong path. In days gone by or, as he liked to put it, in his BC days, this would have eventually led to the bedroom. Maybe not today, but tomorrow or the next time they were alone. But these weren't the BC days. They had just met, and Jack wasn't sure how strong Emily's faith was, and until he did, it was up to him to keep it together. Jack knew the enemy would love to see him fall and take Emily down with in the process. That would take Jack and his ministry out of the picture for a while, maybe long enough for the enemy to get a foothold in a new territory of his life. Jack respected Emily and loved the Lord too much to consider going down that road.

He pulled away slowly and said, "That was—amazing."

Emily gently touched his cheek and whispered, "You know, I have to confess. I often thought of what it would be like to kiss you. And yes, it was amazing. I can't believe I'm here, holding you like this."

Jack thought, 'Is she kidding? I'm the one who finds this hard to believe.' Jack took the opportunity to say what he hoped would come out right without sounding presumptuous or inappropriate.

"I know we have only been on two dates." He paused and asked, "I guess this is a date, right?"

Emily smiled and said, "I think that's safe to say."

"I want to be upfront. I really like you. It's been a while since I have allowed myself to feel this way about anyone. So—I guess what I'm saying is, I need to take it slow. I know we just met, and we know little about each other—but I want you to know how I feel about..."

It comforted Emily to know Jack was the real deal. She could see he was having an awful time getting out what he wanted to say, so she stopped him right there.

"You don't have to say anymore. I respect what you're saying and I have gotten into some poor relationships and made a few major mistakes in my life. I'm a big girl and yes, I'm really attracted to you, Jack Bennett. It would be easy to go back to the old ways. We both want to honor the Lord with our lives, so we'll work on it together, okay?"

Jack could hardly believe what he was hearing. She had taken the words right out of his mouth. It said so much about her commitment to the Lord. He felt so relieved. "Thank you for not leaving me hanging out there. I'm afraid I'm not too good at this kind of thing. I have had little time for dating. Burying myself in my work was all I allowed myself to think about. Emily, I feel incredibly relaxed around you. You are so easy to talk to, and—that's a rare quality these days. I don't want to appear like some kind of prude." Jack looked into her sparkling blue eyes and whispered, "I do love kissing you, so we'll keep that part, okay?"

Emily laughed out loud. "Oh yes, Mr. Bennett. We'll keep that part. By the way, I think you're doing just fine." Emily put her head back on his shoulder, and they continued to talk deep into the afternoon.

20

MEETING IN THE SKY

Monday morning found Washington D.C. bathed in a steady rain. A black limousine carrying Senator Wellsenburg pulled up to Reagan National Airport, where Dante Adal waited in his private jet. The Dassault Falcon 900LX sat fueled and ready to go. The Senator was traveling alone today, but that was normal procedure whenever he met with Adal. He always carried one small personal bag and a briefcase that held his tablet, a burner phone for calls he didn't want anyone to know about, and a few important documents he was required to review. He wasn't entirely sure why Dante called this meeting, only that some very influential people wanted to meet him and discuss his future.

Once aboard, within minutes, the jet was in the air and leveling off at course altitude. The cockpit door swung open. Dante Adal swaggered down the aisle and sat down next to the senator. He loved flying, not necessarily in this fashion, but when he did, he insisted on taking part in the takeoffs.

One of Dante's personal flight attendants approached Senator Wellsenburg and asked, "Would you like a drink, Senator?"

Dante always had several beautiful young ladies accompany him on his flights. He found them to be both pleasing and useful.

"Yes, I'll have a scotch on the rocks."

"Hennessy Paradis for me," Dante said firmly.

The senator raised his eyebrows. "That is an exceptional cognac."

Dante gave him a smug look. "Why should I drink anything less?"

Senator Wellsenburg loved expensive things, and nothing impressed him more than a man who was a connoisseur of all.

"It is vital that you continue to use your influence in the Senate to ensure that the United States withdraw military aid to Israel. We have grand plans for the Mid-East, and it doesn't include the United States. Think bigger, Senator. The entire world is there for the taking. We are making great strides on many U.S. campuses; anti-Semitism is on the rise, fueled by Muslim activist groups promoting the Palestinian cause. However, we need to make sure all fronts continue to move forward. The American people, especially this new generation, must become completely disenchanted with Israel. I hope you understand what I'm saying."

A small bead of sweat appeared on Wellsenburg's forehead as he formulated a response. "Dante, that is very difficult for me to do. There is still substantial support for Israel in the Senate. Remember, I voted to support Israel in the past. My recent change of position has raised more than a few eyebrows. I have made some inroads, but it is an arduous task."

"I thought you were on our side, Senator? I urge you to keep our little deal in mind. You know, the one that helped you get where you are today. We expect your support. The Jews have been the bane of my existence since they became a people. Do you have any idea how many times we have attempted to eliminate them down through the ages? There is always one that rises and gets in the way. Noah, Abraham, Moses, Joshua, David, Mordecai, Esther—the list goes on. We sat beside Nero and the Roman Empire, Hitler, and the Third Reich. We were there guiding them, inspiring them, and those damn Jews still survived. Do you plan on being the one getting in the way this time, Senator?"

Wellsenburg backpedaled for a moment. He thought, 'Noah? Abraham? Moses? What in the world is he saying?'

"By we, do you mean the society?" he asked cautiously. "I did not know that the Sons of Nimrod had such a place in history. You never mentioned that before. How do you know all of this?"

Dante was in no mood to be cross-examined. His countenance changed drastically. He wasn't about to divulge that he was, in fact, talking about himself and other powerful beings. He gave the senator a piercing look that made his blood run cold.

"We are the Sons of Nimrod, are we not?" he questioned him sarcastically. "Or did you think you and your Washington cohorts came up with that all on your own? If you need a history lesson, Senator, I will give you one someday, but now is not the time."

Dante readjusted himself in his chair and peered into Wellsenburg's eyes. "I asked you a question before. Do you plan on being the one getting in the way this time, Senator?"

Wellsenburg swallowed hard, then took another drink.

Clearing his throat, he answered, "No, I have no other plans. You know that. I need your support to become the next President of the United States. You said a new world order was coming and that as President, I would play an integral part in bringing that about." Putting his drink down, he added, "And that, sir, is my only plan."

Dante sat back in his chair, satisfied he had put the subject to rest.

"Fine. We have other things to discuss, so let's get down to business. There is a rash of new church groups popping up all over America. Not church buildings, but groups of believers using schools and other public buildings for their services. We need a law to keep them out of all public places. I want them shut down. They are wreaking havoc within the spirit world. Wee must discourage their faith and discredit those who would oppose us."

Wellsenburg's ears perked up. And a puzzled look crossed his face. He knew Dante was different and seemed to have some kind of mysterious dark power about him, but he didn't really know much more than that.

"The spirit world? I don't understand."

Dante reached over and took a sip of his cognac. He had revealed a little more than he intended to, at least for now.

"I use that terminology often to express the general atmosphere around certain situations that we have to deal with. It's more like karma. You will become accustomed to its usage as we continue to move forward on future projects." Dante knew what those future projects would be. Wellsenburg accepted the answer, for now, nodded, and decided it best to move on. He knew better than to ask any more questions. Perhaps he would save them for another day.

"Today's meeting is vital to your campaign. My associates have agreed to take time from their busy schedules to meet with you. Some have traveled a great distance." Dante's eyes bore into Wellsenburg. "You need to appreciate the opportunity set before you, Senator."

Wellsenburg was feeling very uneasy. "I can't be away from Washington for too long. "I have important budget hearings to attend. Who exactly are these associates of yours, and what is their agenda?"

"Not to worry. My pilot will fly you back in the morning." Dante leaned into him and cautioned, "You don't seem to understand what is at stake here. If all goes well, you will have more than enough money for your campaign. You want to be president—don't you, senator?"

Wellsenburg glared at him. "That has always been my plan."

"Fine then. There will be enough time to discuss business during the flight, but for now, I think you need to relax and enjoy some female companionship. Ladies?"

The good senator always looked forward to these meetings. Dante Adal knew how to keep his little marionettes happy.

21

CAPTIVE

Frank got out early from his nine o'clock meeting at the J. Edgar Hoover Building and walked out into the light rain that continued to fall in D.C. He was on a mission. Grabbing his phone, he called Jack on his way to the car.

"Frank. What's up?"

"You will not believe what happened. This morning, before my meeting, I got talking to one of my guys about the Lord. He was raised a Christian but hadn't been to church in years. I told him about your church. He said he might check it out."

Jack smiling. "That's cool, Frank. You didn't waste any time sharing your faith. That's outstanding!"

Frank took a quick look around and got into his car. "The Lord is amazing. Whoever thought, right? I heard something this morning that is a game-changer. You know we've been talking about the Sons of

Nimrod and the secret society? Well, during the conversation, he mentioned this up-and-coming tycoon type he read about in Forbes magazine. He said this guy is a big-time player. My man's into this stuff. The article mentioned his connection to some secret society. When he told the name, I freaked out."

"What name?"

"Dante Adal."

Jack's eyes widened. "Dante?"

"How could I forget that name after that night at the church? Dante was the name the angel called that demon creature, right?"

Jack was cautious not to jump to any conclusions. "Yes, it was, but I don't see the connection."

"I'm not done. My guy told me about a hush-hush meeting held at the Hotel Palomar, attended by a dozen high-profile business types and two prominent U.S. senators. And are you ready? This Dante Adal was one of them. It hit me like a ton of bricks. I mean, what are the chances of that name coming up associated with a secret organization here in DC?"

Jack was stunned. It didn't seem possible. The thought of a demon taking the form of a man and interacting with U.S. senators was frightening. Jack knew this was uncharted territory, a whole new level of demonic invasion. The darkness was stepping it up in a bold move to gain greater control in Washington and beyond.

"I have to admit. I don't think that it's a coincidence. Creepy, but no coincidence. Did he mention the senators involved?"

"Here's the kicker. He wasn't sure, but he thinks one of them was Senator George R. Wellsenburg from New York."

"Wow!" Jack managed. "If that's true, there is little doubt that this Dante Adal is our demon prince. If that's the case, we are in for a major battle for the soul of America."

Frank took a deep breath and groaned, "Never a dull moment when I'm around you, Jack. So, what are we gonna do?"

"We have to pray and pray hard. When are you heading back?"

"Well, that's the next thing I have to tell you. We have a fresh case. It seems there is something crazy going on close to where your church meets. A report came in from a woman who said she has been hearing strange sounds coming from her neighbor's house at all hours of the night. She says it's been going on for days. Last Saturday night, she thought she saw objects flying around in the neighbor's backyard. The local police checked it out and dismissed it, so she found the agency's number and called us. The Director wants us to investigate and file a report. I should be to you by noon."

Just then, there was a knock on Jack's front door. "Okay, see you then. I gotta go. I have a meeting with Pastor Eli. See you when you get here."

"Hi, Eli. How are you this morning?"

"Hey, Jack. I hope you've got the coffee on."

Jack laughed and nodded. "Always."

"I got a strange one for you."

Jack's eyebrows went up. "There seems to be a lot of that going around today. What's up?"

"I had a very unsettling experience during the outreach last week. We were going door-to-door handing out postcards, inviting the neighbors to the church picnic, and letting them know there was a new church meeting on Sundays at the school. We came to this one house, and as soon as the man came to the door, I felt an evil presence. And from what I could see from the porch, the house was in complete disarray."

"I got a bad feeling about that guy, Jack. Maybe you and Frank could check it out. I have no authority to force my way in there. But something is not right. I can tell you that. I told the man that if he needed any help to contact the church, but he said he wasn't interested and slammed the door in my face."

Jack quickly put two-and-two together.

"I can't believe you are telling me this. I think this might be the same house Frank just called me about. A neighbor reported objects flying around the backyard and hearing strange noises all at hours of the night. We are heading over there this morning."

"If possible, I would like to accompany you. I have been in prayer all morning about it. I couldn't get him off my mind."

"I can't think of a better person to have with us, but we have to document our investigation, and they only allow authorized personnel to be involved. It's an official federal investigation at this point. Frank will be here in a half-hour. Maybe we could spend some time in prayer together. I would really like Frank to see how we prepare before going out on these missions. Afterward, I should be able to get you involved in the follow-up."

"That would be great. It would be a privilege to pray with you guys. Isn't it wild that the government is getting involved in all this?"

"That's just the tip of the iceberg, Eli. Just the tip of the iceberg."

The two men bowed their heads and prayed, and as they did, time flew by. Before long, there was a tap on the door. "Hey Frank, come on in!"

Frank gave them an odd look. "I could hear you two as soon as I got out of the car. What's up?"

Jack smiled. "We were praying. I guess we got a little carried away. You're right on time."

"Hi Pastor, I really enjoyed your sermon on Sunday, and the music was exceptional."

"Thanks, Frank. So glad you liked it. Good to see you again. Jack tells me you have another case to go on today."

"Yeah, another strange one, for sure."

Frank felt a little uncomfortable interrupting their prayed time. "You have been praying, huh?"

Eli stood up and shook Frank's hand. "Yes. I think you are going to the same house I came to talk to Jack about."

Frank looked surprised. "Really."

"I'll tell you all about it on our way. Pastor Eli would like to pray with us before we head over there. Is that okay?"

Frank glanced over at Eli. "Okay, I've never actually prayed with anyone before, but I guess there's a first time for everything."

"You can pray out loud or silently. It doesn't matter. God hears it all," Pastor Eli said with a reassuring smile.

They stood together and prayed for about ten minutes, Frank silently. It was time to move out. Pastor Eli told them he would continue to pray and asked that they let him know how things turned out.

Jack jumped in Frank's car, and off they went. It only took a twenty-minutes to get from Jack's place to Edgewater Drive, the location of the unusual activity. They walked up to the house of the woman that filed the complaint and knocked on the door.

The door opened, and a large woman, about fifty years old, stood before them.

Frank introduced himself, then Jack. "Hello, ma'am. I am FBI Special Agent Frank Lederman, and this is Jack Bennett, consultant to the FBI. Are you Katie Warren?"

"Yes, I'm Mrs. Warren," the woman responded cautiously.

"We are here to investigate a complaint you filed concerning the house next door."

"Well, it's about time someone took this seriously. Those first two officers never even went into the house. They breezed in and out and did nothing. Nothing at all! I hope you are prepared to conduct a proper investigation."

Frank glanced over at Jack, who was doing his best to keep a straight face.

"Yes, ma'am. Is this the house in question?" Frank pointed to the house next door.

"Yes, that's it. Strange goings-on over there, I'll tell you. When they moved in, there were three of them: a man, a woman, and a young child–a girl. But I never see the woman or the child come out of the house. I know they're in there because I can see them walking around upstairs late at night."

"It appears you keep a pretty good eye on things."

The woman straightened, and her eyes narrowed. "That's right. I got a right to know what's going on next door to me. That doesn't make me a bad person."

"No, ma'am, it doesn't. We'll check it out and let you know what we find out."

"You boys better watch yourself. That place is evil. It's got the hooey on it."

"Yes, ma'am. Thank you." They turned and started down the sidewalk. Jack looked at Frank. He couldn't contain himself any longer.

"The hooey? And what's with all the 'ma'am' stuff? I feel like I'm watching Dragnet."

Frank gave him a sideways look. "When I'm on official FBI business, that's how I roll."

Jack tried not to laugh. "That's how you roll? All I can say is watch out for the hooey!"

Jack's smile disappeared as they approached the front door of the house. It was a two-story building in desperate need of repair, with a small front porch that looked like it could fall at any moment. Jack sensed something immediately; it was a feeling he knew all too well. Frank knocked on the door. They could hear heavy footsteps approaching. When it opened, a large, bearded, barrel-chested man in his mid-forties stood before them. Looking like he hadn't slept in days, if not weeks.

He peered at them with dark, bloodshot eyes. "What do you want?" He growled. "I ain't buying nothin', and I don't need nothin', so get the hell off my porch!"

Frank spoke first, "Sir, are you Raymond Hillerbrand?"

"Yeah, what about it? You some kind of reporter?" The man snapped back.

"No, sir. I am Special Agent Frank Lederman, FBI. And this is FBI consultant Jack Bennett. We are here because of a complaint filed with our agency. May we come in and talk with you for a moment?"

"The FBI?" Hillerbrand stiffened. "We ain't done nothing wrong. Who complained? That old witch next door? She ain't nothin' but an old busybody, always snooping around, looking for trouble. She better watch it. It just might come her way one day, if you know what I mean."

Hillerbrand glanced at Jack. His face twitched slightly. Jack immediately picked up on it.

Frank continued, "Sir, just the same, we need to ask you a few questions."

Hillerbrand positioned himself in the center of the doorway, his large hand tightening its grip on the doorknob. "Any questions you have, you can ask me right here. No need to come in my house unless you got a warrant."

Frank took a more serious tone. "Sir, if you make me get a warrant, I will come back here and search every crack and crevice in this house. Is that what you want?"

Frank knew he would have difficulty getting a warrant in this situation, but he hoped this guy didn't know that.

Mr. Hillerbrand peered at Frank for a few seconds, then back at Jack. This time, his eyes appeared darker and larger than before. Finally, he said, "All right. You can come in for a minute, and then I want you out of here. I don't give a damn who you are. You got it?"

Hillerbrand stepped back and opened the door. The front room was a complete disaster. Clothes strewn all over the floor, discarded food containers scattered all around. The smell was overwhelming. It was pure filth, from top to bottom. They thought it better to remain standing.

He noticed them checking everything out and snarled, "The clock's ticking. What do you want to know?"

As he was about to ask his first question, Frank heard a rustling noise coming from upstairs. He turned to Jack and heard it again. It sounded like feet scuffling on a bare wood floor. Jack heard it too.

"Who else lives in the house with you?" Frank demanded.

"Just my wife and daughter. They're not here right now."

"I hear someone upstairs. Who is that?" Frank pressed.

"It's just my cats. We have two of them."

Frank and Jack looked at each other. They both had a bad feeling. There were no cats.

"Would you mind if we looked upstairs?" Frank probed.

Hillerbrand's face changed abruptly, and his voice got louder and nastier. "I told you a few minutes, then out! You ain't goin' upstairs without a warrant. You've asked enough questions. Now get the hell out!"

Jack knew what was inside this man, and he couldn't leave without testing the spirits. He was truly concerned.

"Sir, I belong to a church close to here. If you ever need anything, we would be happy to help. Jesus changed my life, and Jesus can do the same for you."

At that, Hillerbrand twitched again, this time more violently. Then a voice came out of him that wasn't his own.

"I know who you are and what you're trying to do!" It sounded like multiple voices, all talking at once. "You are one of His followers. He invited here. This man is mine!"

Hillerbrand lifted his arm, a lamp lifted off the table, and shot violently across the room, nearly hitting Frank in the head. Jack ducked, stood back up, and held out his right hand.

"In the name of Jesus, the Christ, the Son of God, I command you, unclean spirit, to come out of him and leave this place!"

The spirit slammed Hillerbrand's body to the ground and went into convulsions, rolling around on the floor as Jack and Frank prayed.

Jack could feel an overwhelming power surging through him; it was like a fire in his bones. He looked down at the man and spoke again to the spirit. "The Lord God Almighty commands you to go!"

The demon shrieked so loud, Jack and Frank thought the windows were going to shatter. Then suddenly, it went quiet. Hillerbrand's body lay perfectly still on the floor. Jack checked his pulse. He was alive.

"Frank, get me a glass of water. I believe he's going to be all right."

As Frank came back with the water, Hillerbrand's eyes slowly opened. Jack helped him sit up, and he took a drink. Hillerbrand covered in sweat, his eyes clear, and pulse steady and slow, looked up at Frank.

Frank glared down at him and demanded, "Sir, tell me who is upstairs?"

Dazed, he mumbled, "My family - my wife and my little girl."

Frank dashed up the stairs. There were three bedrooms, but only one door was locked. Frank could hear someone inside.

He yelled through the door, "I'm with the FBI! If you are able, please move away from the door. I'm going to break it down!"

Frank kicked the door in. To his shock, he found Hillerbrand's wife and little girl gagged and chained to a large hook screwed to the floor. The room was filthy. Piles of paper plates, some with bits of dried food still on them, were everywhere. They looked like they had been in the same clothes for weeks. Frank could see the desperation in their eyes. He ran over and immediately removed the gags from their mouths and yelled down to Jack.

"They're here! And they're alive! Call 911! Ask Hillerbrand where the key is to unlock these chains."

Jack stood up, grabbed his phone, and called 911. He looked at Hillerbrand, still sitting on the floor. "You heard him. Where's the key?"

Hillerbrand pointed to a small jar sitting on the mantel of the fireplace. "I got it. I'll toss it up to you!"

Jack used Frank's ID to call 911. It saved him a lot of time and explanation. "This is Special Agent Frank Lederman with the FBI. I need an ambulance at 95 Edgewater Drive immediately. I have a man in custody and a woman and a little girl who need medical attention."

Jack tossed Frank the key. He walked back into the bedroom and unlocked the large bolt that was binding them to the floor. The mother grabbed her daughter and hugged her, kissing her on the head repeatedly.

Frank, kneeling on the floor in front of them, introduced himself. "My name is Frank Lederman. I'm a special agent with the FBI. The ambulance will be here in a few minutes. They will take you to the hospital to get checked out."

The wife was frantic. With eyes as big as saucers, she blurted out. "Where's my husband? Keep him away from us! I don't want him around my daughter! Do you understand? Get him out of here! I don't want her to see him ever again!"

Frank helped her up. "Don't worry, ma'am. My partner has him. You are safe now. I will stay with you until the ambulance gets here, okay?"

She nodded her head, still holding fast to her daughter.

Within minutes, two police cars pulled up in front of the house. Pulling right behind them was the ambulance and first aid squad. When they came in, they saw Jack standing alongside Mr. Hillerbrand.

"My partner is upstairs with the little girl and her mother. They both need medical attention." He turned to the police officers and indicated Hillerbrand. "This is Mr. Hillerbrand. He needs to go with you. Special Agent Lederman will fill you in when he gets to the station."

The two cops took Mr. Hillerbrand out in handcuffs. There was no simple explanation for this one, and Jack wasn't about to try. Demon possession isn't exactly recognized criminal behavior. Frank would take custody of Hillerbrand, and there would be a full federal investigation into the matter. What would come of it was up for grabs. The EMTs, a woman, and a young man, gently escorted Mrs. Hillerbrand and her daughter to the ambulance. The two police cars roared down the road, with the ambulance following close behind. Jack and Frank stood in the middle of the room, somewhat dazed.

"Wow. Can you believe it?" Frank said, rubbing his forehead. "How crazy was that! It will be a long time before I get the terror in that little girl's face out of my mind. What is wrong with people?"

Jack looked around the room, taking in every detail. "This guy was into some nasty stuff. There are stacks of porn magazines, videos, and books on how to summon your personal spirit guide." Jack walked over to the bookcase next to the fireplace and spied a paperback book with an image of a bizarre-looking man sitting on a throne of gold. "Look at this one. Be Your Own God. Really new age—I mean, the full deal. The amount of depravity that people let into their lives astounds me. It's heartbreaking." Jack shook himself. "Let's get out of here. I haven't eaten all day. Let's decompress over some food." I know this great little place with the cutest server."

Frank put his hand on Jack's shoulder. "Now you're talking my language."

22

A FLY IN THE OINTMENT

It was 1:30 in the afternoon when Jack and Frank walked into CJ's. Emily was waiting at a table at the other end of the café. They found their usual spot vacant, so they sat down and waited for her to notice them. Emily headed back towards the kitchen, pad-in-hand. When she saw Jack out of the corner of her eye. Her face lit up. She quickly placed the order and walked over to their table.

"Well, Mr. Bennett and Mr. Lederman, what a pleasant surprise. I didn't expect to see you gentleman here today. My shift is nearly over." Emily bent over and kissed Jack on the cheek.

Frank chimed in, "Well, I never thought I'd see the day. Jack Bennett has a girlfriend."

Jack smiled, "Times, they are a-changing." He turned to Emily and asked, "How's your day going? Been busy?"

"Crazy. It finally slowed down. Absolutely slammed since seven this morning. What can I get you two? I know you don't need to see a menu."

Frank laughed, "No, I'll have a turkey club and a cup of coffee."

Emily fixed her big blue eyes on Jack and said softly, "How about you, Mr. Bennett?"

"Well, I have to ask you, do you ever date your customers, because I would like to ask you to dinner and a movie tonight? I know this private little place with a magnificent view. What do you say I pick you up at six?"

"I usually don't," she feigned shyness, "but I think I could make an exception in your case. You seem like a fascinating man."

Frank sat there, listening in disbelief. He couldn't take it another minute.

"What have you done to my partner? I can't believe you two. You have only gone out twice, and look what's happened. Let's get back to talking about food. I'm starving."

Jack smiled. "I'll have one of those black Russians and water with lemon. I've had all the stimulation I can handle for one day."

Emily raised her eyebrows, pouted her lips, and said, "Oh, really?" and walked away.

Frank laughed out loud. "You gotta watch what you say now, buddy. You've got a woman in your life."

They both laughed. Frank was eager to discuss what had happened today. He also needed to talk about the Oslow House. He still had plenty of questions for Jack concerning the supernatural.

"So, what am I going to do with this Hillerbrand guy? He seems like a different person since," he paused and looked around, wondering if anyone was within hearing distance,—"that demon thing left him," he finished quietly.

"Well, he's still the same guy who got himself into all that. I'm sure he wasn't the best husband or father before that unclean spirit entered him."

Emily came over to the table with their drinks. She could see they were in a deep conversation, so she put them down and approached another table, not wanting to interrupt them.

Frank poured a cup of coffee and took a sip. "Great coffee. I will find out a lot more once I interview the wife. She will shed some light on things. That poor woman must have some wild stories to tell."

"No doubt. So, I guess you'll have to let him go through the system. I'll hook him up with Pastor Eli. He'll make sure he sees a good Christian therapist. I doubt his wife and daughter are going to want to see him or that house again. They're the ones who are going to need therapy. I know Pastor Eli and the whole church will want to reach out and offer to help them recover. They're great like that," Jack said.

Emily brought their order and quickly picked up on the intensity of their conversation. "Looks like you guys are really getting into it again. You'll have to tell me more about what you do someday. It must be pretty interesting."

Frank pulled his plate of food in close and glanced at Jack. "Yeah, it gets a little crazy sometimes. Jack will explain it all to you, I'm sure."

"It's just our work. It seems more interesting than it really is," Jack downplaying Frank's comment.

"I'm sure," Emily said, giving them a sly smile. She knew these men were up to something, but she could see the food was ready for her other table, so she reluctantly headed to the kitchen.

Frank dove right back in. "So, what happens to this guy now that the evil spirit is out of him? Does he go back to the way he was before?"

"Jesus said that when an evil spirit comes out of a man, it goes through barren places seeking rest and does not find it. It then returns to the person it used to inhabit, saying, 'I will return to the house I left.' When it arrives, it finds the house unoccupied, swept clean, and put in order. That is the state Hillerbrand is in right now. If he does not fill that house with Christ, he opens himself up for an even worse scenario. The Bible says that the unclean spirit will go out and take with it seven other spirits more wicked than itself, and they will go in and live there. So, the last condition of that man is even worse than it was at first."

Frank rubbed his forehead in amazement and mustered, "You think he will get worse?"

"I'm not saying that. He could get worse, but it's really up to him. Here's what has to happen," Jack continued. "Hillerbrand needs to ask Christ into his life. Getting all cleaned up is great, but it's not the answer. That's why so many addicts get clean but can't stay that way. Hillerbrand will have the opportunity to confess his sins and ask Jesus to come into his life. If he does that, then the evil spirits can't get back in because his heart, or the house that Jesus talked about, is now occupied by God."

"Amazing. I can't believe all this stuff has been going on right under my nose, and I never knew it. I have to say it makes sense. There's an actual war going on, and few people realize it."

Jack smiled. "You understand more than many people who have been going to church for years. You're growing, my friend."

Frank looked worried. He finished his cup of coffee and, studying

Jack for a moment, asked, "What do you want to do about this Dante situation? That whole thing creeps me out."

"I don't know. That's a new one for me. Keep your ear to the ground, and if you find out anything more, let me know. It's very troublesome, but as the coming of Christ draws closer, there will be more and more supernatural intrusions. Let's keep praying about it and go from there."

Frank's eyes widened. "The coming of Jesus? You mean, like the end of the world?"

Jack smiled. "No, my friend, I mean the beginning. We can talk about that another time."

They finished their lunch, and while Frank went to the counter to pay the bill, Jack said goodbye to Emily. He wanted to get home and clean his house a bit before their big date.

Frank dropped Jack off at his house and drove to the local police department to follow up on the Hillerbrand case. He wanted to meet with Hillerbrand's wife and daughter, and hopefully, get a statement from them.

As soon as Jack walked into his house, his cell phone rang. He checked the screen and saw Conni's name. "Hi, Conni. How are you?"

"I'm not sure, Jack," her voice sounded troubled.

"What's going on?"

"We just got the okay to resume our prayer meetings, but there's something that's really bothering me," Conni continued.

Jack never expected things to go smoothly. He had been a little wary of the quick turnaround the historical society made concerning the prayer meetings. He was confident God was on the move, but realized the enemy wasn't about to give up.

"What happened?"

"Well, the executive board at my church assigned one of their board members to oversee the prayer meetings. The whole idea was to keep it non-denominational. To make things worse, he is very strict and legalistic, if you know what I mean. I need you to pray with me that somehow it will work out."

Jack knew exactly what she meant. He had encountered many Christians who had lost their passion somewhere along the line and had instead filled their hearts with rules and regulations. But he didn't want to get her more upset, so he took a different approach.

"I understand completely. I will be praying. Let's see how it goes. Maybe the Lord has this man there for a reason. Keep me updated. I will try to get there this Wednesday if I can."

"Thanks, Jack. I'll talk to you later."

"Okay, Conni. You take care."

Jack hung up and thought. 'Just a fly in the ointment, Hans. A monkey in the wrench.'

* * *

The light rain that fell earlier in the day had cleared out, dropping the temperature from the mild mid-seventies to a cool fifty-five. Jack picked Emily up, and the two of them talked the entire way back to his house. She was very interested in hearing more about what Jack and Frank did for a living.

Once inside, Jack decided it would be nice to make a fire, seeing that it might be the last one of spring. He had everything ready beforehand, so all he had to do was light it when he came in the door. He walked over and got it started, much to Emily's delight.

"Oh, I love a fireplace. I'm so glad it cooled down tonight. This is so nice!"

Jack smiled. "I thought you might like it. It's a perfect night for it."

Emily sat down on the couch and asked, "So, what's for dinner? I thought you only cooked breakfast?"

Jack hoped she wouldn't mind, but he had taken it upon himself to order dinner and have it delivered.

"Well, I ordered out. It should be here soon. Is that okay?"

Emily laughed, "That's fine. What are we having?"

"Well, I heard you say something about Mexican food the other night, so I ordered a bunch of different dishes for us to choose from."

Emily was impressed. Jack had been listening. "Wow! Mexican is one of my favorites."

Jack got the fire going just how he liked it and sat down next to Emily. She looked incredible in her white-lace top and jeans. "I hope you don't mind eating in tonight."

Emily wrapped her arms around him and whispered, "This is perfect. A nice quiet evening, a fire, sitting on this couch with you... I couldn't be happier."

Jack loved the sound of that as Emily laid her head on his shoulder. They both stared into the fire, wondering where this would lead. Emily turned toward Jack, her soft eyes speaking volumes into his heart. She paused for a moment as if there was something she wanted to say and then tenderly kissed him on the lips.

Time melted away until there was a knock on the door.

The food had arrived. "I hope you like what I picked out. I think it looks good."

Emily came in, looked at all the food, and smiled. "Wow! You sure bought a lot of food. Do I look like I eat a lot?"

Jack got nervous and quickly answered, "No, I just wanted to make sure I ordered what you liked."

"I'm just kidding, Jack. I love this stuff." Emily, not one to lose focus, said, "So, this job you and Frank have seems fascinating. What kind of paranormal activity do you guys investigate?"

Jack really didn't want to get into this discussion, but he knew it was inevitable. "All kinds of stuff. Some cases turn out to be nothing, and some turn out to be—let's say, very unusual."

That only piqued Emily's interest. "How unusual?" she asked.

Jack shook his head. He knew it was going to be next to impossible to derail Emily from her mission now.

"Let's take our food into the other room, and I will tell you about it," Jack suggested.

Jack wasn't sure how much he should tell her; there weren't too many people that could handle this kind of stuff. He wanted to be honest with her, but he didn't want to scare her away, either. He had strong feelings for Emily and didn't want to ruin a good thing. Hoping to give himself an out, he smiled and said, "Some of it is classified, you know. I can't tell you everything."

"Classified, huh?" Emily flirted. "That sounds very intriguing,"

Jack lifted his eyes to the ceiling and thought, 'We have the weirdest conversations.'

23

A DARK GATHERING

D ante Adal and Senator Wellsenburg got off the elevator and walked into Dante's office suite. Dante's secretary met them at the door.

"Mr. Adal, everyone has arrived for the meeting, sir. They are waiting in the conference room. Is there anything else you require?"

Dante kept walking, the Senator following close behind.

"Not now. Make sure the servers are ready when it's time to assist with lunch. I will call if I need anything else."

The double doors opened into a large, beautifully decorated conference room overlooking downtown Los Angeles. An elegantly dressed set of tables was along the back wall—a spread rivaling a king's feast. Dante walked in with Senator Wellsenburg in tow, nodded to the group, and proceeded to the head of the table to receive his guests.

"Gentleman, thank you for coming. Senator Wellsenburg and I appreciate you taking the time from your incredibly busy schedules to join us today. I hope you found the coffee and fresh fruit to your liking. If you require anything else, please be sure to let me know. I don't want to waste any of your time, so let's get right to it."

Dante cleared his throat and confidently continued, "The senator has a hectic schedule and must return to Washington tomorrow morning, but I felt it imperative, as you did as well, that we get together and discuss next year's presidential campaign. You will have ample time for questions and become more acquainted with the senator while enjoying the exquisite lunch we have provided for you. I would like to introduce our special guest. Please welcome Senator Wellsenburg, the next President of the United States. Senator..." Dante extended his arm and welcomed Wellsenburg.

Dante's introduction sent an unexpected rush surging through Wellsenburg's veins. President of the United States? The sensation was exhilarating. All the guests at the table gave him a warm, though subdued welcome as he stepped forward to speak.

Wellsenburg felt like he was in a whirlwind. Although he and Dante had time to plan a basic strategy and put together his opening statement, he still felt rushed and unsure about the meeting. But his overwhelming desire to be the next president was a powerful motivator.

Wellsenburg began, "Gentleman, as Mr. Adal mentioned, I appreciate your time and your interest in my candidacy. I am Senator Wellsenburg from New York, and I am thrilled to be here with you today."

Dante's high-profile guests dripped of wealth and prosperity, and they expected to be impressed. All of them were humanists sympathetic to the Society but were not members. In fact, several of them were not United States citizens. Their interests varied, but their goal was the same—world domination through financial manipulation. Wellsenburg, easing into his message, continued, "I believe that a robust economy is the heart and soul of this nation. It keeps the people of America happy and motivated. The world is getting smaller every day, and we must keep pace with the ever-changing economic and moral landscape. As you know, profits are the wheels that turn the engine of progress, and whatever it takes to increase those profits is of vital importance to this country and you and me.

"There are many issues that confront us today, and I will address the ones I know you are most concerned about: regulations governing the spread of religious philosophies, the state of Israel, and the implementing of a universal monetary system.

"Religion has become a thorn in the side of humanity. Most of our problems stem from blind obedience to a so-called god that those of us in this room know does not exist. Christians pose the greatest threat with their narrow thinking and archaic belief system. In a move towards a more secular science-based society, I would like to see a ban on all religious broadcasting and removing all religious entities' tax-free status. This will not eliminate the propagation of religious beliefs, but it will be a big step in the right direction."

He quickly glanced around the room, trying to get a read on their reactions. There were a few nods of agreement, but most were waiting to hear more.

He continued, "Second, we need to label Israel for what it really is —an aggressive terrorist nation. A new survey by the United Kingdom think-tank, Chatham House, finds that 35% of the UK public has an especially unfavorable view of Israel. This is double the 19% who held such a view during the previous survey. In the US, it's 17%. We are working hard on changing that through our university and college campus initiatives. If elected, I will push for a reduction, and ultimately a complete withdrawal of our support for Israel, both financially and militarily."

That statement struck a chord with those in attendance. There were many nods and looks of approval among Dante's guests. Wellsenburg's confidence level spiked.

"On the third and most significant issue, my position has always been the same. I am a vigorous advocate for a universal monetary system based on digital currency. If I am elected, I will do all in my power to expedite such a system."

Wellsenburg spied Dante out of the corner of his eye. He appeared pleased with his performance.

"I look forward to talking with each one of you in greater depth this afternoon. Thank you." Wellsenburg closed, hoping he had hit the mark with Dante's guests.

Dante stood up and addressed the gathering. "Gentleman, as you can see, Senator Wellsenburg is the perfect candidate to lead our cause." Dante slowly and purposely scanned the room. Making sure he made eye contact with each one of his prominent guests. "I am confident you will follow my lead and give the senator your full support. I encourage you to speak with him about any concerns you may have. This is a crucial moment in history. One we must not allow to slip through our grasp." Satisfied, he had made his point; he moved on. "I invite you to enjoy the wide variety of foods provided." Dante signaled, and the double doors opened. Four neatly dressed servers entered the room.

As the servants began their tasks, Marcel Faber, a member of the European Union Parliament, approached Wellsenburg. He was a short, wiry man with close-cropped gray hair in his mid-forties. Well known for his intense enthusiasm for global unity. "Senator, what is your position on one-world government? As President, would you be willing to relinquish the sovereignty of the U.S. to form a new world order?"

The question caught Wellsenburg off guard. The absolute power of the presidency was something he dreamed of obtaining his entire political life. It was what he craved and desired above all else. Now, this man was asking if he would give it up. He thought for a second, knowing full well what his answer must be. "Under the right circumstances, I would be amenable to it."

Faber stood motionless, staring at him. Finally, he nodded and then walked away. Wellsenburg shrugged it off. There would be plenty of time for that conversation when and if he made it to the White House.

The meeting continued long into the afternoon, with those in attendance asking the senator questions and discussing issues among themselves. Dante had been successful in assuring that the senator would have plenty of financial support for his campaign. He was always fond of the idiom, "The devil is in the details." Here, he was in everything—and that's the way he liked it.

* * *

With the senator on his way back to Washington, Dante turned his attention to another meeting. A gathering of a much different type. His guests were coming from all over the world. He would not have to supply any garnishes for this group, only the cloak of nightfall. He wasn't sure the reason for the meeting or what the agenda was, but he didn't mind the company.

It was now nine o'clock on the West Coast. Dante's guests would arrive soon. He sat at the conference table perusing the Internet, catching up on the news from the Middle East. He envied those of his cohorts assigned to that area. They had very few obstacles to overcome and were free to do just about anything they pleased. After all, they were so close to home, the place where it all began. He missed the days of ancient Babylon and all the open worship he and the others received. He looked forward to the time when the entire world would be back under their control. Darkness was on the rise on every level, and he knew soon he and the gods of Babylon would rule the world once more.

Suddenly, the room filled with a reddish-orange mist. It started at the floor and rose, swirling to the ceiling, snaking and twisting upon itself. Dante watched and waited, content in his chair. The mist grew heavier and thicker. Dante breathed in deep, like someone delighting in a deep breath of fresh spring air. It seemed to rejuvenate him. His eyes glowed a hideous reddish-orange. A series of wheezing and hissing sounds emanating from the corners of the room grew louder. It resonated off the walls and ceiling. So much so, Dante could not distinguish one from another. Slowly, the mist fell to the floor, revealing five tall figures, each with damp gray-streaked skin and leather-like wings. They folded their wings behind them in unison, like soldiers standing at attention.

Dante welcomed them, "Marduk, Anshar, Kishar, Nabu, and Asaru. How was the journey?"

Anshar rolled his head on his shoulders, creating a dull, crackling sound. He spoke with a deep, muttering voice that trailed off to a hiss after each word. "It is so much easier moving about Asia and Europe than here."

Kishar leaned forward, twisting and stretching his body. He spoke much clearer but in an intense tone, "There is still much work to be done here, Dante. However, I see and sense some progress."

Nabu and Asaru traveled from Iran and Iraq, where they had been since the days of the Babylonian and Persian Empires.

Nabu spoke, "We prefer to stay in Babylon. It is still very taxing to enter this country."

Dante smirked. "Marduk, you seem to have no problem. What's your secret?"

Marduk was confident. "I have more experience. It would be best if you came in from the North. Stay away from the Bible belt. It's not as bad as it used to be, but it can still pose a problem."

Dante called the meeting to order, "Kishar, what are the reports from the Middle East?"

"The spirit of fear reigns throughout the area," Kishar responded. "There is little resistance at this point. We have had very few angelic incursions. There are a few pockets of believers in certain areas, but nothing to be concerned about. There have been a handful of conversions, but we're keeping a close watch on it."

Nabu looked around the room at the others and then back at Dante. "We hear you are having some trouble with a cell group in a place called Virginia. We all know about it. You know prayer travels fast and knows no boundaries. If you don't put a stop to it, we could have major problems everywhere."

Dante glared at them for a moment, trying to stay calm.

"You have nothing to worry about. It's one small cell. I have it under control."

Asaru hissed and spoke in a foreboding, ominous tone, "I am sure you remember that the First Great Awakening in America started with a few people praying and resulted in a quantum leap forward in the church's life and the nation. I was here. I remember it reshaped America's religious, social, and moral landscapes and determined its destiny for the next two centuries." He glared at Dante. "There is no such thing as one small cell."

Dante stood up. He was visibly furious. He slammed his fist down on the table. As he did, his physical appearance instantly changed into the mythical dragon of ancient Babylon. His eyes, his skin, and finally, his jet-black wings appeared. He stared out at them, wisps of red vapor trailing out his nose.

He thundered, "I told you I have it under control! You tend to your own business, and I to mine."

Marduk stepped forward. "We must stay united if we are to do the Master's will." No one there dared to compromise the dark one's plans, including Dante. "We have met, and we have voiced our concerns. Now, let's get back to our assignments."

There was a general uneasiness to Marduk's statement, but everyone knew there would be hell to pay if they stayed away from their posts much longer. One by one, their wings unfurled in eerie silence. They leered at Dante, their red, bulbous eyes glowing through the rising mist around them. Suddenly, in labored hisses, each one twisted and turned and vanished into the swirling mist. Leaving only Marduk and Dante in the room.

Marduk, bathed in deceit, bowed slightly. His eyes scanned the room. There was no allegiance between them. If Dante failed, Marduk knew he would ascend to his position. "I must also return."

Dante merely glared at him. Wrapped in his shroud of darkness. Marduk collapsed his wings. Wrapping them around himself, he vanished.

Dante turned and stared out the window overlooking the city. His huge menacing reflection mirrored in the glass. He was furious. 'How dare they challenge me? They have it easy over there.' he thought. Dante elevated a foot off the floor and moved from behind the conference table, leaving a trail of red-orange mist in his wake. He drifted to the middle of the room, his eyes glowing red. Unfolding his large leather-like wings until they scraped against the walls of the room. Filled with hate and frustration, Dante tilted his head back, roared like a wounded beast, and vanished.

24

MR. DOUTIERE

The good news about the prayer meeting spread like wildfire. Conni's prayer warriors drove in from all parts of the area, excited about what God had done. There was a renewed sense of expectation throughout the group. Conni was once again at her post, welcoming each person as they came in. Out of the corner of her eye, she could see Mr. Robert Doutiere, dressed in his usual suit and tie, making his way in from the parking lot. He was sixty-three years old, tall and thin, with graying hair that was turning white.

Conni knew Doutiere well, and she was not happy about him coming to oversee the prayer meeting. Conni knew he did not intend to pray, but to make sure she did everything correctly and in proper order. Some in her home congregation sarcastically called him Mr. Doubter because, although he was a knowledgeable man and held a doctorate in theology, many considered him to be a Pharisee, a real stickler for the law. He believed in an extremely conservative interpretation of the Gospel and enjoyed his position of authority in the church. However, Conni had prayed about it, and after talking to Jack, she did her best to trust the Lord. She smiled and extended her hand as Mr. Doutiere walked up the steps. She was so nervous she might slip and say the wrong thing, so she kept repeating his name in her head.

"Hello, Mr. Doutiere. How are you tonight?"

"Doing well, Conni. We start at seven, correct?"

"Yes, we like to start on time. We might wait a few more minutes because some people come a long way to be here."

"If it's important to them, they should make allowances for that. Don't you agree?"

Conni was trying not to let him upset her. In her mind, she thought about locking him in the closet until the meeting was over, but she quickly snapped out of it.

"Everyone does their best, sir. It always works out fine. The Lord is good. He understands."

Robert stared at her and headed downstairs. She silently prayed, "Lord, You're really going to have to help me tonight!"

Conni waited for those she knew were running late, welcomed them with a joyous smile, and then proceeded downstairs. She looked around, excited to be in such good company again. People were greeting one another and laughing. Seventy people gathered for prayer; by far, the most they had ever had.

Mr. Doutiere approached her. "I would like to address the group before we start and make sure we are all on the same page."

Horrified, Conni turned her head away for a moment. She thought, 'What page is that?' Conni was getting upset. Everyone expected him to sit in the back and observe. She took another look. Mr. Doutiere's expression remained the same. He hadn't moved an inch. Doutiere stood firm in his usual authoritative manner, waiting for a response.

Conni took a deep breath and said softly, "Do you really think that is necessary? I usually open in a brief prayer, then hand out the list of prayer requests so that everyone can pray for the needs. It is very orderly."

She thought it clever to throw that in, knowing how he loved order. Unfortunately, the expression on Mr. Doutiere's face did not change. He stood staring at Conni for a few more seconds and then said, "Very well. I will only intervene if I feel things are getting out of control. You may proceed."

He turned and walked towards the back of the room. He picked up a chair, moved it off to the side away from the group, and sat down. Conni couldn't believe it. She closed her eyes for a moment and thanked God for answering her prayer.

Conni returned her attention to the group. "Welcome, everyone!" Conni shouted enthusiastically. "I am so happy to see so many of you here tonight. Let us take a moment and put our hands together in praise and thanksgiving to God for all He has done."

Everyone stood to their feet and broke out in thankful applause and praise. Conni saw Mr. Doutiere out of the corner of her eye. He was the only one sitting with his Bible and notepad on his lap. She wished she hadn't looked. Conni was more determined than ever to block him out and look only to Jesus.

Once seated again, Conni asked a few of the women to help hand out the sheets of prayer requests that had come in over the past week.

"Please keep in mind the main reason God has brought us here is to pray for a spiritual awakening in our country. All the needs in front of you are important, but without a sovereign move of God, our friends and families will continue to suffer under the influence of the kingdom of darkness."

Conni bowed her head and opened in prayer. "Father, thank You for allowing us to be here tonight. Guide us all as we pray and seek Your will for our lives and our country. Amen."

A unified amen rang out and bounced off the concrete walls. They prayed. Some stayed seated, some walked around the room, while others knelt on the floor in front of their chairs.

Mr. Doutiere sat quietly in his chair and carefully scanned the room from one side to the other. He had seen nothing like this before. There were so many people from different denominations and ethnic backgrounds, but all praying in the unity of spirit. Fifteen minutes went by, then thirty, and then at approximately forty-five minutes into the meeting, he felt something he hadn't felt in many years. A strong and overwhelming presence filled the room. At first, it was a little scary, but as it grew, he bowed his head and close his eyes. Mr. Doutiere felt like a small child afraid to open his eyes.

Suddenly, a warm light breeze began blowing through the room. He wanted to open his eyes to see if someone had opened a window or door, but somehow he knew that wasn't it. The presence of God grew stronger, so much so he could no longer stay seated. He felt overwhelmingly compelled to drop to his knees. Mr. Doutiere buried his face in his hands. Suddenly, he had a strange feeling that someone was standing alongside of him. He wasn't sure if he should open his eyes at all. Opening them a crack, he focused on the floor, but saw no one. Then, out of nowhere, he heard a very soft yet very clear whisper.

"Robert." No one in this group would ever call him that.

The voice called a second time, this time a little louder, "Robert." Mr. Doutiere was shaking inside. He closed his eyes, squeezing them tighter.

"Do you remember me, Robert?"

He hadn't heard that voice since he was eighteen years old. On the day he came to the Lord and promised to dedicate his life to reaching people with the message of God's love. He knew who it was–and it made him tremble all the more.

"Why do you wish to hinder My Spirit, Robert? Who put out the fire I started in you so many years ago? The path you have chosen ends in destruction. The enemy has placed you here, Robert, to oppose Me. Return to Me, and I will bless you."

Mr. Doutiere put his head in his hands and wept uncontrollably. Tears poured down his face for the first time in years. He had convinced himself over the years that emotions had no place in a mature Christian's life or the church. It had been so long since he felt that presence in his life—so long. He had filled the void with education and religious positions of authority, avoiding the genuine issues within. He knew what he had to do and decided he could not and would not run anymore.

He opened his eyes and quickly glanced around the room to see if anyone saw what had happened to him. However, everyone was still praying, captivated by their own experience, each deep in their own communication with God. He pulled a handkerchief out of his jacket pocket, one he hadn't needed for years, and wiped his face. He slowly got up off his knees and sat back down in his chair. There remained a wonderful, sweet, calming presence in the room. It washed over him again and again, each time causing a new gush of tears, renewing his faith, and giving him strength. He wiped his eyes again, opened his Bible to the Gospel of John, and read.

"In the beginning was the Word, and the Word was with God, and the Word was God. He was with God in the beginning. Through Him, all things were made; without Him, nothing was made that has been made. In Him was life, and that life was the light of men. The light shines in the darkness, but the darkness has not understood it."

Mr. Robert Doutiere, the one Dante had been so confident in, the one he thought would throw a monkey wrench into this prayer group, dividing it and rendering it useless, sat reading his Bible, bathed in the prayers of those around him.

The meeting continued for another thirty minutes, but it didn't bother Robert. As far as he was concerned, it could've gone on all night.

25

A LITTLE DOUBT

J ack lay in his bed, staring at the ceiling. He glanced at his alarm clock. It was 5:39 a.m. The morning light had chased the last remnants of the night sky. He liked that his large bedroom window faced east and let in the first rays of morning light. Jack slept very little last night. His mind filled with thoughts of Emily. They had an enjoyable evening, that is, until Jack explained all that he and Frank did. Well, some of it anyway. He didn't want to get into it, but Emily seemed interested and had many questions. That was something he didn't expect. I mean, what young woman wants to hear about demons and paranormal activity on the first date, or any date for that matter? Jack was worried that maybe Emily had gotten more than she bargained for. Even though the conversation in the car and the kiss good night were amazing, Jack had convinced himself that Emily had left with mixed feelings about the future of their relationship.

Emily hadn't been totally shocked. She knew he was investigating paranormal activity, but confrontations with demons and angels? That took it to another level. Emily had read about such things in the Bible, but knowing that Jack lived this bizarre reality every day was unnerving. Jack knew he had to give her some space to digest it all, but that was easier said than done.

Despite it being only their first date, Jack had intense feelings for Emily, and the thought of losing her was not something he cared to entertain. All night long, Jack dozed off and on, waking up and praying that everything would work out. Jack realized that confronting demons was an easier task than dealing with his newfound love life.

Jack bolted up. He couldn't bear to stay in bed another minute. There were blogs to write and phone calls to make. He got up and walked across the room and straight into the shower, hoping to shake off all the doubt and negativity he had been battling all night long, his mind racing from one scenario to the next. Emily was a smart girl; she knew this spiritual dimension existed. Jack took solace in the words she said and the way she kissed him. What if she decides that it's all too weird? That it wasn't worth it, that he wasn't worth it?

Jack stood in the shower for a while, letting the hot water pour over his head and tired body. He needed to refocus. 'Jesus, this relationship has to be you. If it's not, I don't want it.' He slowly got his appetite back and decided it was time to get dressed and head to the kitchen for some hot coffee and a couple of eggs.

The sun streamed through the open kitchen window, accompanied by a gentle warm breeze, helping Jack to feel a little more hopeful. The early morning rays fell across the kitchen table, where Jack's Bible laid open to the book of Proverbs. He walked over to the table and glanced down at it. He remembered he had been reading in the book of Psalms before he went to bed. The sun's rays providentially landed on two verses, highlighting them in bright golden sunshine. The verses jumped off the page at him.

"Trust in the LORD with all your heart and lean not on your own understanding; in all your ways acknowledge Him, and He will make your paths straight."

A chill ran up his back. Some might say it was just happenstance, but Jack knew better. It was no accident, not in his world. He put two scoops of freshly ground coffee in his old-style percolator, sat down at the table, and opened his laptop. He figured he might as well get started on his blog.

First, he would check his email. A lot of his mail was advertisements and special offers for all kinds of stuff he didn't want. He deleted them one by one and went through his blog-related questions and comments when a new message appeared on his screen. It was from Emily. Jack's heart skipped a beat. The first thing that came into his head was, 'Why is she sending me an email?' He breathed deeply and read it:

"Good morning Jack! I have been up for a while, but I didn't want to alarm you by calling you early in the morning, so I sent you an email hoping you might be up early. I've been praying about us, and the Lord has given me a real peace about all the things you shared with me. I know He has called you to be a force for Him, and I would like to be a part of that, too. Please call me as soon as you read this.

Love, Emily."

Jack breathed a sigh of relief. He could feel the dark cloud that had been hanging over him lift and instantly disappear. He picked up his phone and called her immediately.

Emily answered, "Jack, are you okay?"

"I am now," he said with a big smile on his face. "I could hardly sleep last night thinking about you, wondering what you were thinking."

"I'm sorry for making you so crazy last night. I just needed to get a handle on everything we talked about. I believe in you and your calling, and I want to know all about you and what you do. You are the kindest, most amazing man I have ever met. I can't get enough of you, Jack Bennett."

Her words wrapped around him like a warm blanket. The thought of losing Emily made him realize how much she meant to him and how serious he felt about her. It seemed surreal. It had only been two weeks, but he knew she was the one. Jack counseled many couples not to jump too far ahead in a relationship without praying it through and getting to know one another. Now, he was on the verge of saying something; it was definitely too early to say. Jack found himself groping for the right words, yet he wanted Emily to know how much she meant to him.

"Emily, I don't have the words to express how much that means to me. Even though we have only been together for a few weeks, I took a chance that you would understand what God has called me to, even if it meant you might decide to walk away. I know I can get a little too intense. I don't have room in my life right now for anything but an honest relationship. As you are finding out, my life is a bit complicated."

Emily was smiling from ear to ear on the other end of the phone.

The pure honesty and transparency of this man was overwhelming. She was falling for this guy, and there was no way she was going to walk away.

"I'm not going anywhere, Jack Bennett. In fact, I called out of work today. I hope you don't have any pressing issues to deal with because as soon as you called me, I got in my car and started driving to your house. Is that too weird?"

Jack laughed out loud. "Absolutely not. I will sit on the front porch and wait for you."

Jack put his phone back in his pocket and walked outside onto the porch. He felt like he could fly. With all the other not-so-normal things going on in his life, it comforted him to know that he and Emily were moving forward. After all, where was he going to find a woman who loved the Lord so much that she was to put up with all his craziness? That she was incredibly beautiful didn't hurt his feelings, either.

26

THE PLOT THICKENS

I t was ten o'clock Wednesday morning on an unusually warm spring day in DC when Senator Wellsenburg walked into his office at the Hart Senate Office Building northeast of the Capitol. The Hart Building is the largest of the Senate office buildings and named for Philip Hart, who served eighteen years as a Michigan senator.

A quick stroll through the office's outer rooms revealed scores of mini-museums doubling as waiting rooms. The content of the exhibits varied widely, ranging from historical artifacts and sports memorabilia to expansive ego walls featuring himself pictured with famous political figures, sports stars, and Hollywood personalities. It was obvious Wellsenburg had built his presidential library in advance.

His personal office featured a moderately sized mahogany desk in front of a floor-to-ceiling library of books ranging from revolutionary war journals to general myths and legends of Babylonia and Assyrian religion and culture. He was very proud of his historical literature collection and considered himself somewhat of an expert on such matters. He was brimming with renewed energy after his meeting with Dante. His focus was clearer than ever. In his mind, he would be the next President of the United States, and no one or thing was going to stand in his way.

The senator closed the door behind him, put his briefcase down next to his desk, and sunk deep into his high-back leather chair. He closed his eyes and replayed the last forty-eight hours in his mind. A smile crossed his face, which grew larger and more sinister as all the possibilities danced through his mind. Just the thought of having all that power sent a rush through his body and reminded him of a quote from Henry Kissinger, whom he had met and talked to many times. "Power is the ultimate aphrodisiac."

He had, of course, tasted it from all his years as a U.S. Senator, but now he wanted more. His dream was one step closer to reality.

A knock on the door interrupted his thoughts of grandeur. It was Ms. Venoldy, his secretary.

He quickly sat up in his chair. "Come in."

Ms. Venoldy was thirty-five years old, with black hair, green eyes, and, as he often remarked privately, very well put together.

"Senator Wellsenburg, Mr. Toller, is here to see you. He said it is urgent, sir."

"Send him in."

Harry Toller, a tall, well-built man of thirty-eight, was Wellsenburg's eyes and ears around Washington. He was part private eye and part enforcer, depending on the situation, but whatever needed to be done; he performed discretely and to the letter. That was what the senator loved about him. What he did not like was what the senator called his dirty habit. Harry loved cigars. Not just any cigars, but fresh off the boat, 100% authentic Habanos. He would, however, have to wait until he got outside to light one up.

"Hello, Harry. What have you got for me?"

Toller sat down on one of the two vintage leather club armchairs positioned strategically in front of Wellsenburg's desk.

"I found out who's been snooping around, asking questions about your relationship with Dante and your involvement with the Sons of Nimrod. It's some agent from the Paranormal Division named Frank Lederman."

"Paranormal Division?" the senator asked, bewildered. He wondered how such a classification could exist without his knowledge? The more he thought about it, the more enraged he got. To think that something like that could've gotten by him.

"What the hell is this Paranormal Division, and who is this Frank Lederman? Does he work out of DC?"

"Well, to answer your last question first, sir, yes. He works out of the Hoover Building here in DC, and from what I've been able to gather, he answers to George Donovan, the head of this new division."

Wellsenburg was getting antsy and more irritated every second. "What about this paranormal nonsense? Who's responsible for that?"

"The director of the FBI apparently created it two years ago. It seems there has been a lot of interest in paranormal activity here in Washington lately. It reminds me of the Germans in World War II when Hitler went wild looking for strange artifacts that were supposed to have some mystical powers. Crazy stuff."

"What the hell is going on in this country? I'd like to know who approved that budget?" In his head, Wellsenburg was thinking, 'I need to talk to Dante about this.'

"Listen, I want you to monitor this Lederman," Wellsenburg instructed. "No guns, no rough stuff. Remember, he is a Federal agent. I don't want to kick off a large-scale FBI investigation that might lead back to this office. Find out where he goes, who he talks to, and what he knows about the Society and get back to me. Understood?"

Toller nodded confidently. "No problem. I'll handle it."

Wellsenburg put both hands flat on his desk and leaned in. "This has to be our last meeting at my office." He grabbed a pen, wrote a phone number on a notepad, tore it off, and handed it to Toller.

"Call me on this number from now on, and if need be, we'll set up a place to meet. We need to be careful from here on out."

Toller nodded, put the number in his pocket, turned, and walked out the door without saying another word. The senator sat back down in his chair and thought, 'The game is afoot.' He reached into his pocket, pulled out his burner phone, and immediately called Dante. He hoped Adal would know what to do about all this.

"My good senator, good to hear from you. Trouble?"

Dante knew there had to be a good reason for him to call on this line.

"I just found out that the FBI has a new division looking into paranormal activity. They are poking around, asking questions about the Society and me. I thought you should know."

"I am aware of some interference around DC, but it's nothing I can't handle."

The senator was more than a little nervous. He couldn't afford to have anything interfere with his run for president. "Listen, Dante," Wellsenburg said, "This thing needs to be handled right away. It will get sticky around here if this gets out."

Back in L.A., Dante rolled his eyes, already weary of Wellsenburg's antics. "Senator, I have taken care of every detail up to now, so there's no need to worry. You need to learn to leave these minor details to me." In a slightly agitated tone, Dante asked, "Is there anything else?"

Wellsenburg felt extremely uneasy speaking to Dante in this way. It was akin to walking a tightrope over a pit of alligators. Yet, he could not afford to have someone expose his connection with the Sons of Nimrod. That could be disastrous.

"I agree. You have taken care of everything so far. I need to know for sure that you are going to take care of this. I hope you understand." The senator held his proverbial breath.

Dante let out an exhaustive sigh. "Let me put your mind at ease. Frank Lederman and Jack Bennett, right? These are the two men you are so worried about?"

Shocked, the senator responded. "Yes. How did you know about Lederman, and who is Jack Bennett?" Bennett was a wildcard. Wellsenburg hated being blindsided.

"Lederman is not the problem, at least not right now. Our biggest nemesis is Bennett, but like I said, I am working on it. Whatever trouble they create, we can fix. I am coming to DC next week. We'll talk more then."

Dante wanted to say, "Bennett and the prayer group," but he didn't want to confuse Wellsenburg. He wouldn't understand it, anyway.

"I've got to go. Just relax. There's no need to jump the gun. I'll be in touch."

With that, Dante hung up. Senator Wellsenburg put his phone back in his inside jacket pocket, swallowed hard, and hoped Dante was right. He sat up in his chair and stared out into space. He picked up a pen, slid his notepad over, and wrote two words. Jack Bennett.

He would have to find out just who this guy was and how Dante knew him. Ironically, Wellsenburg did not like being kept in the dark.

The silence was broken by Ms. Venoldy's voice over the intercom.

"Senator Wellsenburg, Senator Daniel Colson is here to see you, and, I must warn you, he seems very agitated, sir."

Colson was a conservative senator from Arkansas, which would have been enough to qualify him as Wellsenburg's number one nemesis. To make matters worse, he was also a "Born Again Christian" who believed there was a conspiracy afoot to suppress Bible-believing Christians like himself. This would not be their first confrontation.

"Fine. Send him in," Wellsenburg said reluctantly.

Colson came storming through the door and stood right in front of Wellsenburg's desk. He looked as though he was about to explode.

"Senator, we need to talk! There is a battle brewing over religious freedom laws. I understand you plan on sponsoring a bill that would demand that churches all over America marry any gay couple that petitions them, despite their biblical and foundational beliefs that marriage is between a man and a woman. If any church does not comply with the law, they will lose their right to operate as a place of worship? Is this accurate, sir?"

Wellsenburg sat back in his chair and smiled like the cat that just ate the canary.

"You need to calm down, Senator," Wellsenburg's condescending tone was designed to be disrespectful. Wellsenburg cared little about gay rights or anyone else for that matter, but it was a tool he learned to wield well. "You know you can't listen to every idle rumor that makes its way down these hallowed halls in Washington. I admit I am concerned for every American's rights, and I am endeavoring to protect my gay constituents' and secure the rights of the LGBTQ+ community to marry as they wish. I am merely doing the job they elected me to do."

Colson's eyes widened. He was a seasoned politician, and he knew when he was getting a snow job. He grew more enraged.

"You and your leftist cohorts, sir, have gotten very good at hiding your true agendas. You wish to divide this country and put the blame on those who love the Lord. What about their rights to worship God and live according to the gospel of Christ? My sources have confirmed that there is a movement on the state level to revoke non-profit status for religious organizations that do not abide by same-sex marriage. I know you and your associates won't stop until there are no more churches, until there are no more people spreading the Gospel of love and forgiveness through Jesus Christ. And I'm talking now about the unabridged, unapologetic gospel; the one that tells both sides of the story; the one you want to see abolished."

Wellsenburg didn't think it was possible, but he hated Colson a little more every time he opened his mouth. He knew Colson could see right through his rhetoric, but now was not the time to confirm or reveal anything. In his heart, he couldn't wait for the day when Colson and all those who thought like him were behind bars or...

He stopped himself and refocused.

"Senator, I assure you I have never heard of such things, nor do I believe anyone else has any such plans. I simply believe that we should ban all discrimination from our great country. Are you against all gay people, sir?"

Senator Colson stood up straight and looked directly into Wellsenburg's eyes. He knew the senator would love to paint him as a crazed, hate mongrel. Colson's eyes burned like lasers. Wellsenburg felt the heat of his gaze.

"No, I am not, Senator! Hate has no place in my heart. I associate and am friendly with a number of gay community. I represent all my constituents, sir. All I'm saying is, let's have equal rights for all Americans. I may not agree with the court's decision, Senator, but I am sworn to uphold it, and I will do so. 'They ask for equal dignity in the eyes of the law,' I believe that is what Justice Anthony Kennedy wrote. I am a US senator, and I abide by the laws of this great country. Freedom for all Americans, Senator, that is all I am saying."

It is the judicial system that you and others like you have perverted that I have an issue with. "I'm sure you remember those poor people in Oregon that refused to make a wedding cake for a lesbian couple. It wasn't about hate, senator. It was about their belief system. If that couple desired a cake for their birthday, I'm sure they would have sold them one. They lost their business and their very livelihood because of their religious beliefs. They didn't have any rights, did they, Senator? You say there is no conspiracy, then let me ask you a question. Suppose it was a

Muslim family who owned that business? Would everyone have acted in the same manner? Islam is clear in its prohibition of homosexuality. I assure you, Senator, there is a conspiracy. There is a growing element to highjack religious freedom in this country, and I will not let you or anyone else get away with it. I will be watching. You can count on that.

In case you have forgotten the first amendment, Senator, I leave you with this: Colson quoted, 'Congress shall make no law respecting an establishment of religion, or prohibiting the free exercise thereof; or abridging the freedom of speech, or of the press; or the right of the people peaceably to assemble, and to petition the Government for a redress of grievances.'"

With that, Senator Colson headed for the door. As he put his hand to the doorknob, Colson glared back at Wellsenburg. "I know you're affiliated with a secret society senator. And when I find out what you are up to, there will be hell to pay." Colson then stormed out of the office.

Wellsenburg, seething with anger, slammed his hand down on the intercom. "Ms. Venoldy, call my driver. I will be out of the office for a few hours. I do not wish to be disturbed unless it's a genuine emergency."

"Yes, sir. Very good." There was no mystery in Ms. Venoldy's mind why he was leaving the office.

Wellsenburg needed to get out of the office and gather his thoughts before saying or doing something that would endanger his ultimate plans. He walked out of the office and down the hall that overlooked the lobby and got into the elevator. He desperately wanted to call Dante again, but knew it would only make him look weak and needy. Wellsenburg's pride wouldn't let that happen. He would hold off until the next week and talk to him in person when he arrived in Washington.

The elevator door opened, and Wellsenburg walked out onto the large marble-floored atrium, passing the huge 39-ton steel "Mountains and Clouds" sculpture. Above it, suspended from the roof, matte black aluminum clouds, the largest of which weighed a ton. It was quite a sight to see for most visitors, but it had become invisible to him. He had many thoughts running through his head as he walked out the entrance doors onto Second Street, but the thing that kept repeatedly playing in his head were the haunting words of Dante Adal. "Our biggest nemesis is Bennett."

His driver pulled up on cue. His driver quickly got out and opened the door.

"Where to, sir?"

"Take me to the club, Ralph. I need a break."

"Yes, sir. No problem."

Wellsenburg sat back, and thought, why would someone as powerful as Dante Adal concerned himself with a nobody like Jack Bennett? He had to know. He pulled out his phone and quickly Googled his name.

A picture came up and then a brief description. "Jack Bennett, author of Understanding Paranormal Activity and the daily blog, The Growing Evil on Planet Earth."

Suddenly, he made the connection. Paranormal Activity, he thought. That's what Harry Toller was talking about. He mentioned Frank Lederman and said he was an agent with the new Paranormal Division of the FBI. He remembered Dante had put those two names together. Now it was coming into focus. Jack Bennett must work with

Lederman. He couldn't let them connect him to the Sons of Nimrod. Not yet, anyway. Not until he became President. After that, it wouldn't matter.

His mind was racing. What kind of power does this Jack Bennett have? Is he an actual threat, and why didn't Dante tell him about Bennett before this? Wellsenburg would look into it himself, and, if need be, take care of the situation. He sat back and stared at the image displayed on the screen, the face of his new adversary.

27

A SHORT TAIL

I t was nine o'clock on a Saturday morning, and CJ's was hopping. Emily had her hands full trying to keep up with all the orders when Jack came through the door carrying a briefcase. Jack had asked her to save them a table towards the back of the café, away from the windows. Emily showed her concern, especially now that she knew what they were involved in. Emily knew Jack would tell her if he could.

Emily motioned to Jack, pointing to the table against the wall in the back corner of the café. Jack sat down and put his briefcase on the floor next to him. Things were getting stranger by the day. 'Sitting against the wall away from the windows? What was this about?' Jack wasn't sure what to expect next. He didn't have to wait long. He spied Frank getting out of the car in full FBI mode, carefully scanning the area.

"Hey, Frank, we're getting a little mysterious. I got this weird text message last night to meet you here for breakfast like it's the first time we've done this. You got Emily all freaked out. What's up?"

"I'm being followed."

Jack looked puzzled. "Followed—by whom?"

"I'm not sure just yet, but I picked up on it yesterday afternoon when I was in DC."

"Are you sure? Maybe we're all getting a little paranoid. I mean, there's a lot of crazy stuff going on lately."

Frank gave Jack an are-you-serious look. "I know when I'm being shadowed. It must be because of my questions concerning Senator Wellsenburg and the Sons of Nimrod."

"Do you think they followed you here?"

"Yes, I do. That's why we're sitting here on a busy Saturday morning. It's more much more difficult to use audio listening devices in a small crowded room like this, especially with us sitting so far back from the street."

Jack put his elbow on the table and rubbed his forehead. "So, you believe someone is using full-blown surveillance techniques on you?"

"Possibly. We know Wellsenburg has his eye on the White House, so it makes sense that he wouldn't want anything to surface that could damage his chances. Think about it. What if our brief investigation somehow proves that Wellsenburg had something to do with the deaths of the Oslows? We know they were big contributors to his senatorial campaign thirty years ago, and involved in the Sons of Nimrod. I can see the headlines now—Dead, Middle-Eastern Mystery Couple Gave Millions to Wellsenburg Campaign."

Frank saw Emily approaching with coffee, and he stopped talking.

"Good morning, guys. Sorry, it took so long. It's crazy in here today."

Emily put two cups on the table and poured their coffee. "So, what's all the mystery about? Are you all right, Frank?"

"Yeah, yeah, I'm good."

Emily raised her eyebrow and said, "You guys are up to something. I can feel it. Whatever it is, please, be careful, okay? I gotta go. Do you guys know what you want?"

Frank took a sip of his coffee. "I'll have two eggs over easy, a side of bacon, and rye toast, please."

Jack looked up at her and said, "You look great in that outfit."

Frank rolled his eyes.

Emily smiled. "Thank you, honey. Order, please, before I get fired."

"I'll have the same, but with wheat toast."

Once Emily left, Jack asked, "How much do you think they know?"

"I'm not sure, but my inside source tells me they have already linked you to me, so our meeting this morning isn't giving them anything new, but I am worried about Emily. After all, honey,"—Frank tilted his head and fluttered his eyes, "—you seem to be so much in love."

"There is definitely something wrong with you. You know that, right? We're sitting here talking about the fact that a powerful man is prying into our private lives, and you make jokes? What do you think he would do? Would he really come after Emily? Do you think our lives are in danger?"

Frank looked worried. "I don't know. Maybe we should lie back for a while. There are other cases we have to look into. Maybe if the trail goes cold, he will think it's a dead end and leave us alone."

"I don't know if I like that idea." Jack was skeptical. "Do we really want him to become President? What if we stop investigating, he gets elected, then comes after us with guns blazing as the President of the United States?" Jack paused. "We need another plan."

"Okay, gentleman. Breakfast is served." Emily looked at both of them. "Don't think I don't know, you stop talking when I come to the table. You better tell me all about it later, Mr. Bennett."

Jack smiled. "Your hair looks amazing today."

Emily gave him a sly smile. "Eat your eggs,"

"You better be careful what you say to her. She might freak out on you. This isn't the kind of thing most people have to deal with."

Jack's eyes followed Emily as she delivered the food to another table. "That may be, but Emily is not your average girl. Don't worry. I'll figure it out." Jack refocused. "Okay, here's what I think. I agree we need to take a break from our Wellsenburg investigation, but a long break. Just for one case, and then we go back at it. If someone wants to follow us around, then let him. Maybe he'll get bored and move on."

Frank finished the last bit of eggs on his plate, took another sip of his coffee, and said, "Fine. I'll go along with that, but with one condition. If it doesn't go away, we lay off until he does."

"How about we play it by ear? Let's agree to reevaluate after this next case."

Frank knew he would not win this discussion, so he reluctantly agreed. "Fine. Let's move on."

Frank bent down and pulled his iPad out of his briefcase.

"This next case is a little unusual because of a so-called professional ghost hunter cable TV show."

"Really?" Jack disliked paranormal shows with charlatans pretending to be experts, creating counterfeit scenarios for TV ratings and profits. In Jack's mind, a situation involving true paranormal activity was no place for thrill-seekers. Being in the crosshairs of powerful supernatural beings was extremely dangerous, especially without the power of God. Jack vehemently opposed the idea of cameras or onlookers that would attempt to turn a spiritual confrontation into some three-ring circus. "Are you proposing we share the case with this ghost hunter team? You know how I feel about that!"

"No, the FBI has taken over the case. Their team wanted to go back in but were denied. The owner of an old abandoned inn originally called them to verify a ghost sighting and other possible paranormal activity. During their so-called investigation, something attacked one of their cameramen and seriously injured him. He's still in the hospital. The agency heard about it and assigned the case to us."

"Who are these so-called TV investigators?"

"This is their website, and I quote: The Virginia Paranormal Society's sole purpose is to help those experiencing paranormal activity by investigating claims in a professional and confidential manner. We use the latest in paranormal equipment and techniques, and with our professional tools, we have changed the field of paranormal investigating."

"That's quite a statement. So, when we investigate, there will be no cameras, no audience, and no interference, correct?"

"Stop worrying. This is an FBI investigation. Remember, any interference is against the law. The only audience we will have is our tagalong spy. I'm sure he'll find it more than interesting. They would like us to look into it ASAP. How about tomorrow? I can pick you up around nine if that works?"

Jack was a little leery about the attention this case was getting, but he trusted Frank and knew he was a pro. "Yeah, okay. I can do that. I assume this guy knows where I live, so there is no use in trying to hide it."

Frank smiling, "You know that it's the twenty-first century, right? He knew where you lived ten seconds after he linked us together."

Just then, Emily walked up to their table and asked, "Are you gentleman finished?" She looked at Jack, then Frank, and back at Jack. "I mean, with your breakfast."

Jack looked up at her and said, "You're too funny. I'll fill you in later." Jack stood up, took the check from her hand, and kissed her on the cheek.

"I got this. I'll see you tomorrow morning." Jack turned and headed for the cashier.

Frank stood there for a moment and said, "Take care, Em. Don't let Jack drive you crazy. He can do that, you know."

"I'm working on it. Whatever you guys are up to, please be careful."

Frank winked at her, smiled, then turned and walked out the door. As he walked down the sidewalk to his car, he felt eyes on him. He didn't want to tip off whoever it was. It wasn't the first time Frank had dealt with this kind of thing. He always allowed his tail to think they had the upper hand. He liked it that way.

Jack paid the check and watched from a distance to see if he could catch a glimpse of the person following Frank. He waited and watched as Frank got into his car and drove off. At first, he didn't see anyone, but then he noticed a man sitting in a late-model gray Acura sedan about two hundred feet from where Frank had parked his car. The man watched Frank drive away, then pulled out and headed off in the same direction. Jack immediately picked up his phone.

Frank was listening to his favorite album when the call came in. He had a feeling Jack would be watching.

"Did you get a good look at him?"

"How did you know I was calling about that?"

"You're kidding, right? I picked him up as soon as I got out of CJ's. He's not very good, whoever he is. He won't be too pleased because I'm headed back to the office in D.C. Too bad he came all this way for nothing. You keep your eye out, buddy. Things are going to get very interesting from here on out."

Jack quipped, "Like they haven't been interesting until now? Do you think this guy is dangerous? Shouldn't you let someone know what's going on?"

"Not yet. It's a fact-finding mission. Whoever hired this guy is not interested in attacking a federal agent. You watch yourself and take care of that beautiful girlfriend of yours. You're not getting any younger."

"Yeah, thanks for the reminder. I'll be careful. You do the same." Jack hesitated, then said, "Listen, why don't you call me when you get to the office?"

"What? Now you're my mother or something? It comes with the territory, Jack. You know, if you're going to get like this every time we run into a little trouble, we're going to have to stop seeing each other."

"Hilarious. Fine. Forgive me for being concerned. I'm not a super FBI agent like you. This stuff freaks me out, okay? I'll see you in the morning."

"No worries, man. Life in the fast lane."

Jack took a deep breath, put his phone in his pocket, and headed home.

28

REALITY TV

A relentlessly steady rain fell across northern Virginia. The weather forecast called for scattered thunderstorms and heavy rain off and on all day. It only added to the strange atmosphere surrounding the day's assignment.

Jack locked his front door and made a mad dash for the car, doing his best not to get soaked. "Unbelievable. We're on our way to investigate a ghost sighting, and it's pouring rain with thunder and lightning in the forecast. You can't write this stuff."

Frank shrugged his shoulders. "Some people do."

Jack couldn't wait to ask, "So, how did it go yesterday? Did your shadow follow you all day?"

"I don't think so. Once we got back into DC, he gave up for the day. I'm not sure if we'll see him today, but you never know. A face-to-face coming real soon. I will not let this go on much further. How did you make out with Emily last night?" Frank quickly caught himself and added, "You know what I mean."

"She's great. I told Emily about the person tailing you, and she didn't seem surprised. I guess she figured being an FBI agent, things like that happen all the time." Jack paused, and a big smile broke out on his face.

Frank glanced over at him. "Emily's gotten under your skin, dude. You got it bad. You didn't tell her we're both under surveillance, did you?"

Jack made a face and shrugged his shoulders. "Why get her all freaked out before we really know what's going on? Maybe it will just blow over, and that will be it."

"I can't believe you. Senator Wellsenburg sent this guy, remember? We don't know how far he will go to get what he wants. You need to tell her what's going on."

Jack knew Frank was right. He loved Emily, and of course, wanted to keep her safe, but didn't want her to live in fear, either. Jack stared out the window without saying a word. Then said, "Yeah, I know. I'll tell her tonight over dinner. If she sticks with me through all of this, then I guess it's meant to be."

Frank laughed. "Are you kidding? This is my job, and most times I'm ready to bail. I can't believe the things you get me into. I told you from the beginning that day at CJ's that she liked you, my friend. A woman can fall in love with you, but it doesn't always mean she likes you. You buy this girl a big diamond ring and make it forever."

"Hey, this isn't some Hollywood movie. We are just getting to know each other. I can't ask her to marry me just like that."

"You love her, right?"

Jack smiled as Emily's face flooded his mind. There was no doubt about how he felt. "Yeah, I do. But these things take time."

Frank continued, "You told her you talk to demons and angels, and she still can't get enough of you. Let me ask you this—have you slept with her?"

Jack snapped his head around and glared at Frank. "What? No, I haven't slept with her! You know how I feel about that. That's my old life. You should know better than to ask me that."

"Well, I wouldn't wait too long. I see the way you look at each other. There's fire there, brother. Just saying."

"You're too much. Can we change the subject?"

Frank nodded. It was important for Jack to remain focused. "So, what do you think is going on in this place?"

"I don't know, but a lot of this stuff is usually bogus. You know, people love to say they saw this or that, and it turns out to be nothing but overly active imaginations. We could be wasting our time or..."

Frank jumped in, "... or, we could be dealing with a real live demon! All I know is something or someone attacked the cameraman. That part is real."

Jack took a deep breath. "There is no doubt about that." Jack sat back and closed his eyes. He didn't like to think there was a demon around every corner, but unfortunately, that seemed to be the case lately.

Frank knew Jack needed some time to get his thoughts together. He could use a little time to clear his mind as well. They continued silently down the highway towards their destination.

Half an hour later, they came to the turnoff for Hardon's Inn. Frank nudged Jack. "Hey, we're here. At least, I think we are. I almost drove by it. Look at that sign, will you?"

An old beat-up wooden sign hung precariously from one side of a rotted post. It would have fallen over years ago if not for the overgrown brush. The sign swayed in the windswept rain like something from an old Alfred Hitchcock film. Frank turned down the long dirt driveway. The pouring rain had transformed it into a river of mud and slop. A split-rail fence on either side of the driveway led to a large oval turnaround at the inn's front. It was a Georgian style, two-story building with multi-paned sliding sash windows in a 6-over-6 pattern. Many of the panes were broken. However, the gray slate roof appeared to be in decent shape.

Jack scanned the building as they pulled up to the front of the inn. "Wow, are you kidding me? Look at this place. Are we sure it will not collapse the minute we get inside?"

Frank stopped the car but kept it running if, for no other reason, to keep the wipers going so they could see through the windshield. The rain continued to pour down hard, with flashes of lightning in the distance.

Jack looked at Frank like a lawyer cross-examining a witness. Frank was notorious for leaving out a detail or two.

"Is there anything else I should know before we go in there?"

"Well, it was Nancy Stonehouse, the real estate agent, who called in the TV team. "

Jack interrupted. "You're making this up. Nancy Stonehouse? Really? Can you please be serious? I need you to be serious right now."

Frank grinned. "I am serious. I'm telling you the truth." He looked at Jack's face and laughed hysterically. The tension that was so much a part of their everyday lives snapped like an over-turned guitar string, unleashing a flood of laughter that Frank could not contain. Jack kept staring at Frank, which only made him laugh that much harder. Jack tried to keep a straight face, but it was impossible. He lost control and began laughing along with him. They both felt like two idiots, but there was no doubt this insane hysteria had eased the tension.

Finally, Frank got a hold of himself. Smiling, he said, "This real estate agent came to look the property over before listing it and heard a growling sound coming from the second floor. When Ms. Stonehouse looked up, she saw a dark image peering out the window. She called the police. They searched the entire building, but they came up empty. When the story got out, that's when the paranormal team showed up to do their thing."

"Wow! That would have been nice to know before this. Maybe if you weren't so busy getting into my love life, you could have shared that information."

Frank shrugged. "Maybe,"

Frank reached around to the backseat and grabbed two flashlights. He handed one to Jack, then pulled his 9mm Luger out of his shoulder holster and quickly checked it. Jack's eyes lit up.

"Do you think you'll need that?"

"Well, if I do, I want to make sure it's ready to go. We don't know who or what is in there, so better safe than sorry."

"Okay, you've checked your weapon, now let's ready our other weapons. We need to pray before we go in there, and hopefully, this rain will let up a bit before we get out of the car. I prefer not walking around soaked to the skin, if possible."

Frank put his gun back in its holster. "I'm still learning how to pray, you know, but I've been working on it."

Jack smiling, "There are no magic words. God just wants to hear what you have to say. Remember, it's a matter of the heart."

Jack and Frank prayed intensely for about fifteen minutes, asking God to guide and anoint them as they searched the inn for whatever attacked the other team. Although Jack had faced similar situations, he depended wholly on the Spirit of God to get him through.

Although the rain had let up slightly, the lightning and thunder had intensified. As they approached the large wooden door, Frank pulled out the key given to him by the realtor. They looked at each other, both wondering why anyone would bother to lock the door, considering the state of the windows. As they entered the foyer, Frank braced his gun and flashlight in his two hands, sweeping the area from one side to another. Jack prayed silently for discernment as his eyes scanned the murky surroundings.

The air, which had been sweet outside, was stale and reeked of mold and decay. There was a double staircase that went up to an open hallway, leading to second-floor rooms. Frank motioned for Jack to follow him up the stairs. If there was someone up there, they would certainly not surprise them, because each step moaned and groaned from age and neglect. As they reached the top of the stairs, they heard an eerie sound coming from a room off to their left. They walked slowly down the dark hallway until they got to room 201. The door was open a crack. They could clearly hear a low-pitched moaning. Frank motioned to Jack that he was going to kick it open the rest of the way.

He raised his foot and kicked the door open while simultaneously identifying himself. "FBI. Don't move!"

Jack and Frank nervously scanned the room with their flashlights, searching for the source of the disturbance. Suddenly, something jumped out of the open closet. Frank spun around, flashlight and gun securely gripped in both hands. They heard a squeal. A large black cat flew past them and ran down the steps just as a tremendous clap of thunder rattled through the old inn.

Frank relieved glanced back at Jack with a look of relief and disgust. "Damn cats. Did I ever tell you how much I hate cats?"

Jack took a deep breath and rubbed his forehead. The two men continued down the hallway. The only other illumination came from an occasional bolt of lightning that split the sky overhead, followed by a huge thunderclap. As they approached room 210 at the end of the hallway, Jack felt the spiritual atmosphere change dramatically. He couldn't put his finger on it, but it felt like a mixture of depression and hopelessness. It was so deep and suffocating that he could barely breathe. The door to room 210 was shut but not locked. Jack slowly opened it with Frank right over his shoulder, gun in hand.

Suddenly, they saw it standing by the window. The room was a murky gray, the dark stormy weather allowed just enough light in for them to see the outline of the huge dark figure, its head only inches from the ceiling. It looked like a man, but its eyes glowed an eerie orangey-red that cut through the gray shadows. The creature had what appeared to be two large wings folded behind it. It stared straight at Jack, standing in the open doorway. When Frank saw it, his pulse clicked up a notch, and his mouth became dry, making it hard to swallow. He knew at that moment that his gun would not be the weapon of choice. Their flashlights were of no use. To their amazement, the dense darkness simply swallowed up the light.

Jack stared right back at it. He could feel cords of depression, like a giant python trying to wrap around him. He addressed the creature, "Who are you, and what's your name?"

The creature moved a little closer. A trail of reddish mist kicked up as it went. The demon's eyes bore into Jack. "I AM DESPAIR." The words penetrated Jack's heart. The demon swayed from side to side, studying Jack carefully. "What are you doing here? Have you come to die?" It mocked, "—or don't you realize you're being hunted?" Its eyes grew larger and turned a deep red, then orange, and then red again.

Jack straightened up, knowing that demonic spirits most powerful weapon—was fear.

"I have not come to die! The Lord Jesus Christ sent me here to cast you out of this place. Dare you to stand against the King of Kings and Lord of Lords?"

The creature hissed again, only louder. Its breathing became labored and more intense. It spoke slowly in a loud hissing whisper that sounded like a snake. "You have a target on your back, Jack Bennett. You and your apprentice."

Jack knew better than to have a conversation with an evil spirit. The longer he stood there, the greater the danger and the deeper the darkness felt.

"I will not speak with you. By the power given to me by my heavenly Father, I bind you and cast you from this place in the name of Jesus, the son of the Living God!"

The creature winced in pain, but wasn't going until it truly tested Jack's resolve. The next thing Jack knew, the creature was standing over him. It bent over until it was face-to-face and eye-to-eye with Jack. The putrid scent of sulfur hissed and oozed out of the demonic creature. It was doing its best to strike fear into Jack's heart and undermine his faith. Jack felt like he was having an out-of-body experience, but he held his ground. Then suddenly, he felt the hand of God upon him. He shouted, "Leave this place, you spirit of despair. In the name of Jesus, the Son of the Living God! The Lord rebukes you!"

The creature roared like a ferocious wild beast dealt a mortal blow. It spread its enormous wings and let out a chilling howl. It circled the room, then in a cloud of reddish mist vanished from their sight.

Frank looked at Jack, his eyes as big as saucers. "What the heck, Jack? My heart can't take much more of this crap! Whatever happened to flesh and blood bad guys?"

Jack turned to him, his heart still racing. "Our God is an awesome God. That's all I can say." Jack could feel the rush of adrenaline surging through his body. He took a couple of deep breaths and glanced out the window. "That was intense. Hey, look! The rain stopped. This would be a good time to get out of here." Jack had no desire to stay in the room.

Frank stood right where the demon had vanished, totally amazed at the incredible power of the name of Jesus. He looked around the room for a minute and then turned to Jack. "What do you think about what that demon said about us being hunted?"

"I will admit that was weird. Especially since you and I seem to be under some kind of surveillance. However, I've never known a demon to be truthful. Jesus said the devil is a liar. He said that he is the Father of Lies, the very originator of the lie. I don't think we can put too much stock in anything one of his demons told us."

Frank glanced out the window and saw something about

a hundred yards down the driveway. He motioned to Jack. "Look at this."

Jack walked over to the window. His eyes widened. "That's the car I saw back in town!" He looked again. "Yes, definitely. That's the car that followed you. How did he know where to find us? Do you think he followed us?"

Frank checked his weapon one more time. "No way. I would have picked up on that. No, somebody tipped him off—somebody on the inside. That's not good, Jack. It means somebody in the FBI is giving Senator Wellsenburg info on our cases. It won't be long before they connect all the dots."

Jack looked out the window again. "He's leaving. We should follow him and find out who hired him."

"Not now. When I get back to DC, I will find out what's going. Let's get you back home and to that beautiful girl of yours. We need a break anyway, don't you think?"

Jack nodded. "Yeah, this place gives me the creeps."

The two men walked down the steps and out the door. Jack opened the car door and stood there for a moment. He turned and looked back at the old inn, raising his eyes, checking the upstairs window one more time. He knew God had taken care of the situation, but he couldn't help taking one more look.

Frank started the car, waited a few seconds, and then said, "Are you getting in, or do you want to book a room?"

Jack took one more look, then got in. Frank had a bewildered look on his face. "I know I am new to this stuff, but aren't demons supposed to be invisible to mortals?"

Jack let out a deep sigh. "The times they are a-changing."

29

A POST

Jack decided to do a little work around the yard, pulling weeds out of the flowerbeds and watering his tomato plants. Working outside always helped Jack relax and clear his mind. To Jack, there was nothing like getting his hands dirty in the fertile, black, Virginia soil. It always reminded him of the lessons Jesus taught. In the Gospels, there is a story about a man who sowed good seed, and during the night, the enemy came and sowed evil seed alongside it. Jack knew how important it was to keep up with his garden so the weeds wouldn't overtake his plants. He learned to apply that to his spiritual life as well. It helped him remember to pray and read his Bible every day, and it kept the evil seeds of life from taking root in his heart.

Jack had plans to pick Emily up for dinner at six. He knew he had to tell her about the person who was following Frank and him. He was pretty sure that Emily would take it in stride, considering everything else he had told her.

It was five o'clock when Jack got out of the shower. He decided he had time to add a special entry to his blog before he left to get Emily. After today's experience, he felt compelled to write something.

Special Edition

The Growing Evil on Planet Earth

There is much being said today about terrorism, and rightly so. We see brutal killings in Syria and attacks on our sons and daughters in the military and law enforcement all around the world. What drives people to do such awful, brutal acts? What do you think? Is it religion? Politics? Or is it just plain hate? When it happens here in the West, people say it's because the person wasn't in their right mind. Really? That seems to be a no-brainer, don't you think? Well, enough questions. How about some answers?

This world is a battlefield. You and I are in the battle somewhere, if we like it or not. We have two choices.

1. We can bury our heads in the sand. We can continue to live our lives avoiding this truth, in the belief that it won't touch us or someone we love. Hoping it will all somehow magically disappear. (Most of us are doing this now.)

2. We can decide to learn the truth about the forces of evil and fight back.

Now, you may say, "That's easy for you to say, blogger man, but I have a life and a family, and I can't get involved in some crazy spiritual battle."

Trust me, I know it sounds like a sci-fi novel, but allow me to continue. Evil was birthed in the depths of eternity a long time ago. The devil is real, and he hates you. Why? Because God loves you, and Satan hates the fact that God loves us! There is an evil in this world that influences every aspect of life on planet Earth, and when more people embrace the spirit of evil, the more evil they become. God told us how He wanted us to live and how He wanted us to treat each other, but somewhere along the way, we all thought it better to do our own thing and go our own way. You can't put truck parts in a washing machine and expect it to run, just like you can't live on sugar only and expect to feel good. God has a plan for you and me, and we need to follow it.

Evil comes from the master of evil, and no—he doesn't wear a red suit and carry a pitchfork. It's much worse than that. He comes as an angel of light, promising that you will have everything you want if you will only follow him. Sounds like some politicians. However, like the mouse tempted by the cheese, once you're in the trap, it's too late.

What's your opinion? Do you think those poor guys in ISIS and other terror groups, mass murderers and the like, simply had unfortunate childhoods, or do you believe what the Bible has to say?

"We struggle not against flesh and blood, but against the rulers, against the authorities, against the powers of this dark world, and against the spiritual forces of evil in the heavenly realms."

Let's read what John, the beloved Apostle of Jesus, told us in I John 5:19. 'We know that we are of God, and the entire world is under the power of the evil one.'

We need to remember, this is not our home. When Jesus returns, He will redeem not only our bodies, but nature itself.

Until next time,

Jack Bennett.

Jack read it over, hit the enter key, and sent the post off. It was now 5:20 p.m. It was time to get dressed and head out the door. Jack wasn't looking forward to telling Emily about the surveillance, but seeing her overshadowed everything else. As he got ready, Frank's words kept swimming around in his head: 'You buy this girl a big diamond ring and make it forever.'

Jack hoped to do that someday, but it went against commonsense, against everything he counseled everyone else not to do. He knew deep in his heart that the day would come. All he could think about was how crazy he was about her. He grabbed his car keys and rushed out the door.

30
———

DINNER FOR TWO

I t was five o'clock by the time Frank got back to D.C. He was hell-bent on finding out why he was being followed. On the ride back, he made a call to Jeff Callaport, his inside source. Jeff was the one who had given him the info on Wellsenburg and the Sons of Nimrod. He was a longtime friend and a genuine character. He was short at five-two, with a master's degree in sarcasm. Jeff was an excellent agent and called things as he saw them. He spent most of his time at his desk in D.C., running leads and gathering info for other field agents. Jeff knew the ins and outs of Washington better than anyone. Frank figured he might have some idea about what was going on.

They had agreed to meet at the Old Ebbitt at six o'clock. It was one of Frank's favorite spots in D.C. Established in 1856. It was a favorite of Presidents Grant, Cleveland, Harding, and Theodore Roosevelt. Frank was a bit of a history buff, so he got off on the entire experience.

The Old Ebbitt served a diverse selection of food. Jeff liked the crab cakes there, while Frank was all about their steaks. He owed Jeff at least a dinner after all the help he had given him.

Frank parked his car on Tenth Street across from the FBI building and walked half a mile to the restaurant. It turned out to be a nice evening, and Frank needed time to sort through what had happened at the old inn. Hanging with Jack was challenging and a growing experience. He had to admit that he was kind of jealous of Jack's newfound love. He knew Jack and Emily were about to have dinner and hang out, probably until the wee hours of the morning. Having someone like Emily in his life was something Frank often thought about, but for now, he had a job to do. He needed to learn as much about Wellsenburg's plans as possible.

He reached the restaurant on the corner of G and Fifteenth. Jeff was sitting at the bar, waiting. When Frank came in, Jeff motioned to the server. There were many rooms and bars in this historic restaurant, but Frank preferred to sit in Grant's barroom because it was quieter. He loved the high-back mahogany velvet booths. All the bars were gorgeous, with marble, brass, and beveled glass. Frank didn't come here often, mostly because it was a little pricey and always crowded. However, the atmosphere and the food were wonderful.

"Hey, Frank. How are you? Still, in one piece, I see," Jeff joked.

Frank snickered. "Yeah, and I hope to keep it that way."

The server came over to the table in the trademark Old Ebbitt uniform of a white button-down shirt, bow tie, suspenders, and a long, white apron and asked if they would like a drink. Frank ordered a glass of the house red, and Jeff stayed with his Scotch on the rocks that he'd brought from the bar.

"Did you ever wonder who painted that oil painting hanging over the bar?"

Jeff looked at him, noticeably uninterested. "You mean the one of the naked lady? No, not really."

"Are you all right? You seem on edge. I mean, more than usual."

Jeff took another sip and plunked his glass on the table. "Divorce sucks!"

Frank sat back, a little surprised at Jeff's opening salvo.

"Whoa, what's going on?"

Jeff peered down into his drink. "Seven years with this woman, and it's like she forgot we used to be in love. Now it's all about the money and the house. Thank God we didn't have any kids. I wanted kids, but she wanted to wait. Now I see why. Maybe this was her backup plan all along. Sorry, Frank. I know you had a bad one, too. I've had a terrible day!"

Frank felt his pain. It had only been two years since his divorce, and it was not an amicable one. His wife left him for her yoga instructor. She told him it was only a onetime fling, but he found out, with a brief investigation, that she had been seeing him off and on for six months. Fortunately, neither of them had children to drag through it all.

"No worries, my friend. You're right. There ain't nothing good about it." Frank checked Jeff's eyes. "How many Scotches have you had?"

Jeff picked up his glass and studied it. "Just two. I'm not hurting from alcohol, just misery. By the way, you look pretty good for all you've been through lately. What's your secret?"

Frank looked at Jeff and simply said, "I have the Lord in my life now."

Jeff stared at him for a minute, then responded. "You? Mr. FBI?

Frank 'The Lawman' Lederman. Wait a minute! I thought you were Jewish!"

Frank smiled. "Well, I am by birth. I never was a practicing Jew, but yes, I am Jewish. A few weeks ago, I had an incredible experience with God. I felt Him like I never thought possible. I prayed to Jesus for the first time. He changed my entire way of thinking. He gave me supernatural peace. I feel great. I mean, I still have tough situations like the one we're discussing, but I can feel Him leading and guiding me through them."

Jeff sat back in his seat, taken aback by Frank's honesty and openness.

"Wow, I think that's amazing, Frank. I've heard others talk like that, but I never thought I would hear those words coming out of your mouth. I mean, that's great and all, but I don't understand. How does something like that happen? One day you're one way, and then the next day, you're...? "

"I think the word you're looking for is saved. It can happen to you. I'll tell you what my buddy told me. Go home tonight and talk to the Lord Jesus. Talk to Him like you're talking to me. Tell Him all about what's going on in your life and ask Him to forgive you of all your sins —your failings and mess-ups. Believe me. You will feel a genuine peace. Everybody needs a new start."

"Just hearing you talk like that blows my mind. You seem different. I can sense that." Jeff thought for a moment. "I could really use some peace in my life. You know what? I'll do it. I promise I will spend some time talking to God when I get home tonight."

The server came back with Frank's cabernet. Frank ordered the New York Strip, and Jeff ordered his favorite crab cakes. Once the server left, Jeff collected himself and refocused. "Now, tell me more about this shadow of yours?"

"I haven't seen his face, but he followed me out of Blackstone two days ago. And then he showed up this morning at my assignment outside of Merrifield. I figured he's connected to you know who."

Frank was very careful not to throw out any names. After all, this was Washington D.C., and you never knew who was listening.

It was no mystery to Jeff. He knew he was talking about Senator Wellsenburg, and he also knew how dangerous an adversary the senator could be. Jeff reached down, pulled a manila folder out of his briefcase, and placed it on the table.

"Well, there's no doubt about it. I have something else to tell you that will thicken the plot." Jeff lowered his voice a bit as not to draw attention from the surrounding patrons. "I was given something the other day, a paper file that I'm sure was supposed to be destroyed a long time ago. I found it stuck in between my storm and front doors. It appears someone's guilty conscience got the best of them, and from what I've read, it looks like our man might have had something to do with the deaths of your mystery couple."

Frank's eyes widened. 'The Oslows!', he thought. Frank wasn't naïve. He knew this wasn't the first time a file magically disappeared, but it was the first time he was privy to it. Jack was right. Wellsenburg had something to do with the Oslows' deaths. No wonder Wellsenburg had put someone on them. Talk about a skeleton in your closet. This was big. Scary big.

"What does the report say?"

"It seems our man had a big blowout with Mr. O. the night before they found he and his wife murdered. The two men met in Montrose

Park, where they apparently thought no one would hear their conversation. They didn't know that a couple of young lovers were sitting on a park bench just out of sight of their dispute.

"The report says they heard two men talking loudly. They couldn't see who it was, but they heard the whole conversation. Mr. O. wanted out of the society. Our man tried to convince him it was not the right time, that he should be patient, and everything would work out once he won the senate seat. But the dispute grew worse to where our man threatened Mr. O. He said, and I quote from the report. 'You have no idea what powers you are dealing with, O. Even I don't fully understand how things happen. The only thing I know for sure is that they do. If you do this, I cannot guarantee you or your wife's safety.'

"Mr. O screamed at him and said, I quote, 'Listen to me, George. My wife and I are getting out! Do you understand? There are awful, terrifying things going on that we didn't sign up for, and we can't deal with it anymore. We are done!'"

Jeff shrugged his shoulders. "That's it. That is where the report ends. The couple said they never saw them or heard anything else after that." Jeff closed the file and put it back in his briefcase.

"So, you're telling me they never officially filed the report? This happened thirty years ago when our man had yet to be elected?"

Jeff took another drink and answered, "It was common knowledge that our man was receiving large sums of money from the Oslows, so there was a provable connection, but if this report had ever seen the light of day, you could only imagine the ratifications. Granted, there is no last name, but come on! Someone named George threatening the Oslows like that on the day before they were murdered? The press would've had a field day. Wellsenburg was a rookie. That alone would have cost him the election."

Intrigued, Frank. asked the obvious. "What happened to the young lovers on the park bench?"

"Nothing. I suppose because they hadn't really seen anybody, they just left them alone."

Frank's mind was going a hundred miles an hour. He couldn't wait to tell Jack about all this. In fact, he would have called him right then, except he knew he was out and probably having a great time with Emily.

"That is amazing. It's hard to believe someone kept that file all this time. How did they know to give it to you, I wonder?"

"That's the scary part. I don't know. I'm hoping it's because of my reputation as a straight shooter. Oh, that's not all, my friend. You remember the other name I gave you?"

How could Frank forget that name? Dante Adal. Just the thought of his name sent a chill up Frank's spine.

"Yes, you said he was part of the society."

Jeff leaned in over the table and spoke in a hushed tone, "He's more than that. I checked him out. He's a big-time business mogul from out in L.A. Our man flew out there with him last week on his private jet. I'm not sure what went on out there, but I heard through the grapevine, our guy has suddenly inherited a pile of money from some new Super PAC for his potential run at the presidency."

Jeff's demeanor was somber. He knew Frank's life could be in danger. "Here's the situation. The closer you get to link him with anything that would hinder or eliminate him from the presidential race, the hotter it's going to get for you and your buddy Bennett. Having you followed may be just the beginning. Until we find out more about this Dante Adal, maybe you and Jack should lie low for a while. You know, give me a few weeks."

Frank put his elbows on the table and massaging his forehead with the tips of his fingers. He knew that Dante Adal was more than a powerful business mogul, but how could he explain that to Jeff without thinking he had lost it? He could hear the angel saying Dante's name over and over in his head, but it was Dante's response that he remembered most: 'I will have my day and this world, and all the fools who live in it will obey me.'

He had to warn Jeff. If something were to happen to him, he could never forgive himself. He decided the best way was to say it. Subtlety wasn't one of Frank's attributes.

"Listen, I have to tell you that this business mogul, as you call him, is very dangerous. I know it might be hard to believe, but he's over-the-top, more dangerous than our man. Be very careful about what you say and what questions you ask. I'm not sure who we can trust in the Bureau at this point. Somebody tipped this guy off about our mission today, and the only ones who knew the details were in my department. Others may have known about the case, but few knew the day or the time. I made sure of that because Jack wanted no press, no agents, and no ghost chasers."

The server brought their dinners and asked if they would like another drink. Frank said yes to a refill of his cabernet while Jeff drew a bye on the Scotch.

Jeff patiently waited for the server to walk away. His curiosity was killing him. "Okay, you've got my attention. What do you know about this guy that I don't? Because if I need to be careful, I'll need to know why, and I need all the info."

Frank stood up. "Give me a minute. I have to tap my bladder. I'll be right back."

On his way to the men's room, Frank glanced around to get a handle on who was close enough to their booth to pick up on their conversation. On his way back, he checked again just to be sure.

He sat back in the booth and asked, "How are the crab cakes?"

"Good, as usual. Are we clear?"

"I think so. What I have to say will be hard to grasp, so I will take it slow. And because I can't wait to eat this incredible steak." Frank cut a piece and put it in his mouth. "Man, that's good. I've been thinking about this all afternoon."

Jeff stared at him from across the table, waiting eagerly for an answer. Frank cut another piece, stabbed it with his fork, and was about to stick it in his mouth. Jeff sat up. "Really?"

"Sorry. So, this guy Dante. Well, he's kinda not like a real person."

"You mean he's a fraud," Jeff said with a matter-of-fact expression.

"Well, kind of. He's an evil angel. A demon. You know, a spirit thing."

Jeff stared across the table, with a half-smile on his face, waiting for Frank to laugh, but he didn't. He just cut another piece of steak and stuck it in his mouth.

"What the hell are you talking about, Frank? You are telling me with a straight face that this..."

With his mouth full of steak, Frank lifted his hand, holding up one finger. A signal for Jeff to lower his voice.

Jeff took a deep breath, leaned in, and spoke in a quieter tone.

"You're really saying that you believe this Dante Adal is a demon or something?"

Without hesitation, Frank said, "Yeah. That's what I'm telling you. The guy is a demon thing."

"I don't know what to say to that. How can you be so nonchalant, so cavalier about something like that, and expect me to believe what you're saying? Frank, I think you have gone a little overboard with this newfound religion of yours. How do you know this? Did Jesus tell you?"

Frank stopped chewing for a second and said, "Look, your dinner is getting cold. Eat your crab cakes."

Jeff gave Frank a look of disbelief and then motioned for another Scotch.

"Yes, sir. Right away."

Jeff freaked out. "What the hell do you want me to say, Frank? The next thing I know, you'll be telling me you see angels, too."

Frank almost choked. Lifting his napkin off his lap, he placed it on the table. Frank owed Jeff a more detailed explanation than that, but it had been a rough day and he was still new to this kind of thing.

"Okay, I know you think I've lost it, but listen, Jeff. You would not believe the day I had today. However, I'm praying that you will. Oh, and by the way, that wasn't nice to say about Jesus. If you must know, I have seen him."

Frank paused, looked back down at his steak. A slight grin slowly came across his face as he realized what he just said. "Not Jesus. Dante. And if you want to stay ahead of all this, you better get on board with the truth. What I'm telling you is real and, knowing all this, just might save your life one day."

Frank put his fork down and leaned forward. With his arms folded and both elbows on the table, he said, "Listen, we've gone as far as we can with this conversation here. Let's finish our dinner. It's a nice evening. We'll take a walk around town, and I'll tell you what I know."

The server came over with Jeff's drink and placed it on the table. "Is there anything else, sir?"

"No, thank you. That's all."

Jeff never looked at the server. He just kept staring at Frank. He was completely dumbfounded. The server gave them a weird look and walked away.

Jeff reluctantly went back to his crab cakes. He couldn't help but wonder what his longtime friend wanted to tell him. Frank didn't miss a beat. He went on with his plan to demolish his steak. The explanation would have to wait.

* * *

Frank wasn't the only one having a nice dinner and soaking in the historic atmosphere of D.C. Jack surprised Emily and took her to the Chart House in Alexandria, a picturesque little town and the hometown of George Washington. It was now eight o'clock. Jack and Emily were just finishing their dinner outside on the patio, enjoying the gorgeous panoramic view of the Potomac. The decor at the restaurant was beachside. A laid-back nautical theme with bubble lighting fixtures throughout. Jack and Emily loved seafood, and the Chart House made a great baked shrimp stuffed with crab. They were enjoying the clear, late evening sky and the pleasant breeze off the water when a woman in her mid-thirties sporting a tight green floral lace dress, cut just above her knees, walked towards their table. Her hair was light brown and styled in a way that said I'm sexy and smart.

Every man looked up as she walked by, but she didn't seem to mind. She was the type of woman that was accustomed to causing a stir.

She walked right up to Jack. "Hi, I'm sorry for interrupting, but I have to ask. Are you, Jack Bennett?"

Jack looked up at her and smiling. "Yes, I am."

The woman barely gave him time to answer. "My name is Lisa Hill from the Washington Post. I read your blog and follow you on Twitter. I had to come over and meet you. Your posts are quite interesting. I would love to interview you sometime."

Emily glanced at Jack from the corner of her eye, watching to see what kind of reaction he would have to this beautiful woman raining compliments down on his head. Jack had little experience with this sort of thing. He was friendly to most everyone, even beautiful women, and was not ready for this relationship test.

Staring into her big brown eyes, he said, "Oh, thank you. I'm flattered. I'm glad someone is reading them. I'd hate to think I was only talking to myself."

Lisa tossed her hair and laughed, showing off her sparkling smile. "Oh, you have so many who read your posts," she said flirtatiously. "Here's my card. Call me at your convenience. I would love to get together with you." She glanced at Emily, then back at Jack. "You know, for that interview, I mean."

Jack smiled politely and took the card. "Thank you."

Lisa gave Emily a quick, patronizing glance and walked back to her table.

Jack had no idea what had just happened or what this little encounter was going to cost him. He was about to get a lesson on how to ruin a wonderful evening in fifteen seconds.

Emily stared at him in a way he had never seen before. "What was that?"

Still in the land of I Don't Have a Clue, Jack said, "Wow, that was pretty cool, huh? An interview for the Washington Post."

Emily was more than a little perturbed. "You do realize that you didn't introduce me or recognize the fact that I was sitting here."

"I didn't really have time. She was just here for a few seconds."

Emily thought, 'You mean you didn't have time because you couldn't take your eyes off her long enough to remember that I was here?' "A little, this is my girl friend Emily would have been nice. She looked at me like I didn't matter to you."

Jack wasn't finished digging his hole, his inexperience threatening to bury him. "She only wanted an interview, that's all. I think you're making too much of it. Why would she look at you that way? She seemed very nice."

Jack wasn't getting it. He had yet to learn that a man should never defend another woman to his girlfriend or wife and expect to live to tell about it. Jack had just committed one of the cardinal sins in relationships.

In her mind, Jack had just chosen this woman over her. The last thing she wanted was Jack sitting alone somewhere with this hot, career woman pouring his heart out and telling her his life story.

Emily looked at Jack, her big blue eyes speaking volumes, "We haven't been going out that long, so I don't want to appear like some kind of jealous freak, but Jack, you didn't think that was a little suspicious? Listen, no one believes in what you do more than I do. I know you have tens of thousands of followers on Twitter and your books make the bestseller list, but really. That woman is up to something."

Emily glanced over at Lisa's table. She was in a deep conversation with two suspicious-looking men. Something was up. "Why is a woman like her sitting with two guys who like hit men for the mob?"

Jack took a quick glanced at Lisa's table and had to agree. He was a little rusty when it came to the ladies, but he knew two things. One, he was set up by an enemy that he was used to dealing with in a much different environment, and two, Emily's discernment had proven to be on point.

Jack took her hand. "I apologize. I should have been more aware, and introduced you immediately. You're right. Something's up. I should have seen that."

Emily reached out with her other hand, tilted her head slightly, and said, "And?" She was waiting for a confession.

Jack knew what she wanted to hear. It killed him to have to admit it, "And because she was pretty."

Emily smiled. "Pretty? She's super-hot, and was falling all over you. Sorry, I guess I'm not used to hanging out with a celebrity."

Jack laughed, "Oh yeah, that's me.

Emily leaned in, placed her hand on his cheek, looked deep into his eyes, and kissed him. Not just a kiss, a long, incredible kiss, one that let him know she was hot too. Emily also knew Lisa was watching from afar. By the time she let Jack go, Lisa was a distant memory.

Emily flipped her beautiful blonde hair back over her shoulders. Knowing she had made her point, "Let's get out of here. It's a delightful night. I would love to go for a walk."

"That sounds good to me. It's a great little town."

Emily and Jack walked out of the Chart House smiling, hand-in-hand. As they approached Lisa's table, Jack felt something in his spirit. When he glanced back at Lisa, he saw something he hadn't seen before. There was a dark figure, a shadow or shroud, hovering around her. When he turned and looked again, it was gone. It was a gentle nudge from the Lord reminding him he was not meant to do this alone for a multitude of reasons. Jack was blessed with the faith to dispose of demons face-to-face, but the enemy had many covert ways to destroy a life. Jack understood, at that moment, that the Lord had given Emily her own special gifts.

Once outside, they walked along the sidewalk on North Union Street, passing the Torpedo Factory Art Center. Emily looked up at the building and noted, "I've heard about this place, but I have never been in it. Was it really a torpedo factory?"

Jack knew all about it, of course. He loved history and was happy to be talking about something else. "Yes, the Torpedo Factory Art Center was once an actual torpedo factory. It began the day after Armistice Day, the day marking the official end of World War I. It was November 12, 1918. On that day, the Navy began construction on the original building. It was called the U.S. Naval Torpedo Station, and it was fully operational. Now it's home to over 165 professional artists who work, exhibit, and sell their art."

Impressed, Emily could listen to him all night. Jack's knowledge of so many subjects amazed her. They turned down Kings Street, old town Alexandria's main street, paved with cobblestones and amazingly picturesque. It was a beautiful night under a perfect moonlit sky.

Jack knew they had a lot to talk about, including that someone powerful was following Frank and him.

"I have something I have to tell you."

Emily kept walking, her expression unchanged. Expecting the unexpected from Jack was the new norm. Considering their brief history and outlandish adventures.

"Okay, what is it?" She braced herself.

"Well..."

"You know I hate it when you start with well, but go ahead."

"Someone is having Frank and me followed. It started a couple of days ago."

Emily stopped walking. "I knew it! It was that day in the café, right? I could tell something was wrong. I expected you to say something last night."

"I was going to, but we were having such a great time."

They had stopped in front of a bench under one of the many trees that lined King's Street. "Let's sit for a minute."

Emily looked at him, knowing something big was coming.

Jack took her hand and said, "We think it is Senator Wellsenburg."

"Oh, Jack." Emily's face turned ashen. "You've made an enemy of a U.S. senator, and not just any senator, but a powerful one? Is that what you're telling me?"

Jack had a sheepish look on his face. "Yeah, I guess so, but there's more to it than you might think. There is a good possibility the senator is involved in things that could cost him his senate seat and possibly earn him prison time. Remember me telling you about that night when Frank prayed and gave his heart to the Lord?"

Emily nodded. "Sure, how could I forget that? The night you faced the demon, and the angel came and saved you and Frank. That doesn't happen to everybody, Jack."

"Well..." he caught himself. "Sorry. We believe the senator is somehow connected to the demon we saw that night."

Emily sat straight up, her eyes growing wide. "How can that be? How can a U.S. senator, someone who is supposed to be helping people and protecting the country, be involved with a demon? Jack, this is way out there, even for you. I mean, I believe you, but wow! He's the one keeping tabs on you and Frank?"

"It looks that way."

Emily took Jack's hands and held them tight. "What are you going to do? Do you think someone is watching us now?"

Jack wished he had a more comforting answer to give her. "I don't know." "There is only one guy following us we know of, so I think he has his eye on Frank more than me right now. Frank is in D.C. tonight. He's meeting with an old friend from the Bureau. Hopefully, he will give us some additional insight."

Emily was in uncharted territory. She prayed and read her Bible daily, but this—this was beyond anything she had ever encountered. The situation was becoming extremely dangerous, and she needed more details.

She brushed her hair back, sat up straight, and said, "Okay, Jack. It's time. Tell me how and why this kind of thing happens? I know there is evil in the world, that's easy to see, but this is different. I mean, this is in-your-face New Testament stuff and beyond."

Despite the situation, Jack was loving it. Here he was sitting next to this smart, incredibly beautiful girl, who couldn't get enough of God and, for reasons unknown, couldn't get enough of him.

"Okay, I'll do my best. Some of this you already know, but I need to start from the beginning for it to make sense." He took a deep breath, praying it wouldn't be too much for her. "The world is racing down a road that will soon end in a great battle called Armageddon. Now just about everyone has heard that term. Most see it as the end of the world, caused by an alien invasion, natural catastrophe, or God only knows what. But most do not understand that this coming battle between absolute evil and the Creator of the world was put into motion thousands of years ago. Satan is now in the final stages of grooming the nations, including the U.S. to rebel against Christ. Satan, that ancient serpent known as the devil, believes it is possible to defeat God and rule the world."

Emily stared in amazement. She was familiar with the subject because of the teachings she had attended over the past few years, but never heard it explained so clearly. Jack had a knack for explaining things.

"Where in the Bible does it say that?"

"In many places, in different ways, but one of the oldest writings may be in the book of Psalms."

Jack reached into his pocket and pulled out his phone. It had several Bible apps on it, along with a ton of his favorite research apps and websites. He paged to Psalms chapter two and read it.

"'Why do the nations conspire and the peoples plot in vain? The kings of the earth take their stand and the rulers gather against the LORD and his Anointed One. Let us break their chains, they say, and throw off their restraints...'" Jack put his phone down and explained, "The scripture is telling us that in the time before Christ's return, there is going to be a move away from God and His commandments. Eventually, the devil will convince the world that they can defeat Christ and do away with all his moral laws and teachings."

"Is that when the Antichrist will come?" Emily asked.

"Yes, but first the Apostle Paul tells us there will be a falling away, meaning that even Christians who may have followed the Lord at one time will completely fall out of love with God and go back to their old ways, embracing the message of the coming world leader."

Jack saw the troubled look on her face. He sat back on the bench and put his arm around her. Emily put her head on his shoulder, and looking up Kings Street towards the Capitol Building, asked, "Is that why there is more demon activity? Because we are getting closer to this great battle?"

Jack wished they didn't have to have this discussion on such a beautiful evening, but he understood how important it was for Emily to understand what was going on.

"Demons, fallen angels, and unclean spirits have always been around. The difference is that there are now over seven billion people on the planet, and a great number of them are entertaining spirits and inviting them into their lives. Not only individuals but also entire nations. Sadly, many don't realize it. The devil doesn't show up in a red suit with horns and say, 'Let's make a deal.' It happens when they turn their backs on God and the truth of God's Word to follow their own lusts. It creates a spiritual vacuum that Satan is more than happy to fill."

"I guess I always knew this stuff existed, but it gets a lot scarier when it's happening to you or someone you love." Emily pulled Jack closer. "But how can fallen angels and demons materialize as regular people? Is that in the Bible?"

"It happened in the days of Noah. Angels came down and took the form of men. They captured other men's wives and took any women they desired and had children with them. They planned to rule the earth. That was one of the main reasons for the flood."

Emily whispered, "So, you and Frank believe that Senator Wellsenburg is working with a demon, like in the days of Noah?"

Jack looked around to make sure no one was in earshot. The thought of being heard made him uneasy. After all, who in their right mind would believe a story like this? If it got beyond their little circle, they would all find themselves in a padded room somewhere.

Jack chose his answer carefully. "Yes, and no. I'm not sure Wellsenburg knows who or what Dante is, but this much I can say with confidence. He has made a deal with the devil, whether or not he realizes it. I know he would do anything to be President of the United States, and his agenda targeting religion, especially Biblical Christianity, is well known on the hill. Let's just say it would serve him and the prince of darkness well if he got elected." He looked into her eyes and said emphatically. "Frank and I can't let that happen."

Looking a little confused, Emily said, "But didn't you just say that the Bible has predicted all this? How can we stop it from happening?"

"The Bible is clear that we are in the last days before Jesus returns and that these things will happen, but He also gave us the command to occupy until He comes. In the original Greek, it means to continue or busy oneself. As followers of Christ, we are to continue the work He started. As you know, the Apostle Paul told us we do not fight against flesh and blood, but with spiritual forces of evil in the heavenly realms. That literally means our battle is against the evil kingdoms and the rulers who sit on those thrones. With the Lord leading the way, that is exactly what we intend to do."

Jack felt the good pleasure of the Lord upon him as he spoke. He cherished the familiar feeling and never took it for granted.

Deep in her soul, Emily could feel it, too. She loved that about Jack. Emily stood up, and as she did, the wind caught her hair and whirled it around her face. Brushing back her hair from her eyes, she looked down at Jack, feeling proud and happy.

"You know, Jack Bennett, my life sure has changed since I met you. But as scary as all this might be, I want you to know something." Emily paused, and took a deep breath. "I believe God has His hand on you in a special way. You are so different. I can't explain it. I didn't think guys like you really existed." Emily's soft touch on Jack's face made his heart race. With a look Jack had never seen before, Emily said, "I think I'm falling in love with you, Jack Bennett."

Jack was stunned. He stood up and, looking into her beautiful eyes, said, "I'm happy to hear that, Emily Richardson. Because falling in love with you was easy. You are amazing. I thank God every day that He brought you into my life."

He put his arms around her waist and pulled her close. Her hair gently blew around him. He breathed in deeply. The scent of Emily's hair filling his senses. There wasn't anything he didn't love about her. Their lips met. Jack loved kissing her. She knew how to make him forget about everything else.

She curled her arms around his neck, tilted her head, and gazed into his eyes. Jack loved it when she did that. When her lips touched his, they were warm and soft. It was a long kiss, one that each would remember because of the things they had shared this night. As they gently pulled away from each other, Jack said, "Kissing you takes me away to another place."

Emily, smiling, said, "I know. I feel it too. I love that feeling."

"What do you say we forget about all this for a while? How about we walk down to Pop's Old Fashioned Ice Cream? I heard they make an outstanding banana split."

Jack took her hand. They continued down the sidewalk, relieved to be thinking about other things.

Parked across the street in a gray Acura sedan was a large, rough-looking man, smoking a cigar and talking on the phone. He studied them closely as they walked west on Kings Street. Taking a long drag off his large cigar, he said, "Yeah, that's right. Her name is Emily. And she obviously means a great deal to him. Do you want me to hang around?"

He took another puff and waited for his orders.

"Okay, then. I'll head back to Washington."

He listened intently and was about to pull out when the caller asked another question.

"I can't be sure, but yes, there's a good chance she knows what he knows. Yes, sir. I'll wait to hear from you. Thank you, sir."

He watched Jack and Emily walk into Pop's Ice Cream, then put the car into drive and slowly pulled away. Confident he had once again done the job they sent him to do. He wondered what his boss had in mind for the happy couple.

* * *

It was eight o'clock when Frank and Jeff stepped out of Old Ebbitt's onto Fifteenth Street. The traffic was picking up, but there were fewer people on the sidewalk. They turned onto G Street and began their walk back to the FBI building where Frank had parked his car. Jeff's car was in the Colonial Parking Garage on Eighth Street. It was a relatively short walk, about half a mile, so he would have to talk fast. Jeff had lots of questions he needed answered.

"Okay, Frank. Lay it out. What is going on?"

"It's best if I start with Jack. You've heard me mention Jack many times, but you have never met him." He glanced at Jeff. "He is a different guy."

Jeff looked at him funny and asked, "So, what? You mean like he only has one eye and two butts?"

Frank laughed out loud.

Jeff talked with his hands most of the time. Using hand gestures helped him to make his point.

Jeff laughed. "Yeah, yeah, I know. He's the consultant slash writer that the FBI hired to investigate all that paranormal crap, right?"

"That's right, except it's not crap. It turns out a lot of that stuff is real. You have heard of people performing exorcisms? Well, that's kind of what Jack does—sort of — I guess." Frank wasn't really sure himself. When he thought about all the things he had seen God do through Jack, he had to keep reminding himself that it was real. "I know I'm not explaining it well, but it's hard to describe."

Jeff rubbed his forehead. He was searching for a reference, "You mean, like The Exorcist?" He felt stupid saying it, but that's all he had.

Frank laughed. "No, that's Hollywood's version or the devil's version, as Jack would put it. You know those movies where good struggles to overcome evil, and the priest or minister gets all beat up and thrown out the window or something. I really don't know. Never really watched it all the way through. I thought it was a lousy movie. Anyway, that's not how it goes, at least not with Jack. He confronts these demon creature things and sends them on their way."

Jeff was having a difficulty digesting it all and keeping up with Frank's long strides. "Hey, would you slow down? I feel like I'm having a foot race with an ostrich!" he said, his arms flailing away.

Frank laughed out loud. Jeff always cracked him up. He slowed his pace.

"Let me get this straight. You have witnessed this yourself?"

Frank, still smiling, answered, "Yes, I have seen it with my own eyes."

Jeff's next question was the one he was dying to ask from the beginning. "So, what do they look like?"

"One night, Jack and I were in this old, empty church investigating some crazy reports of lights going on and off and objects flying around inside the building when a huge, ugly, demon thing confronted us. It had black leather like wings and eyes that glowed orangey-red. Every time it moved, it left a trail of reddish mist. It got so close to me I could feel and hear it wheezing as it breathed in and out. It had thick legs covered in scales, and its feet looked like the claws of a lizard."

Jeff's eyes were as big as saucers, like a kid listening to someone telling ghost stories around a campfire. "What did Jack do?"

Frank had to admit he was enjoying telling this story. He wasn't sure why, but he felt good all over. It was the same feeling he had the night he prayed in the car.

"He prayed in the name of Jesus and told the creature to leave, but this one was more powerful than the others he had faced, and it was doing its worst to fight against Jack's prayer. Jack then called on God the Father to remove the demon from that place. But this time, when Jack prayed, a powerful angel appeared and banished the demon."

Frank paused. "I was there, and just telling the story gives me chills."

At that, Jeff abruptly stopped walking, turned to Frank, and said, "I knew there would be angels! I said it in the restaurant. I said, 'Next you'll be telling me you saw angels.'" Jeff began walking in circles, his arms flaying about. "Frank, you are freaking me out right now." Jeff was hyper, to begin with. This took him to a new level. He started talking faster and faster, "If I didn't know you, I would think you'd lost your marbles. Let the genie out of the bottle. You know what I'm saying." He walked a few feet away and then turned and walked back. "Okay, okay. I can't believe I'm saying this, but I believe you. Somehow, I always knew deep down inside that these things existed, but I guess I never wanted to think about it or admit it." He took a long breath and tried to refocus. "Okay, I'm ready. What else do I need to know?"

They resumed their walk at a slower pace, with Jeff hanging on every word that came out of Frank's mouth.

"There are dark forces at work right here in D.C."

Jeff interrupted with a chuckle, "That's not exactly a news bulletin."

"No, but what is, is what the Lord has taught me through Jack. There are darker forces at work, greater than what man can muster. Spiritual realms, with princes and rulers, with an agenda that mortal men are not aware of, and these beings are the ones who are inspiring and leading them on. Trust me, they are the ones who are really in control and this so-called entrepreneur, Dante, is definitely one of them."

Jeff's head was spinning. "This is incredible stuff. What do you and Jack plan on doing? We can't let this guy become President." Jeff realized he had just included himself in this frightening quest.

"So... it's we now?" Frank observed with a grin. "Jack's got the lead on this one, but I'm sure he'd agree that we could use all the help we can get."

As they approached Frank's car, Jeff had a worried look on his face. "Wellsenburg obviously has his eye on you and Jack, so you better be very careful. He is a powerful man, even without Dante or becoming President. I will keep my eyes open and let you know if I hear anything."

Frank put his hand on Jeff's shoulder. "Remember what I told you and spend some time talking to the Lord tonight. You need to have Him in your life. Jesus is the answer to everything you are going through."

"Are you kidding? I was praying off, and on the whole time, you were telling me that story. The Lord and I have a lot to talk about. My life is full of screw-ups. You know I can be a real jackass."

Frank grinned. There were so many ways he could respond to that, but he thought better of it. "Compared to God, we're all screw-ups. That's the whole reason for the cross. Besides, I heard He likes little people."

"Yo, what ya saying? So, you got jokes. Hey, I'm in good company. You know, Mother Teresa was only five feet tall." They both laughed.

Frank needed to add one more thing, "About Wellsenburg, please do not do anything stupid. Let Jack and me run with the ball on this one. I will be in touch."

"Yeah, yeah. Okay, okay. I'll follow your lead."

Jeff nodded and walked off to get his car. Frank was genuinely concerned about his friend. They would have to stay in close contact from here on out. Only God knew what the next move was.

31

VISITORS

The morning sun found Jack beside his bed on his knees, asking God for His divine protection, strength, and discernment. He knew he had to become even more dependent on the Lord's touch and protection. Jack prayed for Emily and their future together and thanked God for Frank's salvation and his strong desire to follow the Lord.

Unbeknownst to Jack, someone, or in this case, some thing, was on his front porch. It made no sound as it moved about, for it lived in a different dimension. The creature stood five feet tall and had arms and legs, but it moved quickly, smoothly, back and forth without using them. Its feet were enormous, with sharp claws protruding from the ends, leaving deep scratch marks on the wooden porch floor as it moved. It reared up on its rear legs, reaching its full height, and peered through Jack's picture window. Wisps of red vapor trailed from its twisted mouth and nose, and an eerie smirk grew on its distorted face as it studied the layout of the house. It's bulging, reddish eyes searched back and forth and then grew wide as it looked down the hallway and spied Jack kneeling by his bed.

Suddenly, there was a loud thump. And another wisp of red vapor twisted and turned, and an identical creature landed beside the first. They lowered themselves into a coil of sorts, their shoulders hunched over like two old men. Each carried short, black daggers strapped to their sides that dripped with an oozing black slime that burned like a toxic acid when it hit the porch floor. They grinned with vile expressions of anticipation. The creatures glared at Jack through the window, their own disfigured images reflected in the glass. Slowly and carefully, they pulled their instruments of terror out of their sheaths. They intended to stab Jack repeatedly with their poison daggers. It would not be a physical stab, leaving deep wounds and flowing blood, but a spiritual one that would leave Jack discouraged and fearful. The effects of their attack could last for days, weeks, or even longer. Their task was to distract, discourage, and eliminate the threat to their master's kingdom.

Like a bolt of lightning, they took off and flew around the house in an eerie demonic ceremonial dance. Drooling with expectancy, they shot straight for the front door when suddenly an object of incredible brilliance fell from the sky and appeared on the porch. The creatures hit the wall of light with tremendous force, propelling them head over heels onto the front lawn, hissing and spewing red and orange vapor as they went. When they opened their eyes, they found themselves staring at Uriel, thrown a hundred feet from the porch. The angelic warrior had planted himself right in front of Jack's door.

Uriel put his hand on his sword, staring into their crazed eyes, and with all the authority of God himself, pronounced, "You cannot enter here because of this man's prayer. Be gone or be destroyed!"

The creatures looked at each other and grinned. Intoxicated by their overwhelming hatred and desire to destroy Jack, they convinced themselves they could defeat Uriel.

"There is only one of you, and there are two of us!" They hissed in a voice so evil that it silenced the birds in the nearby trees.

Uriel's sword glowed as he pulled it from its sheath. He knew that these were lesser demons sent to discourage Jack and do damage to his spirit. They did not have the power to do anything more to Jack, but it would have been enough to disrupt what the Lord had for him. Uriel would not let that happen. Their plan was no secret to him. He knew why they were here and who sent them.

The creatures leaped to their feet, flew straight up into the sky, and circled around and around above the front of Jack's house, screeching in a fit of rage and fury. Their eyes burned red hot. The thought of not completing their mission was intolerable to them. With daggers in hand, they flew with great speed towards Uriel.

But they were no match for the warrior of righteousness. Uriel knew that one of them would try to distract him while the other attempted to get at Jack. He would have to move quickly, but he was used to moving in and out of time. In the blink of an eye, they were on him. Moving with incredible strength and speed, Uriel slashed one demon across its chest, sending it spinning back onto the front steps, red vapor spewing everywhere. The second one flew towards the front window at lightning speed. Moving between the seconds, Uriel swung his sword to his right and cut the creature in two.

With a high-pitched wail, the creature vanished in a wisp of smoke. Seething with hatred, the remaining demon with red vapor oozing from its chest snatched up its poison dagger and came at Uriel a second time. Uriel swung his sword high and, with one mighty stroke, severed the creature's head from its body in an explosion of red mist. The vapor cloud rose, briefly taking the slain creature's shape, before being abruptly swept away by a gust of wind. When it vanished, a great feeling of peace instantly surrounded Jack's house. Uriel sensed that the area was clear, but he scanned the skies above just in case. He heard the birds singing once again in the nearby trees. He loved to hear them praise their Creator.

Uriel turned and walked up to the window to check on Jack. He was still praying and pouring his heart out to the Lord, unaware of the battle that had just taken place. Uriel was pleased. He walked out onto the green lawn in front of Jack's house, took one more look around, then unfolded his large, powerful wings. Smiling, he whispered, "Carry on, Jack Bennett." He shot straight up into the crystal blue sky and disappeared.

Jack's prayer suddenly to turn to praise, and, as it did, he could feel an overwhelming peace sweeping over him. In his heart, Jack knew he had received the answer he had prayed for. Either God had answered his prayer, or He was about to. Either way, Jack felt a sweet release in his spirit and inner joy he couldn't explain. He finished praying, stood up, wiped a few tears from his eyes, and made his way into the kitchen. He always felt connected to the Lord when he prayed, but this time, it was different. It was one of those special times that rarely happened. He felt refreshed, but hungry, not having anything to eat for the last twenty-four hours. He walked into the kitchen, filled his percolator with water and fresh ground coffee, and stepped outside for some fresh air.

Jack immediately noticed the deep grooves in the wood flooring of his porch. He was alarmed and puzzled. He bent down and ran his fingers over the marks. As he did, a chill ran down his spine. Not out of fear, but blessing. He had seen enough demon-like creatures to know something alarming had happened here, either overnight or early this morning. Jack ran out onto the front lawn to get a better look at the front of his house. He looked high and low, but there was no other damage or evidence of any conflict. Jack walked around the rest of the house to see if he could find any other evidence of a demon incursion. He found none. There had been a battle of some sort between the forces of darkness and light. He knew it was the Lord who had kept him safe. Jack's heart overflowed with gratitude and praise. He clearly understood why he had such an amazing time in prayer. An unexplainable surge of fresh energy and faith pulsed through his mind, body, and spirit.

Jack loved the Lord, but to have God come down and touch him like this was beyond anything he had ever experienced. He walk to the middle of his front lawn, stretched his arms up to the sky, and with only the birds and the crystal blue Virginia sky as his audience, shouted at the top of his lungs, "Thank you, Jesus! Thank you, Lord! You are incredible!"

Tears of joy ran down his face. God had carried him from despair to a place of great joy and renewed vision. In his mind, the mission was clearer than ever. He was to continue to expose the powers of darkness without fear, trusting in Almighty God to lead, guide, and protect. The Lord had given Jack many impossible tasks before, but this path led him into far deeper water. Jesus knew what he needed. It reminded him of what an old pastor friend of his used to say. "God equips those he calls."

He stood there with hands raised, gazing up into the sky. It was as if he could see in the Spirit, right through the atmosphere and straight into Heaven. His spirit was soaring. He felt like he could fly, and he knew, in his heart, that one day he would.

32
_____

A TINGE OF GUILT

D ante's private plane landed at Reagan National at 4:35 p.m.
Dante traveled alone and without security, at least none
that anyone could see. Dante felt it was important to travel
as mortals and loved disguising himself as a human. He particularly
liked the way women looked at him. At six feet, three inches, with jet-
black hair and an athletic build, he was very good-looking. He moved
quickly through security, carrying his briefcase and a small travel bag.
He continued out to the concourse level in terminal A and through the
doors to the sidewalk.

Senator Wellsenburg arranged for a limousine to pick him up. It
was waiting for him as he walked out. The driver walked around the
back of the limo and opened the door. Dante got in without saying a
word. He had no interest in speaking to a human of little significance.
The driver closed the door, returned to his seat, and the limousine
quickly pulled away. The driver instructed to keep silent unless spoken

to, did as he was told. He was to bring Dante directly to the Hart Senate Office Building.

Dante sat in the back of the limousine, checking his email messages on his phone. He was a powerful being, but could only be in one place at a time. He wasn't God, although he liked to think of himself as one. For now, this was the best way for him to keep up, especially with those on the Hill. He enjoyed flying for many reasons, but absolutely hated being driven around in cars. He would much rather appear at his destination than waste precious time getting frustrated in traffic. However, he had to continue to play the part if he hoped to be successful.

It was a relatively short drive to the Hart Senate Office Building from Reagan National via the George Washington Memorial Parkway. It was just over five miles, and, on a good day, you could make it in eleven minutes. Today was a good day.

The limo pulled up to the destination on Second Street. The driver jumped out and opened the door for Dante. As he stepped out, his devilish grin appeared. The driver had explicit orders to wait for him, then take him to the Palomar Hotel on P Street. He had told the senator that whenever he came to Washington; the Palomar is where he wished to stay. Dante left his briefcase in the Limo, knowing he would have to go through security before entering the building. He lifted his head, scanned the building, then moved swiftly up the steps and entered the westernmost doors.

He passed through a door, then through another, to a security checkpoint. Dante lifted his arms high, showing he had nothing to place on the conveyer belt. The guard didn't care for his dramatic display and looked him up and down. Annoyed, he motioned for him to walk through the metal detector. Once on the other side, Dante, amused, smiled triumphantly. The guard, not so much. Dante continued into the lobby. He looked up at the atrium ceiling that rose high above the first floor, revealing the eight balconies of the floors above him. The ninth, and very top floor, used for meetings, did not have a balcony.

The north area of the building had six elevators, three on the west wall and three on the east. There was no seating in any part of the vast lobby area. Dante made his way towards the elevators on the east side. Senator Wellsenburg expected a text when he arrived, but Dante like doing things his own way and thought it best to soak in the surroundings. He pushed the button for the floor of the senator's office and grinned. Mere mortals did not impress him, but he loved and respected power and control, and it was in abundance here.

Senator Colson stood in the hallway discussing a bill with Senator Rimersol of South Carolina. Rimersol was a tall, thin, grey-haired man and, like Colson, a staunch supporter of religious freedom. Hearing the elevator announce its arrival, they temporarily paused their conversation. Colson glanced over as the elevator doors opened.

Dante stepped out. Their eyes instantly met. They both felt a jarring jolt to their spirits. Dante's eyes widened, immediately drawn to the mark on Colson's forehead. He instinctively took a step backward. The small, glowing, gold, circular mark on Senator Colson's forehead appeared to have some type of ancient writing on its perimeter.

Dante knew what it was but didn't expect to find it here, in what he mockingly referred to as "The Den of Iniquity." The mark was invisible to humans. Only spirit beings could read it. No mortal could, not even those who wore it. The seal of the Spirit of God came upon those who were loyal followers of Jesus Christ. It was a seal of ownership, a symbol of the redemption of body and soul in the future. Dante jerked his head away quickly and acted as nothing happened.

Senator Rimersol looked at Colson. His face said it all. It was obvious he felt something, but he couldn't explain what or why. He had an eerie feeling that started at the hairs of his head and ran to the soles of his feet. Dante didn't have the time, nor was he interested in a spiritual encounter. Making a mental note of the man's face, he stepped out of the elevator and continued down the hall. Colson's eyes never left him. Dante turned into Wellsenburg's office.

"Do you know that, man?" Senator Rimersol asked.

"No, I don't. I'm not sure what that was all about, but I saw him go into Wellsenburg's office, so I have my suspicions."

The senator nodded in agreement. "I don't know him either, but I felt something odd when he looked at me."

The senator sensed Wellsenburg was up to no good, which usually meant trouble. Colson knew that he and this mystery man, whoever he was, would cross paths again. The two senators took their conversation to Rimersol's office.

Dante introduced himself to Ms. Venoldy, the senator's secretary, "Hello, I am Dante Adal. Senator Wellsenburg is expecting me."

Ms. Venoldy looked up from her desk, a bit surprised and somewhat delighted. "Oh, Mr. Adal, the senator, had every intention of meeting you in the atrium."

Dante smiled at her, "Yes, I was supposed to notify him when I arrived, but I took my time and looked around a bit before coming up. I hope it isn't a problem? May I see him now?"

Ms. Venoldy's smile grew wide. Taken by Dante's charm and good looks. If she knew who he really was, she would have screamed and run out the door. "Yes, of course! I will announce you at once." It was difficult for her to take her eyes off of him.

She picked up the phone, hit the intercom button, and said, "Mr. Adal is here, sir."

Within moments, the door flew open. "Dante. I would have met you as you came in. Did you have any trouble with security?"

Dante jested. "No. Why would I have a problem with security?"

"No, of course not. I just wanted to make sure all went well. Please come in. Ms. Venoldy, I don't wish to be disturbed. For any reason."

"Yes, sir. Absolutely," she said firmly. The senator ushered his guest into his office and locked the door.

Dante sat down in one of the senator's high-back leather chairs. "Would you like a drink? I keep a Deanston Highland single malt scotch whiskey in my desk."

"Yes, pour me one." He smirked. 'Another perk of taking on human form.'

The senator reached for the bottle and held it out proudly. "Interesting fact. The Deanston distillery sits just eight miles from historic Stirling on the banks of the River Teith. The site served as a mill for much of its history until its conversion into a whiskey distillery in 1965. It's very smooth." Wellsenburg thought of himself as a connoisseur of fine whiskey.

"I know the place well," Dante commented. "At the end of the 13th century, a long war began between the Scots and the English. During the war, Stirling Castle changed hands several times. The English invaded in 1296 and captured the castle. However, they were severely defeated at the Battle of Stirling Bridge in the same year. It was a fine and bloody war, as I remember."

Wellsenburg set two of his favorite rocks glasses on his desk. Although the glasses were old school, he thought them perfect for displaying his favorite scotch. As he opened the bottle, he paused. Dante's words intrigued him. Wellsenburg cocked his head to one side and inquired, "As you remember? You speak as if you were there."

Dante recovered well. "I read about it somewhere. You know how I love history." He shifted his body in the chair and quickly changed the subject; "I heard you put a tail on Bennett and Lederman when I specifically told you that I would handle it."

Wellsenburg almost spilled the scotch he was pouring. Surprised and somewhat embarrassed, he had hoped to keep his little investigation secret, at least for the time being.

"Yes, well, I thought it would be best to monitor them. I don't like surprises, and they have been asking way too many questions lately."

As Wellsenburg handed him the glass, Dante grabbed hold of his wrist. Staring directly into the senator's eyes, he said, "I have eyes everywhere. I do not require assistance from you or anyone else when it comes to covert activity." At that, he took the glass and released Wellsenburg's arm.

The senator swallowed hard. Dante continued. "What if they trace it back to you or see you talking with certain unsavory characters? Have you thought about that? We need to get you into the White House. You do want to be President, don't you, George?" Dante put the glass to his lips and took a sip. His dark eyes peering at Wellsenburg over the rim.

Wellsenburg felt like a small child getting a lecture from his father.

He didn't appreciate it. He took a hefty swallow of his scotch and put his glass down on his desk with just enough force to let Dante know he was not pleased. Dante lifted his eyebrow slightly, a bit surprised, yet delighted, at the senator's moxie.

"I will be the next President of the United States." He said with conviction and determination. "There is no doubt in my mind about that. Understand. Sometimes I need to do things my way."

"I respect that in a man," he said with a smirk on his face. "Okay, enough bantering. Let's get down to business. So, you had them followed," he said matter-of-factly. "Tell me what you found out. It might be possible that I missed something. I'm open to enlightenment."

"Lederman has been snooping around the Bureau asking questions about a murder case in Blackstone, Virginia, thirty years ago. They're attempting to connect me with those murders."

Dante knew all about the Oslow murders more than he cared to admit. He wasn't about to let Wellsenburg know about his involvement, especially since he clad himself in a thirty-nine-year-old body, so he played along. "The Oslows..." he said in a low tone, a ponderous look on his face. "I recognize that name. They were members of The Society. I remember reading about them. Such a tragic story. In what way are you connected?" Dante wanted to see how much Wellsenburg actually knew about that night.

Wellsenburg finished his drink and paced from one end of the room to the other. His voice had a nervous edge to it.

"They introduced me to the society when I was running for the Senate over thirty years ago. They donated generously to my campaign, and their considerable influence swayed key political groups. The Oslows convinced them I was the right man for the job. I owed them. One day, he called me and said he needed to see me as soon as possible. The term he used was extremely urgent. I met with him alone that night. He told me they wanted out. Claiming The Society had gone too far, and he didn't like what was going on. He was terrified. I had never seen him like that before. I told him not to leave, that it would all work out, but I couldn't persuade him. The very next night, they found him and his wife dead of unknown causes in their home. I don't know what happened to them, and I didn't ask questions. The elections were only a few months away. I didn't want to ruin my chances of winning a senate seat, so I kept quiet and moved on. It sounds pretty pathetic, I know. But I had my future to think about."

Although it had been three decades ago, the ever-conniving and calculating senator still felt a tinge of guilt. However, this was different. It was the first time he had ever verbalized it to anyone.

Dante sat in his chair, a slight smirk on his face, doing his best to hide his delight. If he wasn't totally convinced of his choice before this, he was now. He knew for certain that he had the right man to do his bidding. He stood to his feet and put his arm on Wellsenburg's shoulder.

With a feigned look of concern, Dante said, "Not at all. You did the right thing. They made their decision, and you made yours. You had every right to protect your political future and the future of this great nation. Don't you worry about Lederman and Bennett. We will convince them it would be better for them and their loved ones to back off and let this unfortunate incident die. We'll make sure this case stays buried along with the Oslows." Dante literally meant that.

He would see to it, and there was no need for anyone else to get involved.

Wellsenburg walked back to his desk and sat down. Dante had successfully washed away any feeling of guilt the senator had. Wellsenburg changed the subject. "You know Bennett has a girl now, and I hear they are getting very close."

Dante grinned, not wanting to address the senator's comment directly. He had his own ideas on how to handle the situation. "My limo is waiting. We will continue this discussion tomorrow at breakfast. Let's meet at the hotel restaurant, say at eight o'clock. I have an appointment tonight that I must prepare for." Dante walked away, then spun around and glanced back at Wellsenburg. "You better chew on a piece of gum, Senator. You wouldn't want your staff to think that you drink on the job."

Dante grinned and walked out, closing the door behind him. He felt good about their little chat. Now it was time to see how the rest of the world was doing.

33

TURNING ON THE LIGHT

Jack and Emily were sitting on Jack's front porch glider, enjoying the gentle evening breeze, when a car came barreling up the long, stone driveway. Emily lifted her head off Jack's shoulder. Recognizing the car, they watched as Frank pulled up in front of them.

"I wonder what's going on," Emily said with a concerned look on her face.

Jack laughed. "Nothing, probably. That's just the FBI in him. He loves to make an entrance."

Standing in the driveway with his elbows resting on the roof of his car, Frank quipped, "I hope you weren't making out or something. I would hate myself if I disturbed you two lovebirds." Frank loved to stir the pot. He couldn't help himself. It was in his DNA.

Jack gave Frank a dirty look. "I assume this is important...?"

"I stopped by because I think we need to compare notes and catch up on a few things. I would have called, but you never know who's listening these days."

He walked up to the front porch steps and stood there for a moment. His expression changed from glib to serious. Jack sensed this wasn't a social visit. He had a bomb to drop. "What is it, Frank?"

"Dante Adal is back in D.C., and my source tells me he met with Wellsenburg late this afternoon."

Jack turned to Emily. She had a curious look on her face. It wasn't the reaction Jack had expected. Emily had hoped that they could put all the craziness aside for a few hours, but it was quite clear that would not happen. If she was going to stay with Jack, normal was not in her future. Emily was falling in love with Jack more each day, and no matter what came her way, she was determined to make it the best life she could.

"I can't believe it, but I guess you guys were right. There is a definite scary connection there."

"Unprecedented, I would call it, but don't worry, the Lord is in control."

Emily seemed more focused than concerned. Jack stood up. "That makes sense somehow, considering what took place here yesterday."

Frank noticed the grooves in the porch. They were deep and jagged. "What happened here?" He looked closer. "They look like claw marks." As the words were coming out of his mouth, he visualized the type of creature that would have made them. His face filled with shock and rage. "Are you kidding me? They came after you? Are you all right?"

"I'm fine. Pull up a chair. We have a lot to talk about."

Emily stood to her feet and, pointing her finger at Frank, said, "Jack can tell you all about yesterday while I go to the bathroom. But I want to hear all about this Dante Adal, so don't start without me."

Frank assured her. "Okay, okay. I promise."

Emily had heard all about the demons on the porch and the spiritual battle that took place. As for Dante Adal, Emily's curious side demanded to hear all about it, her logical side not so much. However, she was part of all this now and needed to know what was going on, no matter how disturbing.

Frank paused and gave Jack a nervous look. When Emily had gone into the house, he asked, "Is she all right?"

Jack sighed. "She's a tough girl, but these are not your run-of-the-mill-life problems. I'm concerned that I could put her in real danger."

"I'm afraid I agree," he said, glancing back into the house. "I have some news that confirms your suspicions, but first, tell me what happened here yesterday."

"I'm not really sure. Obviously, by the look of things, there was a battle on my front porch. I was lying in bed, staring at the ceiling most of the night. I had a real heaviness in my spirit and spent most of the night fighting off waves of depression.

"At one point, I felt like I was fighting for my life. I got up and paced back and forth, praying out to God for help. I knew I was in a battle. I finally knelt by my bed and prayed, as I've rarely prayed before.

"I prayed for an hour with no real release. I still felt like I had a dark cloud hanging over my head. Then, suddenly, out of nowhere, it lifted. I can't explain it, but it was like God put his hand under me and lifted me up. It gave me a whole new perspective. My prayers went from desperation to praise and worship. It is not something I would like to repeat, but it was amazing.

"When I walked outside, I realized what was going on. From the evidence, all I can figure is that while I was praying, God must have sent an angel down to battle the forces of evil that were trying to destroy me. When I saw these marks, I knew God had delivered me from an evil attack."

Even though Frank had been with Jack on many occasions and seen things that few have, hearing Jack's story gave him a chill from head to toe.

"Jack, what the heck is going on with you? Nobody has the experiences you do. I don't know what to say. What an eye-opener. To think I have been walking around totally oblivious to the spiritual world all this time. How did Emily take it when you told her?"

"It freaked her out a little, but she is pretty cool. I keep thinking one day she will say, I love you, Jack, have a nice life, and walk right out of here. By the way, I'm sure we are not the only ones this is happening to. The supernatural world is growing exponentially as we approach the coming of the Lord. The battle will get more intense."

"You've got a good one there. Emily is a keeper for sure. I guess I was right about her, huh?" Frank remarked with a measure of pride. "I don't know anyone else who would hang with you through all this, except maybe for me, but don't get any ideas. I don't love you."

"Ah, although I am disappointed, I'll get over it,"

Emily shouted from the kitchen. "I'm getting a bottle of water. You guys want one?"

"Yeah, sure! Bring a couple out here. Oh, and could you turn on the porch light, please? It's getting dark."

Emily came out the front door and handed them each a bottle of water. "Maybe I'm a little paranoid, but don't you think, considering the circumstances, sitting out here with the light is such a good idea?"

"Emily is right. I should have thought of that. We can't be too careful." Standing to his feet, Frank said, "Nice call Em."

Emily shrugged her shoulders. "You two are rubbing off on me. I don't mind telling you. The whole thing creeps me out."

Frank saw the look on her face, and he said, "Don't worry. There is no reason to suspect anything, but you're right. No need to put ourselves in the spotlight."

With that, they left the porch and made their way into the kitchen. It was a good-sized kitchen with a counter big enough for four with a six-foot, dark oak table off to the side.

Jack kicked it off. "So, what did you find out?"

"I had dinner with Jeff Callaport the other night after we got back from Hardon's Inn. He read me a police report that was never officially filed, detailing a meeting between Mr. Oslow and Senator Wellsenburg the night before they found the Oslows murdered."

"I knew he was involved in this somehow."

Frank paused. He didn't want Jack to jump to any conclusions. "Involved for sure, but I don't think he had anything to do with their deaths from what I heard. From what Jeff read me, it sounded like he knew who was threatening them and who might have been involved, but that's it."

"Well, that alone would keep him out of the White House, and who knows what else he has done over the past thirty-plus years?"

A little confused, Emily asked Frank, "Are you saying Senator Wellsenburg had these people killed?"

Jack quickly interjected, "All Frank is saying is that Wellsenburg probably knew what was going on."

"Listen, Frank said cautiously, we have to be careful. This is a powerful man, and if he finds out we have proof that will incriminate him or tie him to this case, he will stop at nothing to shut us up. He has people everywhere, people that will do anything he asks."

"Where did Jeff get the report?"

"Somebody left it on his doorstep. Think about it. Even back then, Wellsenburg had enough influence to make the report disappear."

"Yeah," Jack said, sitting back in his chair, "And I know who is opening the doors for him."

Emily glanced at them both. "You mean Dante Adal?"

Jack took her hand. "Are you sure you want to listen to all this stuff?"

Emily pulled her hand back quickly. "Yes, Jack! I need to know. You said it yourself; you can't expect me to walk around in the dark. I'm not happy about it, but it's real. I love you, and I want to stand with you, and if I'm going to do that, I need to be kept in the loop."

"I'm sorry. You constantly amaze me. We'll get through this together."

Frank took a long drink from his water bottle and leaned back in his chair. "Since the three of us are sitting around talking openly about this stuff, I need to know more about this spiritual realm - demons, angels, princes. Even though I have seen more than I care to remember, I still don't fully understand what we're dealing with."

Emily agreed. "I'm with Frank on this, Jack. We have had a few conversations, but I would like to know more, too."

"Okay, that's a good idea. I'm not an expert, but the Bible is, so let's look." Jack picked his Bible off the counter and sat back down. This was a deep subject. Jack knew he couldn't cover it in a few minutes or even in one session, but he was more than happy to share what the Lord had shown him.

"It's hard to know where to start, so I guess I'll start at the beginning. In Ezekiel chapter 28, the Lord talks about the origins of evil and Lucifer's rebellion. I'll read it to you."

'You were in Eden, the garden of God; every precious stone adorned you: ruby, topaz and emerald, chrysolite, onyx and jasper, sapphire, turquoise and beryl. Your settings and mountings were made of gold; on the day you were created, they were prepared. You were anointed as a guardian cherub, for so I ordained you. You were on the holy mount of God; you walked among the fiery stones. You were blameless in your ways from the day you were created till wickedness was found in you.'

"Somewhere back in the annals of time, Lucifer got it in his heart that he wanted to challenge God for His throne. That was the beginning of the rebellion in Heaven. He influenced one-third of the angels to follow him and rebel against God. He hoped to defeat and overthrow God and His angels and take over Heaven.

"A great battle ensued, and Satan and his angels' defeated were cast out. According to the book of Job, Satan still has access to the throne of God, where he comes to accuse those of us who follow Christ. He is always trying to convince God to focus on our faults and shortcomings. Lucifer hates us because God has loved us, and that drives him crazy.

Although God allows him to come before Him occasionally, he can never again enter Heaven.

"The Apostle Paul calls him the prince and power of the air, meaning his kingdom is of this world. In John 14, Jesus calls him the prince of this world."

"I thought Earth belonged to God?" Emily asked.

"The Lord God owns everything and is ruler over all, but for now, He has allowed Satan to influence this earth. Paul tells us that our struggle is not against flesh and blood, but against the rulers, against the authorities, against the powers of this dark world and the spiritual forces of evil in the heavenly realms. Those heavenly realms he refers to are the created heavens, the supernatural sphere that surrounds the earth, not the Heaven where God is."

Frank needed a moment to digest what Jack had said. He had seen those spiritual forces and knew firsthand they existed. "I can attest to the phrase' dark world. The reports we get in at the Bureau every day would blow your mind. It's like you say in your blog. The world is getting darker every day."

Emily jumped in, "That's because of the coming antichrist. Right, Jack?"

"Yes, that's true, but I don't want us to get off track here. Let's concentrate on the evil spiritual forces in the heavenly realms. Satan's kingdom is similar to other kingdoms in the sense that there are levels of power and authority. There are fallen angels who the devil put in charge of different regions of the earth. There are princes over countries and cities all over the world. We don't know the number of angels that followed Satan. All we know is that one-third of the angels in Heaven went with him. But we have a reference for how great that number might be.

"In the book of Revelation, chapter five, verse eleven…" Jack thumbed through his Bible and found it. "Here it is, 'Then I looked and heard the voice of many angels, numbering thousands upon thousands, and ten thousand times ten thousand.'"

Emily thought for a moment, then her eyes widened. "That is amazing, but it also means that if the two-thirds who stayed with God number in the hundreds of millions, then the devil has millions of fallen angels at his command."

Frank looked at Jack and smiled. "She's pretty good with numbers."

"Unfortunately," he said, smiling. "Okay, let's all take a deep breath. The Lord is all-powerful and completely in control, and his presence is everywhere. Remember that the devil can only be in one place at a time. He is not God. The Lord said, 'I am with you always, even until the end of time.' He will never leave us alone or abandon us. He just proved that to me again yesterday. God has His people all over the world. We are not alone. He doesn't expect us to take on all the forces of darkness, only what He puts in our path."

Frank said, "I think He has given us a wide path."

Jack nodded. "Everyone is called to pray and be a part of God's army, but not everyone is called to this ministry. If this is our calling, then we must be obedient. I will admit it's not something I prayed for, but it is a true privilege to serve the Lord in this way."

"How about a cup of coffee?" Frank proposed. "I think I need a shot of caffeine to keep up with all this, and I still have an hour's drive back to D.C."

Emily jumped up and headed for the stove. Feeling like a poor host, Jack said, "You don't have to do that, Emily. Let me take care of it."

"I can't help it! It's what I do. Really, it's fine. I need to move around a bit, anyway. I get antsy when we talk about this stuff. Would you like a cup, Jack?"

"Why not? I have a lot of writing to do tonight. I need to put some of what we are talking about on my blog tonight. You two have inspired me with these brilliant questions."

"Well, I've got another one for you." Emily had something in her mind that had always bothered her. It was about a friend that she hadn't seen in years.

"I have a question. What do you think about this? I had a friend at college who said she had a spirit guide that she communicated with, who helped her decide and achieve a higher level of conscious awareness. I realize now that this so-called spirit guide was not from God, but how do you explain this? Was she losing it, making it up, or what? Do you think this spirit was a demon?"

"The short answer is yes. A spirit guide is a term used by the Western tradition of spiritualist churches. Mediums and psychics describe an entity that remains a disembodied spirit to guide or protect a living human being. Evil spirits, or demons, are always impersonating deceased loved ones or masquerading as angels of light. They go searching for people who aren't familiar with what the Bible says about the afterlife, and convince them they are good entities when, in fact, their only purpose is to lead them down a dead-end road and away from the truth. They may disguise themselves as departed loved ones, aliens, or, in your friend's case, spirit guides."

Emily handed Frank his coffee. He took a sip and smiled in

approval. "Okay, we've had several conversations concerning what we have seen lately, but we never talked about this. The beings we have seen so far, were they demons or angels?"

"We don't have the time to get into the difference between angels and foul spirits or demons, but I will say this. All but one manifestation we have seen so far was a demon."

Frank's eyes widened, and his heart rate jumped. "Then, you're saying Dante Adal is a fallen angel."

"I believe so. Angels can take the form of men, but they don't possess people. They don't enter living humans and walk around. That's the difference. Angels have a form. Demon spirits don't," Jack explained.

Before ending the conversation, Jack added, "It's getting late, but I'll share one more thing with you. I don't want to freak you out completely, but this is a true story and a great example of what we're talking about.

"I remember an incident a few years ago that happened in a church where I was invited to speak. It was half an hour before the morning service, and the pastor was showing me around and introducing me to several members of his congregation that helped serve at Sunday service. He took me downstairs, where they usually held their Sunday school classes. Several teachers were preparing the rooms for the children. The pastor introduced me to this gracious lady who had been one of his teachers for over twenty years. We'll call her Ava for now. I remember it like it was yesterday. Ava was widowed, attractive, and nicely dressed, medium height with brown hair. As I approached her, I felt something wasn't right. I didn't want to say anything at first, thinking it was just me. I was a guest and didn't want to go all super spiritual on everyone. When I reached out to shake her hand, I felt it again, only stronger. I sensed the Lord wanted me to pray for her. I asked if that would be all right. She smiled and agreed.

"I invited the pastor to join me. We gently laid our hands on her shoulder and prayed. As soon as we did, her face went blank, her eyes grew wide, and a voice came out of her that wasn't hers."

Emily sat back in her chair and crossed her legs, but never took her eyes off Jack, her heart racing. Frank's eyes widened as he unconsciously tapped on his shoulder holster under his jacket. "That must have blown you away, man. What did it say?"

"I must admit, I didn't expect that, and neither did the pastor. The other three ladies that were there immediately stopped what they were doing. I glanced over at them. They each had a look of complete terror on their faces. The voice was grave and low and had a measure of authority when it spoke. It said, 'You can't make me leave her. She invited me.'

"The pastor and I looked at each other and then back at the woman. Then, suddenly, she jumped backward, and her face abruptly changed from the sweet woman I first met to an ugly, disfigured, tortured soul. I took a step towards her, and the demon spoke again. 'I am an unclean spirit, and this is my house now!'

"I could feel the Spirit of God coming over me. I commanded the demon to set her free in the name of Jesus. The demon screamed. 'No!' but I commanded the spirit once again to release her. The woman screamed and dropped to her knees, convulsed, and then collapsed on the floor."

"Oh my God," Emily said, leaning forward. "Was she hurt?"

"We knelt next to her and continued to pray, and she quickly revived. We helped her to a chair, and one lady brought her some water. When she regained her senses, Ava told us she started watching erotic movies about a year before, and it quickly escalated into an addiction. She began watching them regularly and started reading books she knew were destroying her soul, but couldn't stop. Ava was fooled into thinking she could still follow the Lord while leading a double life."

"We brought her into the pastor's office and prayed for her. She cried and asked the Lord for forgiveness. The Lord beautifully restored her through a series of counseling sessions over the following weeks. She hadn't realized how far from God she had fallen.

"These things don't happen overnight. It's a long process that begins with little things that eventually lead to overwhelming bondage. She did not know she was opening the door of her soul to an evil and unclean spirit."

Emily looked concerned. "Wow, that is some story. I was taught and believed that a demon spirit could not enter a Christian."

Emily was visibly upset. The thought of not being protected from evil spirits was frightening, especially considering that the man she was in love with was front and center in a war with dark spiritual forces. She sat up in her chair, her eyes wide with alarm. "Are you saying that's not true?"

The last thing Jack wanted to do was get her upset or confused. "No, that is absolutely true. I didn't mean to upset you. Please never think that, Emily. Jesus said, 'As the Father has loved me, so have I loved you. Now remain in My love. If you obey My commands, you will remain in My love, just as I have obeyed my Father's commands and remain in His love.'

"We are secure in God's love, but when a person walks away from the Lord and lives in darkness rather than the light, they open themselves up to all kinds of problems. It works both ways. The Lord said, 'If anyone does not remain in me, he is like a branch that is thrown away and withers; such branches are picked up, thrown into the fire, and burned.'

"We must continue in fellowship with the Holy Spirit. The devil is always ready to take a person back. It can be a terrifying scenario."

Emily breathed a sigh of relief. The saying ignorance is bliss came to mind. It would be so much easier to ignore such things, but she also understood the need to study in order to grow.

Her face softened. "It is scary, but I understand. So, these so-called spirit guides are really demon spirits that lead people astray." She thought for a moment and then asked, "Does that mean my friend was possessed?"

"No, not at all," Jack said emphatically. "Possession is a process. You don't wake up one morning and find yourself possessed. I don't want you to think that there is a demon around every corner. Remember, some people unknowingly invite them into their lives out of ignorance, while others openly thumb their noses at God and blindly jump in with both feet. Either way, there is always a price to pay. There is only one spirit we should listen to. That's the Holy Spirit. He will never lead us astray."

"They don't teach this stuff at Quantico," Frank quipped. "I never thought in my wildest dreams that I would learn about things like this. If anybody heard this conversation, they would lock you up and then ship me off to be deprogrammed. I have to say, if I hadn't seen it myself, I probably would have you under constant surveillance."

Jack raised his left eyebrow. "Fascinating. Your comment is quite ironic, wouldn't you say, Agent Lederman?" Jack was a huge Star Trek fan and knew all the old episodes, and had watched all the movies at least five times each. He also did a great Mr. Spock impression. He got a laugh out of Emily, but only a smirk and a head tilt out of Frank.

"You and Star Trek. How can a guy with so much smarts watch that stuff?"

"Come on, Frank!" Jack said with a big grin. "You can't be serious all the time. Remember, all work and no play make Jack a dull boy."

Emily gave Jack a playful smile, one that immediately increased his heart rate.

"That's my cue to get out of here and head back to D.C. By the way. I bought you a new phone. It's secure, so use this when you need to call me. Don't trust anyone, and after what you told me about your uninvited guests, I think we should all be putting more time into prayer."

Jack and Emily walked arm in arm, accompanying Frank to the door. Frank had some last words, "Let me know if anything unusual happens, not that you would be involved in anything out of the ordinary," Frank said sarcastically. "I will let you know what I find out in D.C. tomorrow. Keep an eye on one another, okay?"

"We will. Drive safe and keep your eyes open."

They watched Frank's car disappear behind the trees that lined the entrance to the driveway. As Jack turned to walk inside, Emily grabbed him by his belt. She tilted her head at him and smiled playfully. Wrapping her arms around Jack's neck, she pulled him in close and kissed him long and hard, letting it linger. She pulled away slowly, leaving Jack somewhat stunned. He finally exhaled. "Wow, what was that for?"

"I don't know. I just felt like it. Why? You didn't like it?"

Jack more than liked it, and she knew it. They needed some alone time. Emily had had enough heavy-duty conversations for one night. She had to be at work by 6:00 a.m. and wanted Jack all to herself. Jack put some music on, and Emily made sure the rest of the evening belonged only to them.

34

DARK PLANS

Dasht-e Lut is one of Iran's largest desert basins. 300 miles long and 200 miles wide. It is also one of the driest and hottest places on the planet. Temperatures in the Lut Desert can reach 159°F. It is the hottest temperature ever recorded on Earth. Its surface is covered with black volcanic lava. Scientists claim that no living creature lives in the region, resulting in its nickname: "Emptiness Desert." However, man is not aware of all beings in God's created time and space.

A full moon shone like a small sun in the night sky as a torrid wind howled across the open plain. Although the sun had set hours ago, the air remained brutally hot. Three huge dark figures emerged on the horizon atop one of the many reddish dunes that dotted the desert floor. Marduk, Nabu, and Asaru stood tall and menacing in the stark arid wasteland with their large black and pewter wings outstretched, unaffected by the heat of the desert and searing winds. A stark contrast to the myriad of desert colors illuminated in the bright moonlight.

The desert landscape was a familiar haunt to the three demonic princes. They ruled these regions for thousands of years, flourishing in the days before the Flood and again during the days of Nimrod, also known as Gilgamesh. A vile, filthy man and the inspiration for building the Tower of Babel.

Marduk and Nabu fared well in the time of the Babylonian Empire. Each with a temple built in their honor and libraries dedicated to their worship. After the Ziggurat and the royal palace, Marduk's temple was the greatest of the architectural complexes of ancient Babylon. These princes longed to rule over this region and the world again.

They stood and waited in silence for the one who summoned them. In the distance, they could see his huge, imposing figure moving swiftly and effortlessly across the desert floor. Within moments, he stood before them. They bowed, their knees to the ground.

"Where is Dante?" the voice thundered.

Keeping his position, Marduk lifted his head and spoke, "I do not know, my lord." His voice was strong and deep, yet fearfully respectful.

Suddenly, a swirling, twisting, thick red mist appeared alongside Marduk. It existed in a different dimension, unmoved by the strong wind that viciously and relentlessly blew around them. As the mist slowly dissipated, it revealed a bowing and somewhat humble Dante Adal.

"Master, I apologize. I had a few obstacles in my path that I had to deal with. It won't happen again."

"Stand to your feet!" the master commanded.

Although Dante, Marduk, Nabu, and Asaru were close to seven feet tall, they had to look up to the huge, menacing being in front of them.

"I grow weary of your lack of respect. I fear you are enjoying life as a mortal a little too much, Dante. Maybe I need to make a change. Do you feel I should make a change?" he demanded.

Dante had become enamored with the lusts of the flesh. He found the desires of his mortal body to be a greater challenge than he bargained for. He was becoming more and more addicted to his new form and lifestyle. Lying would't work in this case. That only worked on mortals. He needed to be careful, or there would be hell to pay. "No, master. All is going according to plan. I assure you, I can handle my assignment and whatever comes my way."

The huge, dark figure moved its head from side to side, studying his other princes' reactions. Neither wished to be assigned to the battle for America. While victory in that arena carried the greatest reward, it was also the most difficult spiritual battle to fight. As far as they were concerned, Dante could keep it and, hopefully, lose it. There was no love among the fallen. They hated and envied all created beings equally.

Satisfied that there was no hidden agenda among the others, their master turned his piercing gaze to Dante. "There will be no more warnings. We are in the best position to rid this planet of the Jews since World War II. Russia and the Arab world must keep moving forward. America must continue to distance themselves from Israel. Give me your reports. What have you been doing to move our cause forward?"

Nabu answered first, "Here in Iraq and Syria, we have stirred up the spirits of the Medes and Persians, who have no delight in silver or gold. Their bows will strike down the young and the old.

Asaru continued, "They will have no mercy on infants, nor will they look with compassion on children, and they loathe Jews and Christians and all they stand for."

"Well done!" the master responded with zeal.

Marduk extended his wings and stretched his neck from side to side. "I have awakened ancient Magog to the north. He and his cohorts are gearing up for battle. They are moving troops and military hardware into Syria and sending the needed weapons to Iran. They will be ready when the time comes," he said proudly.

Dante smirked, always looking to outdo his peers. "I have been busy blinding the U.S. to the Russian plan to unite the Arab world for an Israeli invasion and preparing the next president of the United States, along with many U.S. senators. When the new administration takes office, they will denounce Israel's actions and cut off military aid." Dante smirked, "My job is far more difficult than arousing an already militant people to hate and war."

Marduk, Nabu, and Asaru's eyes blazed with hate. There was no camaraderie between these dark beings, only self-edification and pride.

Their lord sneered, "We are done. Make sure you follow your assignments. There is a rustling among the angels in Heaven. I sense the time is short. No mistakes this time. This time we win!"

He vanished without a sound, leaving the four princes alone and uncomfortably silent. One at a time, Asaru, Marduk, and Nabu extended their wings. With their eyes burning with hate, they gave Dante a flaming glance. Then each rocketed straight up into the night sky. Within seconds, the three were out of sight. Leaving Dante by himself in the torrid Iranian desert. He grinned and then let out a deep-throated laugh that echoed through the surrounding mountains. The effects felt on the plains of Megiddo and the hills surrounding Jerusalem. He rolled himself up in his large wings and vanished in an explosion of red mist.

* * *

It was eight o'clock in the morning when Senator Wellsenburg walked into Urbana at the Palomar Hotel. The décor of Urbana restaurant, inspired by 1920s New York, was a favorite of hotel guests.

The restaurant was busy. All but a few tables occupied. At a table In the far corner of the restaurant, Dante waited alone. He was taking great pleasure in a hot cup of black coffee when the senator came in. Dante had developed a real taste for the addicting bean. The more time he spent in human form, the more he envied the many sensations mere mortals experienced. It only increased his hatred for all humankind. He never understood how God could love such inferior beings. They failed constantly, tempted easily, and appreciative nothing. The more he thought about it, the greater his resentment grew. He looked up and saw the senator walking towards him and quickly changed his demeanor.

"Good morning, Senator! Would you like coffee? It's quite good this morning."

Wellsenburg sat down and motioned to the server to pour him a cup. Dante studied him carefully. The senator seemed hassled and a bit frayed. It was important to keep his prestigious pawn focused if he hoped to succeed.

"Did you sleep well? How was your meeting?" Dante asked with feigned interest.

"It went well. Things are moving forward as expected."

The senator took a sip. "I have to be back on the Hill in an hour, but I am hungry. I usually eat before this, but I got tied up." He motioned to the server that he was ready to order. "Do you feel like having breakfast?"

"Yes. I'll have the mushroom, spinach, and goat cheese omelet. I've had that before and found it very nourishing."

The senator tilted his head and smirked. 'Very nourishing?' There were many times when he thought Dante reacted strangely to certain things. It was like he was an alien visiting planet earth for the first time. He wrote it off because Dante had many other traits far more mysterious, but it still bothered him.

"I'll have the Nutella French Toast," Wellsenburg told the server.

The server nodded. "Excellent, sir."

"So, what's your meeting this morning?" Dante asked, always digging for more information.

"Russia is causing concern on Capitol Hill because of the latest military moves into Syria and its growing relationship with North Korea and Iran. They say it's only to protect their interests, but no one really knows their true intentions. It is also making Israel very nervous, and when that happens, Washington gets nervous."

Dante was well aware of Russia's intentions. This was the very opportunity the dark forces of this world were waiting for. Disguising his thoughts, he said, "The world is a dangerous place and always has been. We need to focus on your candidacy and prepare for your announcement declaring your decision to run for President. It's the middle of May, so we shouldn't wait much longer."

Wellsenburg's heart leaped in his chest. He had been waiting a long time to have this conversation. He was anxious and excited at the same time. His mind raced. President of the United States. Wellsenburg inhaled it, savored it, letting the thought saturate his very being. Knowing this could be a reality by the end of next year was nirvana.

"I think I should announce next month. This will give us enough time to raise the needed funds."

Dante smiled. "Oh, I don't think you will have to worry about that. That's my job. But first, we need a plan to slow down Mr. Bennett and his partner, Frank Lederman. You mentioned you have a few men you trust. Is that true?"

The senator's demeanor abruptly changed. He had hoped Dante would take care of all that. Personally, he didn't care what had to be done or to whom, but he would have nothing to do with its planning. He studied Dante, then answered cautiously, "Yes. But I will not be part of it."

Dante was about to respond when he saw their server approaching. The server placed the dishes on the table and poured them another cup of coffee. They nodded their approval. "Don't worry. I wouldn't have it any other way. We need to contact the girl, if you know what I mean. Do you trust your contacts not to screw this up?" Dante asked.

Wellsenburg sat stunned. He put his hand over his mouth, so no one could read his lips, and then whispered, "You mean kill her?"

"What?" Dante said, shocked that Wellsenburg would ever think of such a thing. "No, of course not. What kind of person do you think I am? No. We just want to send a message. I'll have your men follow her and grab her one night. They'll hold her for a couple of days and then let her go as a warning. That's all. I'm sure our two heroes will back off after that."

Wellsenburg looked perplexed, his mind racing. Didn't Dante say the other day that he had people everywhere and all the resources in the world? He wondered, 'Why then, does he need my help?' "I'm confused. Why aren't you using your resources for this operation?"

Dante was attacking his omelet like the Invasion of Normandy. The senator had barely touched his food, yet Dante had nearly finished his breakfast. Another oddity that nagged at Wellsenburg since the day he met him was that Dante ate as if he had never tasted food before in his life.

Dante looked up at him, fork in hand, "I understand your confusion, Senator, but my resources cannot touch Jack Bennett at this time. I can't go into it now, but as long as you have the contacts that can handle this mission, you do not need to worry." Dante finished his breakfast and motioned to the server to bring more coffee.

Wellsenburg raised his left eyebrow. "You might want to take it easy on the caffeine. You're already a little more hyper than usual."

"It does have a curious effect on me, but I do like the way it feels."

The senator was dumbfounded, once again, at Dante's odd response.

"Write the number of your contact. I will arrange a meeting here at the hotel at eight o'clock tonight. I will make it clear to them what I want done."

Wellsenburg reached into his jacket pocket and pulled out a small black notebook. Grabbing a napkin, he wrote the number down.

"Ah, a little black book?" Dante commented with a grin.

"Yes, I prefer old school. No digital footprint. It's much easier to make this little book disappear than any digital device."

Dante reached over and put the napkin in his pocket. Wellsenburg looked at his watch, took one more sip of coffee, and stood to his feet. "I have to run. Keep me updated."

"On the contrary, you'll know nothing of this operation. That's the way it has to be."

The senator nodded, turned, and walked out of the restaurant. Dante motioned to the server. "I would like to try the Nutella French Toast my associate ordered. It smelled fascinating. Please bring another fresh carafe of hot coffee, as well."

The server looked surprised, but nodded and headed back to the kitchen. No one ever asked for a second breakfast before, and he was sure this fellow was too large to be from the Shire. He chuckled to himself. Dante noticed the sarcasm and the server's slight smirk. Dante decided he would not make the server pay for his insolence if the food were good. Otherwise...

The server returned with the new carafe of coffee, and, as he did, he glanced at Dante. Their eyes met, and fear instantly gripped his heart. He couldn't explain it, but it was real. And it was terrifying. Dante's lip curled up slightly on one side in a fashion that sent a chill down the server's spine and made his stomach churn.

"Thank you, young man. I hope the French toast is as good as it smells."

The server's eyes grew wide. "I'm—I'm—sure it will be, sir. We get many com—compliments on that dish." The young man quickly turned and walked away, wishing he didn't have to return. Dante smirked, pleased he had made his point.

At the opposite end of the room, a man sat alone at a table near the entrance, his fingers busy typing on his paper-thin MacBook. He was a rather short man, stocky, but not fat. He had a balding head and was wearing a dark suit. His jacket carefully placed on the back of the empty chair next to him. He glanced over to where Dante was sitting. Then continued typing on his keyboard. He had arrived moments before Senator Wellsenburg.

The man took one more look, then picked up his phone and made a call. He talked only for a few minutes, but the conversation was intense. He closed his MacBook, placed it in his briefcase, and walked out of the restaurant. Dante Adal was unaware of the man who had been watching him. He was only interested in his second breakfast.

* * *

Dante sat in his two-room suite waiting for Wellsenburg's henchmen to show up. He had read the description online. King-size bed with custom 300 thread count sheets, Egyptian cotton linens, a luxury bathroom with a soaking tub for two, and a large working desk with a comfortable ergonomic chair. He mused on the description of the Egyptian cotton linens. They weren't anything like the fabrics on the beds of the Pharaohs. Dante was very pleased with the elaborate luxuries mortals surrounded themselves with, intent on enjoying all the amenities.

A firm, heavy thump on the door broke the silence in the room. Dante got up from perusing the Internet and opened the door. Two men stood in the hallway. One had a large scar on his right cheek. Both were six-two, with medium builds. Dante studied them. They appeared to be Slavic, possibly Russian. Their faces were pinkish-white with grey eyes. They had thin lips and eyebrows and straight noses with the tips rather thick and roundish. They appeared as if they had done this type of work before.

"Come in, gentlemen," Dante quickly discerned that these men had a long and wicked history, and that pleased him. Pointing to his left, he said, "Have a seat, and we'll get down to business."

Dante sat on the edge of the bed, his forearms resting on his knees. The two men sank deep into the two leather chairs facing the bed without saying a word. Their eyes fixed on the man in front of them. Dante did not know if or what the senator might have told them to prepare for their meeting, so he thought it best to go over a few ground rules.

"First, I don't need to know your names, where you're from, or what your favorite weapon is. I just need you to carry out a few simple instructions, and when I say carry out, I mean perfectly and without incident. Do we understand each other?"

The two men glanced at one another and nodded.

"Good," Dante leaned forward. "What I am about to tell you can not repeat, not even to the man who referred you. Are we still on the same page?"

The men looked straight ahead and nodded again, faces unchanged.

"Excellent. Here are your instructions. You are to kidnap a young woman named Emily Richardson. She is a server at a café in Blackstone, Virginia, called CJ's."

Dante reached in his pocket, pulled out a piece of paper and a photo, and handed it to the one with the long, ugly scar on his face. Dante addressed him because he perceived he was the leader.

"Here is a photo and the address of her apartment building. I want you to follow her and note her schedule. Where she goes when she goes, and with whom. From that, determine your best opportunity to take her. You only get one shot at this, so get it right."

Dante's voice grew deeper and more intense. His eyes flared, briefly changing color. From the edges of their vision, the two men exchanged looks. They would talk about that later.

He continued, "You will find a white Ford van parked on the first level in the parking garage at 2135 M Street. The keys are above the front wheel beneath the fender on the driver's side. When the opportunity presents itself, grab her, throw her in the van, and take her somewhere where no one will hear her scream."

He could tell by how they were gawking at the picture they liked what they saw.

Dante added, "You can have your fun with her, but when you're done, put a bullet in her pretty little head."

The two men looked at each other, then back at Dante.

Dante glared at them. "Is there a problem?" He asked in a low, threatening tone.

The one with the large scar fixed his eyes on Dante. With a deadpan expression on his face, he stated in a heavy Russian accent, "We usually get paid more — for something like this."

Dante bent over, reached down, and pulled a briefcase out from under the bed. He placed it on the floor and kicked it over in front of the two men.

"Open it!" Dante said.

They opened it and smirked. Dante stood up, walked over to the desk, and sat down. "There's twenty thousand in there. When I am satisfied you have done the job to my specifications, you'll get twenty thousand more."

The two men nodded, grabbed the briefcase, and stood up. Dante spun around in his desk chair and opened a bottle of scotch. He lifted his right arm, flicked his wrist, and said, "You can show yourselves out."

The two men didn't hesitate. They opened the door and left. Feeling pleased with himself, Dante thought, 'It's not what the good senator expected, but it will do the job.'

Satisfied, he took a drink. "These humans know how to live. Too bad it won't be for much longer."

His laugh pierced the night and traveled to the darkest parts of hell.

35

OUT FOR A RUN

J ack woke up before the first rays of morning sun could stream through his bedroom window. He had gotten a good night's sleep and wanted to make the most of what looked to be one of the best spring days so far. He had prayed, showered, and loaded up his new blog post. It was Emily's day off, and he wanted to drive by and see if he could convince her to take an early morning walk with him. He had been meaning to start working out. Even more so, now that he had a girlfriend. Emily was more than a girlfriend, and Jack hoped to make their relationship permanent.

Jack jumped in his car and drove to Emily's place. He had thought about calling her, but surprised her instead. Emily was an early riser, so Jack figured she would be up and about by the time he got there. One more month, Jack pondered, and if all goes well, maybe I'll pop the question. Jack realized he was moving fast, but it just seemed right. Besides, he wasn't some twenty-year-old kid trying to figure life out.

Women like Emily didn't come along every day, and he wasn't about to let her slip away. That was a chance he was not going to take.

As he turned the corner and pulled up in front of her apartment complex, he noticed a young woman in the distance, out for a morning run. She was athletic, looking, and running at a brisk pace. As she came into focus, his eyes widened, and his jaw dropped. It was Emily. She had on a pair of tiny green running shorts and a top that stopped just short of her belly button. Hair pulled back in a ponytail, and earbuds plugged into an iPhone strapped to her side. He had never seen her like this. It was very revealing in more ways than one. She recognized the car and slowed her pace.

Jack got out of the car and stood on the sidewalk. Emily approached with a pleasant but surprised look on his face. "Jack, what are you doing here? Is everything all right?"

Her outfit completely captured Jack. "I wasn't aware that you were a runner."

Emily realized Jack had never seen her dressed like this before, but she was more concerned with why he was standing in front of her apartment building at seven o'clock in the morning.

"Jack, you didn't answer my question. Is everything all right? Are you and Frank okay?"

"Yeah, yeah. Everybody is fine. I just came by to ask if you wanted to go for a morning walk, but I see that walking might not be your speed."

He couldn't take his eyes off her. She looked amazing from head to foot. Her abs were rock solid, and her arms were tight and toned. She obviously did more than run. It intrigued Jack.

"I didn't realize you did this kind of thing. I mean, I knew you kept yourself in great shape, but…"

Emily interrupted. She had other things on her mind. "Jack, I have to cool down. Walk with me?"

"Sure." He locked the car, and they walked towards the park, a quarter-mile down the street.

"We've only known each other for a few months. I'm sure there are plenty of things I don't know about you, right?"

Jack wasn't so sure. Emily wasn't merely in shape. She was a strong, very confident woman. Jack had a feeling there was a lot more to her than he realized. "I suppose so, but I believe you know more about me than I know about you."

Emily stopped and gave him a quick kiss. "That's probably true, but you have so much to share. You have to admit my life is pretty boring compared to yours. Let's face it. Angels, demons, and all kinds of espionage around Washington. Getting to know you changed my life. Once I knew how I felt about you, I dedicated myself to finding out all I could. I needed to know if our relationship had a real chance."

Jack stopped. "Well, what do you think now?"

Emily's eyes locked with his. She leaned in and whispered, "I've fallen in love with you, Jack Bennett. That's what I think."

Jack took her in his arms and kissed her with all he had. The heat between them was amazing. Emily slowly pulled away. "We need to talk."

They reached the empty playground, captured two swings gently swaying in the morning breeze, and sat down. Jack was overwhelmed. He was so in love with her; he didn't know quite how to handle it.

Finally, he said, "Emily, you're the best thing that's ever happened to me, other than when Christ entered my life. I never thought I could love anyone this much! I want to know everything about you. Things have been insane. Frank and I have had interesting cases before, but now..." he paused and took a deep breath. "...now it seems all hell has broken loose. If we are to grow this relationship, we need to spend more time together."

Jack's heart was pounding. He wanted to know everything about Emily. The sooner, the better. Jack had been with other women before, but when he came to Christ, he promised the Lord, and himself, the next time he was intimate with a woman, it would be within the covenant of marriage. Staying right with God was essential to his relationship with the Lord and his calling.

Emily stood up, reached down, and pulled him to his feet. They stood face-to-face, nose-to-nose. Emily wrapped her arms around his neck and looked into his eyes. "Whatever happens, I want you to know this, above all else..."

Immediately, Jack's mind raced. Wait a minute. What does she mean, whatever happens? Is she leaving? Does she expect something bad to happen?

Before he could open his mouth, Emily kissed him and said, "I told you I'm in love with you, Jack Bennett." Jack loved the way her lips moved when she spoke his name. Emily smiled. "I have to admit something. Although I had not met you, I knew of you before I started working at CJ's."

"You heard about me? How? I'm not exactly famous."

"Actually, in some circles, you are quite famous. Your blog is very popular, not only in this country but in other parts of the world. Someone turned me onto your blog six months ago. I immediately thought it was fascinating!"

Why hadn't she mentioned it before? It was obvious there were many things about Emily he didn't know. "Okay, but why didn't you tell me this when we met?"

"I didn't want you to think I was a stalker or something. I'm sure you've had your share of those experiences before."

"Actually, never. It's not like I'm a movie star. I'm just an author and blogger."

"Oh, yeah—just a blogger. One who talks with angels casts out demons and is being watched by possibly the next President of the United States!

"When I saw you walk into CJ's with Frank the first time, I wondered if you were involved with anyone? I assumed you weren't married because you didn't wear a wedding ring.

"After days of watching you, I wondered what you guys were talking about because you always looked so intense. Now, I know you weren't discussing sports or some movie you had just seen. You were talking about incredible things—things that few people are aware of. So many times, I wanted to walk up and say, hi, I'm Emily. Would you like to have dinner with me sometime? But I always chickened out.

"When you came up to the register and asked me out—I couldn't believe it. In the beginning, I was taken by who you were and what you did, but after a while, I realized I was falling in love with you. I guess I'm telling you this because I want you to know how I feel. I don't want you ever to doubt it."

"I can't believe you feel this way. I've never had anyone crazy over me. Are you sure you're not on drugs or something?"

Emily laughed. "You're funny, but you are like a drug in one way. I'm addicted to being with you!"

Jack wrapped his arms around her waist and held her tight. The kiss was deep and long. They pulled away slowly. "What did you mean when you said no matter what happens?"

Emily dropped her arms and took a step back. "Nothing. Life can take weird turns sometimes. I just wanted you to know the way I feel about you will never change. That's all."

"Okay, sorry. You freaked me out a little when you said that. I feel the same way. I will never let you go or change the way I feel about you, Emily. Ever."

Jack wasn't sure why Emily was worried, but he accepted her explanation. He loved her too much to think about anything coming between them. He took her hand, and they walked back to her apartment. It wasn't the long walk that Jack had hoped for, but it was a perfect morning!

* * *

It was another outstanding spring day in Virginia, and Emily was ready for her morning run. She felt good about the way things were with Jack. Over the last couple of days, they had shared a lot of stories, talking into the wee hours of the morning. Emily had never felt as close to anyone in her life. Jack was so honest and transparent. She thought guys like Jack only existed in romance novels and Hollywood movies.

Emily did her usual pre-run stretches. She was going to add a half-mile to her run this morning, bringing it to five miles. She could do much more, but today she was going for speed. Emily took a deep breath, looked around, and started down the road. Her route would take her by the reservoir, through the park, and then back home.

She was serious about her workouts. The morning run was just the beginning. Every other day after work, she hit the gym. She ignored the machines. Free weights gave her the best workout.

As she turned the corner where the new construction was going on, she noticed a van parked on her side of the road. Not unusual on this block, because of all the new townhouses that were going up. Plumbers, carpenters, and all kinds of contractors were pulling in and out all day long.

The workers always shot her a look when she ran by. Emily didn't mind their whistles and "Hi there's!" No one said anything vulgar. Men will be men, she thought. However, this van looked different. The company name was absent, and it looked too clean to have been traveling the muddy road that led to the construction site. As she drew near the van, her heart pounded. She instinctively picked up her pace. As she ran by it, she looked at the driver, but he was busy looking at his phone. She felt kind of silly and continued down the road towards the reservoir. Emily dismissed it as paranoia, the kind that came from hanging around Jack and Frank.

The area around the reservoir was beautiful this time of year. Surrounded by wildflowers and tall trees. The flower that Emily particularly loved was Arisaema triphyllum. It was exotic with all its curves, petals, and beautiful colors, but that's not the reason she loved it. It was because of its other name: Jack in the Pulpit. She smiled. It fit him to a "T."

As Emily ran past a line of bushes on her right, she heard

something behind her. Suddenly, two large hands grabbed her shoulders from behind. The next thing she knew, someone was pulling a black hood over her head. Emily could feel the string tighten around her neck. She spun around to take a swing at whoever it was when everything went black.

The kidnapper picked her up and threw her over his shoulder as the white van raced around the corner with its side door open. The man threw her inside and slammed the door shut. He opened the passenger door, climbed in, and they sped away. It would be ten minutes before

The captor hit Emily hard enough to knock her unconscious, but for how long? When she regained consciousness, her head was pounding like a drum. She could barely swallow because of the nasty-tasting rag jammed in her mouth. Emily could sense and smell someone sitting next to her in the back of the van. Suddenly, her captor yanked the black hood off her head. It took a few minutes for her eyes to adjust, but when they did, Emily saw two men—the large rough looking man beside her and the driver.

The one staring at her had a large scar on his right cheek and an evil smirk on his face. She tried to get a look at the driver, but she could only see the back of his head. It was enough for her to recognize it was the same man she had seen only minutes before. Emily scanned the inside of the van, calculating the odds of her getting out alive. The tie wraps that bound her hands behind her back were tight, but her legs were free.

"Well, look what we have here," said in a heavy Russian accent. "You're a pretty little thing with your cute little running outfit and those long, beautiful legs. Just the kind of woman I like. We are going to get to know one another real well." The two men laughed out loud.

Emily noted everything inside of the van. Her captor had a large knife strapped to his side, and a handgun jammed in his back pocket.

Suddenly, the van stopped. She couldn't tell where she was. There were no windows, but Emily was sure it was somewhere secluded.

The man with the scar called to the driver, "Kostya! Remember, I have first round." He laughed. "Wait outside. I will let you know when I am done with this pretty little girl."

Kostya groaned. "You better save some sugar for me, Maksim." Kostya opened the door and got out. Maksim positioned himself in front of Emily, his eyes groping every inch of her. He could never get such a beautiful young woman to even look his way, so for him, this was the icing on the cake. Money and sex. He moved in closer, rubbing his hands up and down her legs. He got right in her face and licked Emily on the neck. "You like that? Oh, we are going to have so much fun."

He removed the knife from its sheath and ran the back of it over her face. "Don't make Maksim have to use this on such a pretty girl."

Maksim put the knife down and unzipped his pants. Emily was praying for strength and opportunity. As he leaned over to pull her shorts off, Emily jammed her right knee into his groin. He jolted backward, grabbing himself in agony. When he did, she kicked him in the chest with both feet. With her running shoes on, the impact was hard enough to drive him backward against the side of the van, furious and groaning in pain. Seeing the van rock to one side, Kostya smiled, thinking his friend must be having a good time. He couldn't wait for his turn.

Emily quickly rolled over to the knife lying on the floor where Maksim had dropped it. She manipulated the blade behind her back to cut the cable ties that held her wrists together. Maksim looked at her with fire in his eyes. He was going to make her pay for that. Sex was no longer on his mind, only vengeance. He pulled his pants up and violently snatched her feet, dragging her over to him. Emily stayed focused on setting herself free. He laid his 220 pound body on top of her, pulled his gun out of his back pocket, and put it to her temple.

"It is a shame to kill such a pretty girl, but business is bus..." Maksim's eyes suddenly grew wide, and his face morphed from hatred to terror. Emily pushed him off her and grabbed the gun in one swift motion. Maksim rolled over on his side to see his own knife sticking out of his chest, and blood pouring everywhere. Emily got to her knees, pulled the gag out of her mouth, and yanked the knife out of Maksim's chest.

She bent down, looked him in the eye, and whispered, "I'm Agent Emily Rafel, Mossad."

She thrust the knife into his chest again, killing him. Kostya was outside and armed. She would have to be ready. Emily checked Maksim's weapon, moved to the back of the van, and waited.

Kostya was getting impatient. He walked around and banged on the van door. "Maksim! Come on! We haven't got all day. Someone might see us."

He waited for a moment more and then, shouting Maksim's name, opened the van's side door. He saw Maksim lying dead on the floor of the van, with Emily kneeling off to the side. His eyes widened, and his heart rate jumped. In rage and fear, he frantically grabbed for his gun, but before he could reach it, Emily shot. The bullet hit him in the center of the forehead. The impact threw him out of the van and onto the side of the road.

Emily jumped out of the van to avoid the river of blood now turning the van floor a deep red. She reached to her side, pulled out her phone, and hit a number on her contact list.

"Aaron, it's Agent Rafel. I have a situation."

AFTERWORD

"In the conflict between Satan and the Believer, God's child can conquer EVERYTHING by prayer. Is it any wonder that Satan does his utmost to snatch that weapon from the Christian, or to hinder him in the use of it?" – Andrew Murray 1828 - 1917

I hope you enjoyed Book I of Hidden Thrones. The purpose of this writing is to increase awareness of the spiritual world around us, especially to those who follow the Lord Jesus. The importance of prayer cannot be overstated. When I am asked which is more important, reading the Bible or praying, I always ask, "Which is more important, breathing in or breathing out?"

God bless, Russ Scalzo

Please share your thoughts by taking the time to review this book.

THE SERIES CONTINUES:

Book 2 *Open Warfare*

Book 3 *Face to Face*

Book 4 *The Hammer Falls*

Book 5 *The Cup of Iniquity*

Book 6 *Many Crowns*

Book 7 Redemption

Join the mailing list for podcast episodes, updates and special offers at RussScalzo.com.

The story continues...

Open Warfare!

BONUS MATERIAL CHAPTER ONE OF BOOK 2
OPEN WARFARE

"Where are you?"

Emily checked her phone for her location and sent it off to Aaron. "I'm sending you the coordinates now. I have two dead bodies and a van that needs to disappear."

Aaron was not pleased. She could sense his blood boiling over the phone.

"What? All you were supposed to do was stay close to Bennett, find out what you could, and make sure nothing happened to him. This was supposed to be a covert operation. You do remember what that means."

Emily looked at Kostya's dead body lying at her feet. She was getting more irritated by the second. After a near death experience, all Aaron cared about was the mission. "First off, thanks for asking, Emily are you okay? Are you injured? Do you need medical attention? And second, can we talk about this after you get me out of here?"

She could hear Aaron sigh on the other end of the phone. "Sorry, they are on their way. Are you hurt?"

"I have a super nasty headache and a few bruises, but I'm fine, thank you."

"We have a few minutes before the team arrives, so tell me what happened."

"It appears they were trying to shut Jack up by kidnapping me. Two old-school Russian mobsters grabbed me while I was on my morning run. They planned on raping me, and after that, I'm not sure. Kill me eventually, I suppose. I stabbed one and shot the other."

"You killed them?"

Really? Are we having this conversation?

Aaron took a deep breath. "I'm sorry, Emily. That must have been awful for you." Aaron knew all about Emily's history. Members of the Russian mob killed her mom and dad in broad daylight on the streets of Saint Petersburg, Russia, fifteen years ago, just because they were Jewish and in the wrong place at the wrong time. Unfortunately, thirteen-year-old Emily saw the whole thing from her parents' car window. If they had known she was in the car, she would have been dead as well. Emily's aunt and uncle took her to Israel soon after. It was that devastating experience that drove her to become a Mossad agent. She worked hard, rose quickly through the ranks, and had become a respected agent. Now considered very dangerous - at least to those who were enemies of Israel.

"Yeah, well, I guess they didn't know who they were dealing with." She took another look at Kostya and Maksim. "They looked like a couple of slime balls to me. "

While Emily was talking, Aaron got word that the team was close to her location, and he wanted to make sure she was all right. "Okay, we're going to get you out of there. This is what I want you to do. Two cars are going to pull up to your location. Get in the car with Erick and get out of there. He will have Doc with him. He will check you out and make sure you are okay." Doc, as he was called, was just as good at saving lives as he was at taking them. "They will take you to your apartment while the others clean up the mess. Take some time to rest and get yourself together. Then send in your report."

Aaron didn't want to get into it, but it was his duty to ask. "It appears you and Bennett have gotten very close. I assume you are still in control of the situation."

Emily didn't appreciate the innuendo. She was a professional and had never used the fact that she was a beautiful woman to do more than flirt on any mission, nor was she ever asked to do more by the agency. Getting emotionally involved was taboo for an agent, and Emily knew it. She wasn't about to tell Aaron that as her mind raced to come up with a plan to take down the two Russians, all she could think about was Jack.

Emily heard vehicles coming around the corner. She walked out around the back of the van and saw two late model SUVs coming her way. They pulled up, one in front of the van and the other behind. Two men jumped out of each one.

"My ride is here. You'll get my report later tonight," she replied in a matter-of-fact tone.

That wasn't exactly the answer Aaron was hoping for, but he trusted her to keep her head about her and do the right thing. "Okay, I'll talk to you soon. Be careful."

Two men escorted Emily to the car while two others placed the dead men into body bags and threw into the back of the second SUV. They were good at what they did, and within minutes, they would have everything under control. The two Russians and all evidence would disappear for good.

* * *

It was now nine thirty in the morning, and Dante was pacing back and forth in his hotel room. He was scheduled to meet Senator Wellsenburg downstairs at ten o'clock, and was more than a little concerned about his two Russian hoodlums, seeing that he hadn't heard from them since six-thirty this morning. They were to check-in as soon as their task was complete. You didn't have to be a supernatural being to know that something had gone terribly wrong. Dante was furious with himself. Normally he would have checked on them, incognito, of course, to make sure all was going according to plan. However, the prayer cover coming from the group meeting at the old church was growing exponentially, making it difficult for him to move around without being confronted by Uriel or some other angel protector. It wasn't that he didn't love a good confrontation, but he needed to keep his actions as stealth as possible.

Dante thought, 'I have experienced nothing like this since...' He cringed...'The Great Awakening'. He paused. Dante had tried many times to erase that entire period permanently from his memory. Just the thought of it sent a shock-wave of fear over him. He winced as it slowly came into focus. *Yes, nothing like this has happened since the revivals in the time of Jonathan Edwards.*

In and around 1730, the church discouraged its parishioners from reading the Bible. They taught the clergy were the only ones who could properly interpret it and that they needed to go through the church in order to communicate with God. But, when the awakening came, it opened people's eyes that the bible was for everyone and that they could walk and talk with God themselves. It led to new feelings of freedom and new levels of faith that rocked the spiritual world of that time. History estimates that ten percent of New England made a commitment to Christ. Twenty-eight million people converted in just two years. It is difficult in this day and age to grasp the enormity of what happened.

Dante knew well that the origins of that spiritual awakening were rooted in small prayer groups that gathered and grew larger as the movement expanded. He especially remembered one particular group that gathered in Princeton, New Jersey. It was one of the first groups to gather for prayer daily. He did his worst to destroy it, but to no avail. He remembered it as a devastating setback. Some say it was that spiritual awakening that helped light the fires of the revolution because it got people talking about freedom from the restraints of the controlling Church of England and any other religious authority, including King George. Because of that spiritual awakening, it was years before the forces of darkness could once again gain a firm foothold in America. Now that they had, Dante and his master were determined never to let something like that happen again.

Dante was sure it wasn't an angelic intrusion. If it were, he would have felt it. There was another player in the mix, a wild card. Dante hated to be blindsided. The more he thought about it, the angrier he got. He wouldn't rest until he found out exactly what took place.

Suddenly, there was a knock on the door. There, standing in the hallway, was Harry Toller, Wellsenburg's eyes and ears around

Washington. He had never stopped shadowing Jack and Emily, even after the senator told him to lie low. Dante stared intently at Toller.

"Mr. Adal, I'm..."

Dante stopped him. "I know who you are." Dante's eyes narrowed. "I presume you have news for me. Come in."

Toller walked in and stood in the middle of the room. He had never met Dante, but he had done his research and knew as much as there was to know about this mysterious individual, at least in this world.

"I have been following Jack Bennett and Emily Richardson for the last ten days. I saw what happened this morning and thought you would like to know."

"How did you know to come to me?"

"There's not much that happens around here that I don't know about."

Dante smirked. Refreshed by his arrogance. "So, what did you see?"

"I saw your two men grab the girl and drive off. I followed from a distance. When they stopped, I parked my car and watched from a wooded area close to where they pulled off."

"Are you sure no one saw you?"

Toller smirked, "I'm good at what I do, Mr. Adal."

Dante now realized he had sent the wrong asset to the job. "I saw one man get out and stand outside the van, while the other stayed inside with the girl. I assumed he was enjoying himself. You know, having a little fun. Fifteen minutes later, I watched as the second man walked around to the van's side door and opened it. Immediately, I heard a muffled gunshot, and I saw the second man drop to the ground. A few seconds later, the girl, Emily, walk out of the van unharmed with a gun in her hand. She looked around, then made a phone call. It was getting really interesting, so I figured I'd wait to see who she was calling. Within twenty minutes, I see two black SUVs pull up, two men in each vehicle. The two men in the first vehicle escorted her into the car and drove off, while the other two loaded the body bags into the back of the second SUV." Toller glared at Dante. "Your two guys, I assume."

Dante's expression was that of amazement. One, because of how thorough Toller was, and second, because of what he was hearing.

"So, you are telling me that this one-hundred-and-twenty-pound girl overpowered and killed two large armed men within a few minutes?"

Toller reached in his jacket pocket, pulled out one of his favorite cigars, and stuck it in his mouth. He enjoyed sucking on it even if he couldn't light it. It helped him think. "Yeah, that's exactly what I'm telling you, and that's not all." Toller noticed the bottle of expensive scotch sitting on the desk. "Would you mind if I had a drink?"

Dante shrugged his shoulders. "Be my guest." He knew a great asset when he saw one. He could think of a thousand uses for this guy. Toller poured himself a drink and sat down in one of the leather chairs next to the desk.

"I was in Special Forces for eight years, and I've seen a hell of a lot of stuff in my time, so when I see a team pull up to a scene like these guys did and clean it up like it never happened, I say to myself, these guys are good - top of their game. And this girl, Emily, she ain't no prima donna. She is a highly trained agent. So, my next question is... Who the hell cares about some professor, blog writer type to the point they are willing to commit all these resources to protect him? My first thought was his FBI buddy Lederman, but these guys didn't look FBI.

I've seen this type of operation before, and I'm telling you, it's not the Feds."

He pulled the cigar out of his mouth and took another drink, relishing the moment. Holding the cigar in his left hand, he pointed to Dante and said, "I'm gonna throw this out there, and maybe you can tell me if it makes sense to you." He took another sip, feeling more and more comfortable and confident by the minute. Dante didn't appreciate the drama, but he allowed him his moment. Then Toller dropped it. "I think this girl, Emily...is Mossad."

Dante's back straightened, and his head snapped back as if he had just got slapped in the face. He hated them mostly because they were Jews, but also because they had foiled some very well-planned terrorist attacks that he and his cohorts had inspired. How could he have missed this? It had to be the prayer cover coming from that infernal prayer group. It was becoming intolerable and was now inhibiting his ability to see into certain spiritual realms. His anger was getting the best of him, and when that happened, he had difficulty cloaking his real identity. His head was spinning. What was Mossad doing here? And what connection was there between them and Jack Bennett? He had to know what proof, if any, Toller had. Dante's eyes narrowed and flickered back and forth from human to cat-like, turning reddish-orange and then back again. It was extremely rapid, but noticeable. Toller tried not to react, but his curiosity was peaking. This bizarre display did not shock him. He had his own thoughts about who or what Dante really was. What he saw only underlined his suspicions. He was now convinced that Dante was some kind of alien being. 'How cool is this?' He thought.

Dante's icy stare brought him back. "What makes you say that?"

"As I said, Mr. Adal, I've been around. I know how these guys operate. It's their style. You've got a real problem here. You don't want to mess with these people. If I were you, I would figure a way to get around them. Unless, of course, you have resources I'm not aware of?" Toller was baiting him to see what his reaction would be.

Dante didn't bite. He stood up, walked over to the door, and opened it. "Thank you for the information." Toller finished his drink, put his glass down, and walked towards the door. Dante reached in his pocket and handed him three one-hundred-dollar bills folded in half. "I will be in touch." Toller gave him one last look, hoping to see some more evidence to confirm his theory. Dante motioned with his right hand towards the hallway without saying another word. Toller nodded and walked out. Dante had some work to do.

Made in United States
Orlando, FL
06 August 2022

20659828R00163